Sherlock Holmes and
The Folk Tale Mysteries
Volume 2

The Dyrebury Danger and Other Stories

Gayle Lange Puhl

Paperback ISBN 978-1-78092-806-7
ePub ISBN 978-1-78092-807-4
PDF ISBN 978-1-78092-808-1

Published in the UK by MX Publishing
335 Princess Park Manor, Royal Drive,
London, N11 3GX
www.mxpublishing.co.uk
Cover design by www.staunch.com

For Andrew, Ainea, Anicia, and Brennen

Table of Contents

The Case of the Dyrebury Danger

The cases Mr. Sherlock Holmes accepted throughout his long career as a consulting detective came to his attention in various ways. Sometimes the authorities, like Scotland Yard officials or his brother Mycroft, who was once described to me as being "the British Government", sent for him to request his services. Public servants, not excluding Cabinet Ministers or Members of Parliament, have graced our simple rooms urging Holmes to help them out of their difficulties, either public or private. Humbler clients have written or arrived to our sitting room at 221 b Baker Street in person to request his aid. Occasionally he found something to pique his interest in the paragraphs of the numerous daily newspapers he read, many of them from outside London.

The case I remember as one of our most unusual adventures came to us in a new fashion, shortly after Holmes had finally decided to have a telephone installed.

In my surgery a few streets away I had grown used to the benefits of having a telephone and had urged my friend for months to get one for his exclusive use. Typically he had taken some time to investigate the pros and cons of such a move. I think he thought that such an invention situated in his own rooms might disturb the mental processes he had honed to such fine points while sunk in deep deliberation of clues and observations gathered during his intricate cases. An insistent ringing might also draw him from his chemical experiments at a critical moment.

Finally modernity won out and Sherlock Holmes soon found that the instrument greatly simplified his work. Now experts could be consulted and lines of information opened immediately to him, instead of his enduring the frustrating time spent waiting for answers to the many wires and notes he was accustomed to send out daily in the course of his profession. Mrs. Hudson was saved the trotting up and down the seventeen steps of our staircase to deliver questions and information that arrived via her instrument installed in the lower hall. Holmes himself no longer needed to bestir himself to walk down the stairs to talk into the receiver several times a day. After a week I could see that he reveled in the ease of sitting in his armchair and reaching out a hand to pluck the gadget from a nearby table in order to place his calls.

He also took advantage of the simple act of taking the receiver off the hook to silent the telephone when he engaged in such important work he felt it must not be disturbed by any outside concerns.

This had been a half-day for me at the surgery and I returned to Baker Street at lunch time. I found my friend sprawled in on the sofa, a newspaper spread across his chest, wearing his dressing gown.

He lifted languid eyes to me and acknowledged my presence with a wave of his hand. For a moment I wondered, but a quick glance at his eyes reassured me that the pledge made to me long before still held. Sherlock Holmes was merely resting.

"You solved that case that worried you last night," I remarked.

"You progress, Watson. Yes, I called up the Yard this morning and gave them the last bit of information needed to put Lady Spratt away for the murder of her husband. They thought it was a simple case of voluntary starvation, but the marks on the pantry door told the true tale. But I didn't expect to see you here in the middle of the day."

"I had a half-day today and thought you might like to go out for some lunch."

"I am feeling a little peaked. The last meal I remember was dinner at that vile little café by the docks two days ago."

"Yes, and you haven't had a bite since. Come, get dressed and we'll try that new restaurant you mentioned on Gloucester Street. You said their chef is remarkable."

"Watson, you scintillate today!" He jumped up off the sofa and went his bedroom. A few moments later he emerged, the dressing gown gone. In its stead he wore a smart City suit. He was knotting the tie around his collar when the telephone rang.

"Oh, bother the thing and just when I'm hungry! Hello? Hello? Yes, this is Mr. Sherlock Holmes. Who's this? Lord Owen Sessamy of Dyrebury? What, in Yorkshire? Ah. You want to come here and consult me on a case? What kind of case? Oh, you would rather not say over the 'phone. Very well. Are you in London? I am just going out but you may meet me at the "Gai Souterrain" in Gloucester Street in twenty minutes. You know the place? Excellent. Goodbye.

"Well, this should be a most fruitful lunch, Watson. A meal to sustain the outer man and a murder to occupy the inner man."

"How do you know it is a case of murder?"

"When a busy and important man like Lord Sessamy, who owns several thousand acres of land in the West Riding of Yorkshire peopled with tenant farmers and who controls two coal mines and a limestone quarry currently producing building materials for the Sheffield Cathedral repairs project travels all the way to London to consult with me, you may feel assured that is not because of some trifling robbery or trespass on his estate better handled by the local constabulary. No, it is something grave. That is clearly stated by his reluctance to even mention it over an open telephone line. Ah, Watson, that's a lot of information for you to digest on an empty stomach. The place is close so I think we shall walk. I think for once we both can say that we approach this meal with hearty appetites."

Yet I had one more question. "How do you know so much about Lord Sessamy, Holmes?"

"You have forgotten my subscription to the **Leeds Mercury**, Watson, not to mention those commendable publications the **Doncaster Voice** and the **Sheffield Star**. As a consulting detective it behooves me to keep up with the doings of my old London "friends" when they decide to rusticate in the country. A change of air and scenery may motivate a man to try new variations on certain old tricks and I like to keep up with the latest modes of crime wherever they appear. There has been much in the newspapers lately about Lord Sessamy's involvement in the Cathedral rebuilding, and there was a short paragraph earlier this week about the accidental death of his castle librarian."

The "Gai Souterrain" was set beneath pavement level under another eating establishment and entered by a set of well-trod stone stairs. The space within was lit with flickering gaslights along the drab walls, although it was the middle of the day. A French maître d', solemn in white tie and tails, ushered us to a table and slapped down the hand-written menus on the white tablecloth before us. He motioned for another waiter to attend to our wants and returned to his station by the front entrance.

There were no windows. Despite the flaring flambeaux the restaurant was only half-lit. There were a dozen tables, each with its candle, and the subterranean motif was carried out with a flagstone floor and fitted stone walls. Overhead the ceiling seemed to hang heavily, as if it hadn't decided if it would remain there, or crash down on our heads. The place was filled and the clientele murmured quietly to each other as a trio played softly in a corner.

We had barely picked up our menus when Owen Sessamy, Baron of Dyrebury, was shown to our table. He was a man with broad shoulders and a trim waist, just over medium height. He was about thirty years of age with fair hair smoothed back over a high brow. His dark eyes looked from one to the other of us as he took his seat. His nose was aristocratic, his mouth thin-lipped but backed by a good set of white teeth, and the cleft in his chin gave him a somewhat rakish appearance. He was clad in a dark suit of tweed and wore a striped school tie. His hands gripped the menu with strong fingers and he moved with the masculine grace of a lion. I noticed several women at other tables watching him as he joined us.

We ordered lunch. As the waiter left Sherlock Holmes shook out his serviette and invited Lord Sessamy to explain his problem.

"I am the twenty-first Baron of Dyrebury and my home is Cliffdale Castle in the Yorkshire Dales. We have lived there since Edward III set up the office to fight for and defend the northern Border. My widowed mother and my two younger sisters live there with me. The nearby village of Dyrebury hosts a holy spring, dedicated to St. Galena. There was in olden times a steady stream of pilgrims travelling north to visit it and bathe in its waters, for it was as renowned as a healing spring and many miracles were wrought there. Indeed, there is a little cave hard by the water that is filled with the small stones tradition calls for the pilgrims to leave at the site. The spring still draws visitors to this day."

"Are there many caves in the Yorkshire Dales?" I asked, as Holmes sat fidgeting with a fork.

"Yes, a great many. The base is limestone, you see, with other mineral veins shooting through at intervals. On the estate I have a large quarry for the stone, and also a couple of smaller coal mines. The tenant farmers do well with sheep and hay and some grain, but mostly sheep, because the land is cut up into many little valleys set among the rolling hills and other higher elevations. There are many streams that drain away into the Ouse and the Humber. I may be biased, but I think there can be no prettier sight than the Dales in early morning, when the rising sun picks out the huddled flocks safe within the long, dry stone walls set up by sturdy peasants centuries ago."

"You are a poet, sir," I said.

"There is a literary strain that runs through the family, Dr. Watson, and it plays a part in this problem."

At this moment the waiter appeared with our first course and we took a few minutes to appreciate the chef's efforts.

"Please state the nature of your problem, Lord Sessamy. Leave nothing out. Even the most insignificant detail may prove important to the case." said Holmes. Lord Sessamy continued as the waiter served us throughout the meal.

"Yes, Mr. Holmes. I fear it is a long tale, but I will try to condense it down to the major points. It naturally resolves itself into three parts. The first part starts back in the days of King James II, when the government was corrupt and crime was rife. For a period of nearly two years a band of highwaymen roamed the Yorkshire Dales. There were rumours that over time there were as many as forty men on horseback involved. They covered a large area in their depredations, but their robberies and assaults centered mainly on the pious travelers that came to Dyrebury to take the healing waters, so they were referred to as the Dyrebury Danger. Reports said that their leader, called the Captain, a dashing figure swathed in a blood-red cloak and wearing a wide-brimmed hat festooned with sweeping feathers, rode a great black stallion. He seemed invincible. Officers of the King's Law, along with many local men, organized mounted parties and patrols that ranged over the Dales in attempts to capture or kill him. Occasionally they would find members of his band and summary justice would be done, but the Captain would always escape. It was said that local people helped to conceal him, for he was a romantic figure and even admired by some. Some helped him hoping to discover where he had hidden his cache of ill-gotten gains, a treasure of gold, silver and precious gems taken from the wealthy victims. Men wanted to learn his secrets and as for women…well, he was reputed to have long light hair, a handsome face, dark eyes that could mesmerize a girl at a glance, and a way with a woman unequaled in the district.

"It was his penchant for the ladies that finally did him in. Officials discovered that the Captain regularly visited an innkeeper's daughter, named Bess Boniface, in her room at her father's pub, the "Lamb and Lion". They threw a guard around the building and waited for him to appear. Many a cold and weary night they watched and waited until they wondered if their information was true.

"He must have been watching them, for the first cloudy, moonless night after they had called off the surveillance he was sighted in the courtyard, embracing the girl before he mounted his steed. A cry went up and in a moment six men were running for their mounts. He laughed at them before spurring his black horse down the road that led into the countryside. As they scrambled to follow him, one constable, too fat to join in the hasty pursuit, grabbed Bess and forced open her clenched hand. He found four sovereigns and a gold ring that fitted the description of one stolen from a lady waylaid on the road to Dyrebury only three days before. She was dragged to a storeroom and locked inside, while more help was summoned from the town.

"Meanwhile the ruffian led his pursuers a merry chase. Sparks flashed from his horse's steel shoes as he thundered down the frozen highway. He galloped the animal at such a pace that the plumed hat flew from his head. . The Captain used all his tricks; suddenly turning off onto soft ground to disguise the sounds of his horse's footfalls, standing hidden by shadows as the posse blundered past, and finally, when it seemed he was to be surrounded at last, dashing over a bridge and galloping into a thick wood. It appeared that he had made his escape, but a couple of the officials drew pistols and fired just before the thick trees hid the fugitive. They both swore they hit him.

"The men were not far from Cliffdale Castle, my family's seat, and decided to ride there in order to inform the Baron that the Dyrebury Danger was abroad on his estate. As they clattered up the hill to the front entrance of the Castle, they were astonished to find a fine black horse standing, floundered, by the icy steps. At its feet lay the huddled body of a man, tangled in a blood-red cloak, and bleeding to death from two pistol shots. The Baron was called out and he was horrified to find, when the body was turned over and a horn lantern held up, his youngest son, Jarvis Sessamy, breathing his last under the cold, starless sky.

"The evidence was clear. Jarvis Sessamy, third son of Lord Clarence Sessamy, had led the Dyrebury Danger. He was by all accounts a reckless lad, who was destined for the military. But he resented all authority and resisted his father's half-hearted attempts to get him to enlist, for he was his mother's favorite. She was French and very passionate, by all accounts, and her husband could deny her nothing. She died soon after Jarvis. Bess Boniface pleaded her belly before the Justice of the Peace and was allowed to remain locked in her bedroom at the "Lamb and Lion" until she was delivered of the child. The baby, a girl, was born five months later, but Bess died in childbirth and the infant was handed over to the innkeeper's wife to raise.

"The rest of the gang were either captured or driven from the district, but all suspects questioned claimed that their shares were divided up and given to them immediately. Only Jarvis Sessamy knew the location of the cave that held his lion's share of the treasure they had stolen. Many men went out, armed with shovels and picks, to search the caves and caverns of the Yorkshire Dales in a vain attempt to discover the treasure of the Dyrebury Danger. Not a trace of it was ever found."

The waiter came and cleared away the last course. Brandy was poured and Owen Sessamy and I accepted cigars. Sherlock Holmes, his thin fingers now steepled before him, waited for the Baron to continue.

"The second part of the story occurred about fifty years later. The scandal had receded into legend. Dunley Sessamy, the Baron's oldest son, had inherited the title and estate decades before. His surviving brother, Creighton, had gone into the clergy and raised a family on the estate, having been given the living of the Dyrebury parish as a young man by their father.

"Creighton had a granddaughter, fancifully named Berengaria, whom the family called Berry. By all accounts she was a bright girl, only sixteen, but a bit bookish. She had heard the story of the Dyrebury Danger and took it upon herself to research the tale with the intention of writing it all down as an adventure to read to the younger children in the family as a nighttime story.

"No one saw any harm in that. In truth the people in the area had come to consider Jarvis as a bit of a rogue to be proud of. He had never seriously injured anyone and the local population held him to be a sort of Robin Hood, although there was not much evidence that he distributed more than a few coins among the poor. In any case, much time had passed and memories had softened. Berry interviewed the oldest remaining residents; of which there were only a few. She visited the various places the Captain and the Danger had been known to be seen, the better to describe them. The only people that would not talk to her about the incident were the Bonifaces of the "Lamb and Lion". Yes, the same family still owned and ran the public house. Bess's daughter had lived and it was her family who refused to talk to Berry. The child was a sensible girl and did not press the issue.

"Berengaria carefully wrote out a manuscript of over fifty pages. As a Christmas surprise she presented the entire thing to her grandfather. He was so impressed with the manuscript that he caused it to be set into typeface and had one copy printed. The copy and the original script were bound between covers, making two books in all. The typeset copy was given to the current Baron for the Castle's library, and the handwritten manuscript was retained by the old vicar, with instructions that Berengaria should inherit it upon his death.

"Unfortunately, young Berry didn't live to see her twentieth birthday, and when the household was broken up after the old man died, his handwritten copy of the story was lost. There did remain the copy in the Castle's library and as the years and decades went by it became a favorite of the younger members of the family. As a child I thrilled to the account of my wicked Uncle Jarvis of ancient memory when my nanny consented to read the tale to my sisters and me in the nursery when we had, in her opinion, been especially well-behaved that day.

"Now we come the third and most recent part of the story. My father was no bibliophile, but he did care about the things left in his care from earlier generations of Sessamys. About twenty years ago he decided that the Cliffdale Castle library needed a complete overhaul. The collection was vast and far-ranging, having been added to by generations of the family. Many old volumes were falling victim to neglect and even crumbling away as they sat on the shelves. A complete inventory hadn't been done in decades and in short, the job was well overdue.

15

"He hired a man, Garrett Aydin, a scholar of some repute, who specialized in Highland myths. He had traveled around for years as a tutor to this family and that. He was nearly forty and grateful for the offer of such steady and interesting work. He proved to be a fine librarian, and the good fellow devoted himself to the Herculean task.

"I knew Mr. Aydin well. He had rooms in the Castle, never married, and spent his working hours organizing the innumerable volumes in the large library. It is a tall, broad room, with a balcony circling the main floor half-way up, lined with books. Below the balcony multiple shelves girdled the wide space with a moveable ladder reaching up from the parquet floor. It holds tens of thousands of volumes. Many an hour I spent as a youth at the huge main table, the light from the stained glass windows that bore our family coats of arms falling on a book or atlas whose contents took me far away from Yorkshire to exotic lands where monkeys chattered from palm trees or pirates glared at their helpless victims as with naked blades clenched between their teeth they climbed the sides of treasure ships bound for Spain from the gold mines of South America.

"Mr. Aydin was a fixture of the Castle, a kind, knowledgeable man who not only cared for and preserved the books under his charge, but read them as well. I was educated by tutors, but whenever I had a question they could not answer, Mr. Aydin helped me find the solution. He grew grey in the service of the Sessamys, Mr. Holmes, and he did not deserve the fate that befell him.

"One early morning, a week ago, one of the housemaids found Mr. Aydin lying on the floor of the library at the foot of the ladder. He had been dead several hours. The back of his head was crushed by the edge of a display case behind him that held a collection of ancient knives and daggers. A few books and papers were scattered around his body. The consensus was that he had fallen from the ladder with his arms full of materials. He was unable to save himself, hit his head on the case and died. No one had seen him since dinner the evening before and the library had not been used by the family that night. The police closed the case, the inquest declared it to be "death by misadventure" and poor Mr. Aydin was buried yesterday in the Dyrebury churchyard near the Sessamys he had served so faithfully."

"But you have doubts about Mr. Aydin's death," said Sherlock Holmes shrewdly.

"Yes, I have," replied Lord Sessamy. "The man was devoted to his job, but I, who knew him from when I was a child, never knew him to start work before breakfast. He had a regular schedule to which he adhered. He was a man of method, as behooves a good librarian, and had worked out a routine from which he seldom digressed.

"Garrett Aydin rose each morning at seven, had breakfast at eight and was at his desk before nine. He worked until one, had lunch and then took a walk down to the village or over the fields of the estate. He returned after an hour, resumed his duties and worked until five-thirty. He usually ate dinner with the family. Sometimes of an evening he would play chess, fill in at whist or bridge as needed or discourse on current affairs when asked. During holidays he was always included in the festivities. During Christmas we quite depended on him to get up little pantomimes and plays for the amusement of our guests."

"What about his family?" asked Holmes.

"His parents had died before he came to Cliffdale Castle. He had a sister and a younger brother in Chester. He used to go visit them once a year. His sister was a governess and caught typhoid from one of her charges ten years ago. She died. His brother immigrated to Australia after that. Mr. Aydin then started taking walking tours through Scotland during his vacations."

"Is there another reason you think his death was suspicious?"

"I went into the library after his body was removed and the police were finished with the room. I picked up the books and papers from the floor. To my surprise the papers were just blank note sheets from the desk. The books were all from one lower shelf. There was no need to carry them up the ladder. And strangely, when everything was tidied up, the only thing found missing from the library was the old copy of Berengaria's story."

"Does the library contain many valuable books?"

"Yes, indeed. There are volumes dating back to medieval times, first editions of many famous authors and even an illustrated Bible from an ancient Irish monastery. Berry's book was old and rare, but would hold little interest to anyone outside the family."

Around us the lunch crowd had thinned. A waiter hovered in the background. It was time to leave. Sherlock Holmes allowed Lord Sessamy to pay the check and then led us up to the street level above.

"What is to happen to Mr. Aydin's things?" he asked.

"His personal items are to be packed up and sent to his brother in Australia. I wanted to wait until after I consulted you to have his things disturbed. I wish you to come up to Cliffdale Castle and look into this for me. The Dowager Baroness has gone to visit family in Wales and my sisters are currently abroad. There is plenty of room, I assure you, for both you and Dr. Watson."

"Very good. Watson, do you fancy a little trip to the Yorkshire Dales? Can you leave your practice for a few days?"

"I will make arrangements with Jackson this afternoon."

"Excellent. Lord Sessamy, look for us tomorrow. What is the nearest station?"

"Cragville, about ten miles from Dyrebury. I will send a carriage to meet you. I am leaving from King's Cross this afternoon."

Holmes and I parted on the pavement before "Gai Souterrain". I returned to the surgery where I made arrangements to have my patients covered by another doctor while I was out of town.

The trip from King's Cross to Cragville the next morning was uneventful. I found Holmes on the platform holding the tickets. We secured a compartment and I tossed in my valise. Sherlock Holmes asked me if I had packed my revolver, which I had, then handed in his own bag and swung aboard just as the train began to move. We passed the time reading the papers Holmes brought along and when they were exhausted we talked about the history of the Border region. Holmes discoursed learnedly about Hadrian's Wall and the soldiers who manned the fortifications for centuries until the Roman Empire withdrew from Britain in 410 A.D.

A dog-cart was waiting for us at Cragville and we spun through the soft fall air faintly warmed by sunshine flooding down over rolling hills that led towards Dyrebury. The low mountains that the road wound through were graced by fall-tinged trees, shrubs and dry stone walls enclosing faded fields. Our cart wheels rolled through drifts of fallen leaves. From our seat in the cart we could see some of the limestone caves Lord Sessamy had mentioned, dark holes dotting worn hillsides. Lyell, the driver, a horsy old man who handled the reins with a knowing hand, told us that the route we were taking was the very road which bore the traffic of pilgrims to St. Galena's holy spring back in the days of the Dyrebury Danger.

"Aye, the tales my old granddad used to tell me about the stories his old granddad told him of the rich people who used to come to drink the water and wash their limbs in the pool of St. Galena. From all over the kingdom and even over the sea! Fine ladies and splendid gentlemen, all wearing silk and velvet, traveling with their servants in carriages fit for the King himself. But the rich people, for all their money, suffered just as much as the poor pilgrims that walked beside them, all hoping for a cure from St. Galena. Oh, some people went away cured and left a little stone in the cave next to the holy spring in gratitude. But many were never helped and went back to their homes as sick as when they arrived. There was many a pilgrim who started too late and never reached the spring at all, dying on the way. Look, there is an old monument over there to some ailing traveler who died just a few miles short of his hope of relief from his terrible problem."

He pointed with his whip to a pitiful mound of rocks surrounded by weeds at the side of the roadway. We stopped the

20

cart and walked over to the shrine. It had obviously been there for a very long time and the years and the weather had partially obliterated an inscription on the uppermost stone. I used my pocketknife to scrape away the moss and lichen so that the words could be read. To the best of my ability I made out the words. "'Michel Rattaile, born like his brothers blind. He prayed for a cure, but he was taken before he could wash in the waters. God willing that the miracle be manifested to his brothers Jacques and Leon. In the year of our Lord 1533.'"

We returned to the cart and continued on to Cliffdale Castle. After a couple of miles Holmes brought up the subject of Jarvis Sessamy.

"Oh, you've heard of the Captain! Yes, you can order a pint from any public house within thirty miles and hear legends of him and the Dyrebury Danger. Back in the early days of King James II the government was busy with its own affairs with little time to spend worrying about the people of the Dales. When the Captain and the Dyrebury Danger came galloping down over the hills and struck at the poor sick people travelling to St. Galena's well there were naught to protect them but a few servants and the odd discharged soldier hoping to heal his own wounds in the water.

"Once, it's said, a fat merchant hid his gold and jewels in a cavity under his carriage seat. But the Captain knew about it and had the man thrown out on his nose into the dust of the road. His carriage was chopped to pieces before his eyes. The Captain loaded up the booty and tossed the man a single silver penny before he left, saying 'It's obvious to me that you don't need to eat dinner tonight. Here's a penny to give to the honest labourer who clears this wreckage out of the road. He can buy a bird to roast on the remnants of your fine carriage. Now walk, you lazy glutton, and a better sacrifice you will never make to St. Galena in your life!'

"The merchant walked to Dyrebury but it is not known if he got his healing. What is sure is that he promised a reward of twenty pounds to the man who could bring him the Captain's head. But when the time came the Baron refused to give it over and the twenty pounds were never paid."

The old man was a fount of similar stories and Sherlock Holmes listened to them all as we trotted through the nondescript village of Dyrebury, a collection of local stone houses with slate roofs. At one point the driver interrupted himself to point to a large building of the "coaching inn" type set back in a cobblestone courtyard. "That's the very place the Captain was last seen before he was killed." I looked up and admired the long galleries and the heavy roof. From an iron standard over the front door hung a swinging sign painted with a scene of a golden lion lying on green grass next to a white fluffy lamb. Then the dog-cart proceeded up the mountain to Cliffdale Castle.

It was an impressive old Norman pile of square towers and crenellated battlements. From the road below the leads of the inner fortification's roof rose above the curtain walls that surrounded the keep visible through the wide open portcullis of the main entry. It was not among the largest castles I had ever seen, but everything about it spoke of efficient design and solid construction. Only one corner tower showed signs of destruction from a long-ago war, with crumbling stones around a missing roof over smoke-blackened windows. Surrounded by the trees of burning colour that covered the prominence on which it stood, with the afternoon sun warming its ancient stones, the Castle gave the air of standing guard over the valleys and becks of the

Yorkshire Dales like a stern but loving paterfamilias whom one could never question, for he would always know best.

The approach to the Castle ran in a serpentine manner up the bluff to reach the entrance. The carriage entered the Castle walls and stopped within the keep before a shallow set of wide stone steps that gave access to the great wooden doors of the main Hall. Two men, one a tall, fleshy man, the other our client, Owen Sessamy, twenty-first Baron of Dyrebury, stood on the steps. The Baron came forward with an extended hand.

"Welcome, gentlemen, welcome! This is Mr. Handy, my butler. Handy, please have Mr. Sherlock Holmes' and Dr. Watson's luggage taken to their rooms. I trust you gentlemen had a pleasant trip? Fall days can be tricky as regards the weather, but we seem to be in the middle of a fine stretch of sun. I can offer you tea or coffee or something a little stronger if you wish."

We stood in a marble-floored entry hall with a cheery blaze in the fireplace to the right and an intricately-carved walnut staircase reaching up on our left. Before us were another set of doors through which I glimpsed comfortable chairs and handsome paintings.

Sherlock Holmes brushed off any offers of refreshment or rest. "Please show me Mr. Aydin's quarters, Lord Sessamy," he said. "I think this case may be more complicated that I first thought and I wish to lose no time gathering information."

"Of, course, Mr. Holmes."

We climbed the stairs to the third story. On the way Lord Sessamy pointed out our assigned quarters. Garrett Aydin's suite was just above ours. The librarian had been given a small sitting room, lit by two windows, furnished with a couple of armchairs, a secretary with a straight chair, a bookcase filled to overflowing and a small couch. In the center of the room was a round table. The floor was covered with a patterned rug. To the right of the fireplace was a door that led to his bedroom. It held a narrow bedstead with rumpled sheets, as if the owner had just risen from them, a chest of drawers, an armoire and two plain wooden chairs. A small square table stacked with reading material stood next to the bed next to a lamp. His shaving kit was laid out on the deep window sill.

Holmes began to examine the rooms. He began with the bedroom, methodically going through every drawer, all the bedclothes left disarranged on the man's bed, and every other item in the room. He picked up at the shaving articles and peered at them with his magnifying glass. He opened the armoire and felt and sniffed the clothing within. We stood back and watched silently.

Holmes finished with the bedroom and moved on to the sitting room. He gave it his full attention, going as far as to pick up every book on the shelves and flip through the pages of each one.

Nothing fell out. He ran his hand under the couch cushions and thumbed through the contents of the secretary. He opened a drawer and pulled out a stack of blank note paper. Then he stood up and turned to us and with a triumphant flourish held high a single sheet of white.

"You have found something!" I said.

"A clue! A palatable clue! Answer me this, my friends. When is a man's stationary not stationary?"

Lord Sessamy and I looked blankly at each other.

"When it has been moved! Look at this. I found it tucked in the center of the stack of blank sheets."

Carefully he brought the notepaper to the round table. He smoothed it out on the table cloth and we bent over to see what he had found.

"Read it out loud, Watson," Holmes said.

The handwriting was clear and round, as befitted a man who used words in his profession. "It is dated eight days ago. 'Dear Douglas,'" I began.

The Baron broke in. "That's his brother in Australia!"

I continued. "'I was glad to hear of your good fortune. Amelia is a beautiful girl and why she would consent to marry such an old fool as you I will never understand. However I do send my warmest congratulations. I am glad to hear that your business is going well and you plan to open another store in a few months.

'My work here at the Castle goes well. I have found something unusual. It may have to do with that old legend I told you about years ago. I need to check it out but if it is what I think it may be, I might have enough money to join you in Melbourne before the wedding and even invest in your enterprise. I look to have other news too. You know of whom I refer. Our relationship is coming to a head and if my discovery proves correct, I think the results may finally tip the scales and bring me the same sort of happiness you look forward to for yourself. I will write more tomorrow.' That is all there is." I laid the paper down.

"What could he have found that would bring him money? I don't understand," said the Baron.

"I have finished in here," said Holmes as he folded the incomplete letter and put it in his notebook. "May I see the library next?"

"Of course," replied Lord Sessamy.

The Cliffdale Castle library was as handsome and large as we had been told. I paused to admire the tall latticed windows sporting the coats of arms of branches of the Sessamy family going back centuries. They let the setting sunlight into the long chamber from the right side. The blaze in the fine marble fireplace opposite the windows did much to take the autumn chill off the room. Rows and rows of books lined the walls. Over our heads the balcony floor ran around three-quarters of the room supporting more shelves of books reaching up to the rococo ceiling painted with hunting scenes. Glass-topped display tables stood on Persian rugs that shared space with the long mahogany table in the center. An antique desk occupied a spot on the right. Cases with many wide shallow drawers, like those designed to hold collections of insects or mineral samples, stood in a row against the wall beyond the windows.

Sherlock Holmes quickly examined the contents of the display cases. He paid particular attention to one that held an assemblage of daggers and knives. I realized it must be the one Mr. Aydin had hit his head against when he fell. Holmes spent some time looking at the edge of the case that faced the shelves where the rolling ladder had stood with his lens. Finally he straightened up and cast a glance at the rest of the room.

"The question foremost in my mind, Watson," he remarked absently, "is why did Mr. Aydin put the unfinished letter to his brother back in the middle of a stack of untouched notepaper? What are those cases used for, Lord Sessamy?" Holmes indicated the bank of drawers against the opposite wall.

"Collections, mostly, Mr. Holmes. My great-grandfather began them. He was fond of traveling and brought back many small souvenirs. Let me show you." The Baron pulled open a wide, shallow drawer and displayed a tray neatly divided into many sections, each holding a tiny wooden carving of an animal. There were giraffes, lions, gazelles, apes and other fauna of the Dark Continent. Another drawer disclosed mounted beetles, each labeled in an old-fashioned hand. Drawer after drawer was opened, each containing diminutive treasures like Egyptian scarabs, mineral samples from Asia, origami figures from Japan, and coins from all over the globe, each individual item in its own little compartment.

"I have added to the drawers' contents with my own specimens. This one contains shells that I found on the beach when I was taken on vacation to Cornwall as a child. I was very proud when my father reserved a drawer for them. It was my first contribution to the family collection. I have filled several drawers since with such things as exotic birds' eggs from America and fossils found on the estate."

"And this set of drawers in the far corner? Do they have more baubles in them?" asked Sherlock Holmes.

"This last one contains only maps. My father and my grandfather were fond of maps and here you will find a diverse sampling of ones both modern and ancient. I must confess that these drawers were in a sorry mess before Mr. Aydin began work on them a year ago." The Baron opened a drawer and pulled out a hand-drawn sailor's chart of the coast of Norway. "This one dates from the early 1700s and was reputed to belong to the Greenwich Observatory at one time. There are hundreds of maps in these drawers. They cover all the oceans and the landmasses of the earth. My favorites when I was young were the old ones of unexplored territories with the legend "Here Be Dragons" marked in the blank spots."

Mr. Handy appeared at the doorway. "Dinner is served, My Lord," he intoned.

"Thank you, Handy. Since it will be only us, Mr. Holmes, I thought that we might not stand on ceremony tonight and forgo with dressing for dinner. I frequently eat informally when the women are absent. Each time I do I can see Handy's orthodox soul shrink in horror. His greatest fear is that I shall one day turn eccentric and eat all my meals from a plant-stand in the conservatory while dressed in hunting pinks and bedroom slippers."

After dinner Owen Sessamy offered to show us the rest of the Castle, but Holmes begged off and returned to the library. I took the Baron up on his offer, however, and we spent over two hours traversing corridors and climbing stone steps to various vantage points of the Norman pile. While he showed me the Green Hall and the Onyx Suite Lord Sessamy told me tales of the Castle, including the story of the Grey Yeoman. It was the ghost of a loyal soldier whom after death haunted the ruined tower. He had died fighting during a battle with the Northerners five hundred years before. His body had been ravaged by the fire that had devastated the tower. His specter now inhabited the ruins, forever on the lookout for the treacherous Northerners. Early repairs to the tower had to be called off when the workmen reported several sightings of the ghost and refused to continue the restoration.

The Grey Yeoman was reported to cause red lights to dance within and outside the tower on certain nights, as if the fire that destroyed the tower was still raging. There was a constant cold spot at the end of the Castle corridor that led to the Grey Yeoman's last post. Sometimes cries and screams were heard issuing from the tower. Skeptics said they were the calls of nesting birds but no signs of birds were ever found. The most notable manifestation of the Grey Yeoman occurred during Jarvis Sessamy's funeral, held at the castle's chapel. In the middle of a fire-and-brimstone sermon by the vicar concerning Jarvis' many sins, an earthquake shook the building. It was considered the work of the Grey Yeoman, displeased at the harsh words against a Sessamy in their own castle. I smiled at his words, but I saw by his eyes that the Baron was serious. Lord Sessamy admitted that all his life he had avoided the ruined tower of the Castle for fear of encountering the Grey Yeoman.

When we returned to the main floor, there was no sign of Holmes, although a light glimmered from under the library's door and I could hear the rustle of papers from within. I knew how he got when he was in the middle of a case and I decided it was best not to interrupt him. I explained some of his methods to Lord Sessamy and we finally retired to bed.

Sherlock Holmes was not present at breakfast the next day but Handy announced that he had requested we meet in the library after we finished our meal. Lord Sessamy and I found Holmes seated at the vast table. Before him were three folded maps on the polished surface. It was obvious to me that he had neither eaten nor slept since we had parted the night before, but his attitude was bright and cheerful like it frequently was when he was following a promising clue.

"Good morning, gentlemen! I have spent a most interesting night in this fine old room, Lord Sessamy."

"I am glad to hear it, Mr. Holmes," said our host.

"Yes, and I found the most interesting things in that map case. Everything was meticulously labeled and filed away except for one paper. Look here." Sherlock Holmes unfolded one of the maps and spread it before us. "Do you recognize this, my lord?"

"It's a map of the Yorkshire Dales. Here is Cragville and Summitton and here is Dyrebury. That spot indicates Cliffdale Castle."

"And what of this one?" Holmes opened another paper.

"That is an older map, with Dyrebury in the middle. The Castle is marked on the upper left. The style of cartography is from the eighteenth century, I'd say."

"Finally, what do you know of this one?" Another map, more crudely drawn and on rougher paper, was flattened out on the table top.

Lord Sessamy slowly looked it over then turned to Holmes. "Bless my soul, sir. I don't claim to know the details of every map in the collection, but I would swear I've never seen this one before. Where did you find it?"

"It was filed between two other maps in a bottom drawer. One was a street map of Chicago, Illinois, USA and the other was a detailed map of the Great Lakes area of the Middle Western States. These others I pulled out of their proper places."

"But finding this old map where you say you found it doesn't make any sense. Chicago is located on the shores of Lake Michigan, but that location hasn't any connection with this old map. Mr. Aydin was so meticulous in his filing. He would never leave this paper, which covers the Sessamy estate and the surrounding area, filed between two maps concerning a different area of the globe. It must have been a mistake."

"On the contrary, I think it was deliberate. He…" Holmes was interrupted by the appearance of the butler.

"What is it, Handy?" asked Lord Sessamy.

"I beg pardon, my Lord, but Abigail is outside with her bag. She insists that she is leaving."

"What! Bring her in, Handy."

Abigail proved to be a pretty woman of perhaps twenty-five years, with smooth brown hair and a neat ankle, who was dressed in a brown coat and a straw hat trimmed in artificial cherries. She left her valise in the hall and walked into the library. She faced her employer with a defiant face.

"Now, Abigail, Mr. Handy says you want to leave," said her employer. "You've worked here as a chambermaid for several years. Haven't you been well-treated?"

The woman turned her eyes from Lord Sessamy to Sherlock Holmes and me. I noticed that while she was attractive, with regular features marred only by a dusting of freckles over the nose, her brow was creased and she seemed to be both angry and fearful. Was Lord Sessamy a hard master? Nothing I had noticed about him since we first met indicated such a thing.

"It's not the job or the other servants, sir. I won't work in a place that has detectives in it. I'm a respectable girl and my family never had detectives in the house," she said.

"Mr. Holmes and Dr. Watson are investigating Mr. Aydin's death, Abigail. I went down to London to bring them back just for that. It doesn't have anything to do with you."

"I'm respectable, my lord. I won't stay in a place that has detectives in it. I'm sorry, sir, but I'm going to live with my sister in the village. I have made up my mind to it, sir."

"The police were here last week, Abigail, when poor Mr. Aydin died. You didn't object to them."

"The police were bad enough but I won't stay in a house that has detectives in it, sir."

"You are owed money, Abigail."

"You can send it to my sister's house, sir. I won't stay in this place another minute."

With that, the woman turned and carried her bag out of the Castle. We stood at one of the library's windows and watched a light carriage enter the Castle's ground and pull up in front of the stone steps. Abigail hopped in, the driver lifted in her valise, and the whole rig disappeared down the drive towards the main road to Dyrebury.

Handy had disappeared. Our client turned around. "I'm sorry to have to involve you in our domestic problems, Mr. Holmes. I don't understand her objection to detectives. Abigail has always been a steady, hard-working maid."

"What were her duties?" Holmes asked.

"That question is better put to Mr. Handy." Lord Sessamy rang for the butler. When he returned to the library our client told him to answer any question Holmes put to him.

"What were Abigail's duties?" Holmes asked again.

"She was assigned to the third floor, sir," said Mr. Handy.

"Then she was responsible for cleaning Mr. Aydin's suite."

"Yes, sir."

"Was she the maid who found Mr. Aydin's body?"

"No, sir. That was Harriet, the head housemaid. She was questioned by the police."

"You said Abigail had worked here for several years. Had there been any complaints against her during that time?"

The butler looked a bit uncomfortable and glanced at Lord Sessamy. The Baron nodded and Handy answered Holmes' question. "Abigail was a little standoffish from the other maids, sir. She had the reputation of holding herself above her station in life. She also was caught several times in places where she had no business. She was spoken to about it and promised to stop. Nothing was ever missing, however, so we had no reason to let her

33

go. I think she may have been naturally curious, sir." The butler said the last statement like it was some sort of distasteful disease.

"Whose carriage was that which picked her up just now?"

"It was the hack from the "Lamb and Lion", sir. She must have arranged for it this morning. The mailman comes early."

"She said she was going to her sister's house. So she has family in Dyrebury?"

"There is only her sister, sir, Mrs. Darnell from The Oaks, who is old Mrs. Rikketts' housekeeper. Mrs. Rikkett is quite the invalid and never leaves her home anymore. The two women came to Dyrebury about three years ago from Summitton, I believe."

"Who drove that hack?"

"It was young Boniface from the inn, sir. He took over the place when his father died last year."

"Was he an admirer of Abigail's, Mr. Handy?"

"I wouldn't know, sir. Gentlemen callers are not encouraged at the Castle and Abigail never spoke of one. She talked of spending her free time with her sister and then only when she was asked."

Sherlock Holmes thanked Mr. Handy for his assistance and the butler left the library. The hour chimed from the big ormolu clock on the library mantelpiece and Lord Sessamy pulled out his own watch from his waistcoat pocket.

"You must excuse me, Mr. Holmes. I have an appointment with my estate agent in ten minutes at the stables. Please feel free to call on Handy if you need anything." Lord Sessamy left.

Sherlock Holmes picked up the misfiled map and handed it to me along with his magnifying glass.
"There are several interesting points about this map, Watson. Can you find them?"

I examined the faded ink and the rough paper. "It appears to be very old."

"Yes, Watson, that is obvious. What else can you tell me?"

I was irked at him impatient response to my observation and concentrated my attention on the map. "It looks to be hand-drawn by someone who had some artistic skill but was not an accomplished artist. It is not drawn to scale. The little sketch of the Castle is out of proportion to the cross-hatching that designates Dyrebury. I think these lines show mountains and the darker ones are roads. There is a tiny drawing of what appears to be a horse and carriage on this line. There are several marks on the map that indicate locations marked with numbers. The numbers in the legend on the bottom lists names like "Forest", "Bridge" and "Northern Road". Here's one for the "Lamb and Lion". There are also many "X"s scattered over the landscape. There is no indication of what the "X"s are supposed to mean. I see nothing else." I put down the map and the lens with a feeling of satisfaction.

Holmes took up the paper and held it up to the light that was streaming through one of the latticed windows. "I love maps," he murmured, as if only to himself. "They are little bits of history put to paper. They speak of journeys, of unknown places, of people who once laboured and dreamed of accomplishments, yet now are gone and forgotten. The ink is faded to brown, the paper yellowed and crumbling, but the places spread out on this map have taken on a life of their own. What was so important that someone took the trouble to draw this map of a corner of the Yorkshire Dales over one hundred and sixty years ago?"

"I don't understand, Holmes. How can this misfiled map have anything to do with the death of Garrett Aydin?"

"Mr. Aydin hid an unfinished letter to his brother in the middle of a stack of pristine stationary in his room. He hid this map in the middle of a drawer of unrelated maps in the library. Yet Mr. Aydin was the most methodical of men and a systematic worker who was neat and precise in his work. What does the fact that these papers were hidden away indicate to you?"

"He feared he was being spied upon. And his letter spoke of coming into a great deal of money!"

"Then he was found dead, the back of his skull supposedly crushed by the edge of a display case. I have examined that case, Watson, and I'd stake my reputation that his head never came in contact with it. Garrett Aydin was murdered, and the reason for his violent death lies hidden in the Morley triangle of that letter, this misfiled map and the stolen book written by young Berengaria so many years ago. What do you see marked on this corner of the paper?"

I looked where Holmes was pointing. A faint drawing, made up of a series of half circles heaped up on one another with a thin line underneath curving away to the right, was visible. Another line ending in a narrow oval branched out from the first.

"It is a sketch of some sort."

"It is a rebus, Watson. That is to say, it is a puzzle where a word or phrase is indicated by a drawing. Doesn't that look to you like a berry?"

"Of course!"

"I think this map was drawn by the girl Berry after she had completed her manuscript. In it she distilled every clue as to the location of the Dyrebury Danger loot, but she still didn't know where it was. If she had, the treasure would have been recovered then. Mr. Aydin read the book and then he discovered the map. His letter to his brother indicated that he thought he could decipher the clues and find the riches. Lacking the book containing the story, our only chance to find the treasure and the man who killed for it is to solve the riddle concealed within this map. Come, Watson. A bell is no bell until you ring it and a map is no map until you follow its roads."

He returned the first two maps to their proper places and rang for Handy. In a few minutes we had on our hats and coats and were driving the dog-cart to Dyrebury, the old map tucked into Holmes' pocket.

Just past the village Holmes stopped the cart and pulled out the old map. He studied it for several minutes then turned off into a sunken lane that corresponded to one of the lines on the map marked with three of the "Xs'. He eagerly turned his head from one side of the road to the other and after ten minutes' travel slowed the trotting horse to a standstill.

"Behold, Watson! Our first discovery! What do you see?"

I followed the direction of his pointed whip and blinked. "I see a dry stone wall next to this road, if one could call such a trail a road. There is a gate leading into a meadow holding a small flock of sheep. Beyond that there is another wall and then rising ground that ends in a high hill. Silhouetted against the clear sky on the top of the hill is a thick growth of trees. What is so remarkable about that, Holmes?"

"Man, it is as plain as the nose on your face! On the side of that hill, just to the left of those big boulders! Do you see it now?"

"I see what appears to be a cave."

"Yes! And there, just past that crooked tree is another. There are three "Xs" marked on this road and I have no doubt that if we go down a little further we will find the third cave." He stirred the horse into action and in a few moments we could see the third cave set into the hillside, somewhat separated from its fellows.

"So every "X" on this map represents a cave," I remarked.

"That may be so, but we have uncovered too small a sample to confirm it as a theory. I counted twenty-seven "Xs" on the map. We must continue to check out these other marks." With that Holmes slapped the reins and we turned onto another road.

We drove for hours, back and forth across the countryside, following every line on the old map that had even one "X" marked on it. Every "X" corresponded to another cave. The sun was dipping past its zenith when we finally turned toward Dyrebury after pairing up the last cave with the last "X" drawn on the rough chart. Holmes had been content to locate the caves visually and never bothered to even ask me to leave the dog-cart and climb up to investigate them in person.

"It would be of no use, Watson," he said as we neared the village. "Every one of those caves has already been searched by bands of determined men looking for the treasure the Dyrebury Danger hid over two hundred years ago. Remember that Lord Sessamy told us that after Jarvis Sessamy's death every neighborhood cave was scrutinized for the gold and the jewels stolen from the pilgrim travelers bound for St. Galena's spring. I would not be surprised to learn that every adventurous local youth for generations has spent his summers rummaging about in those caves looking for that cache."

I was tired and hungry and looking forward to a late lunch when we turned into the courtyard of the "Lamb and Lion". Again I admired the large coaching inn with its two stories of open galleries, so rare in the bustling world of the late 19th century in which we lived. Much of the building was original in pale native limestone. Parts of it had been converted to small shops at the north end, but the rest of the structure was devoted to the age-old sale of food and liquor and the renting of rooms to travelers. The cobblestones of the wide courtyard showed heavy wear, but the windows were open and we could hear voices from inside. Cheerful red curtains fluttered from the casements and the inn's sign overhead gleamed with a coat of new paint.

Sherlock Holmes handed over the horse and cart to a young lad who led the weary animal off to a water trough to one side. We stepped out of the fall sunshine into a low-beamed, smoky, interior room that featured a long bar crowded with men well furnished with mugs of ale. Behind it stood the landlord, a wiry man of about thirty with blond hair and a cleft in his chin. He was kept busy as he filled the orders of the men lined up along the bar. An elderly barman assisted him. Along the opposite wall was a large space dotted with tables and chairs at which several parties were eating. I went to the bar and ordered beers and sandwiches while Holmes found an empty table and sat down.

I brought the beers to the table, sat, and took a long, refreshing drink. Holmes sipped at his and eyed our surroundings curiously. The most notable item in the place hung on a peg over the bar, over the rows of bottles, near a door that led to the back of the pub. It was a very old tri-corne hat, decorated with drooping ostrich plumes of a faded, dusty red. The rest of the room was made up of plastered walls, a planked floor, and two large, aged settles on either side of an enormous stone fireplace on the far wall. The tables and chairs available for customers were a mix of styles and ages, with Windsor chairs and gate-legged tables predominating. The clientele appeared to be mostly townspeople and locals, with a sprinkling of travelers visiting St. Galena's well. Soon a middle-aged woman in a long white apron brought us our sandwiches and Holmes thanked her.

"You seem to have a prosperous business here," he remarked. Holmes dropped a half crown by his plate. She gave him an appraising glance, then scooped up the money and dropped it in her pocket.

"Bless your soul, sir; I don't own th' "Lamb and Lion". I just do some of th' cookin' and work out front a bit. The Bonifaces have owned this place for generations an' made a good living at it, too. Mind you, they've had their problems, what with ol' Orion Boniface dyin' last year an' his son young Linus havin' t' pay death duties to keep th' inn goin'. He shook out ever' sack and dug into ever' drawer t' find th' money t' satisfy th' tax man an' now he goes about with a sharp eye on th' costs ever' day. More than once he's come into th' kitchen an' questioned th' cook, who's been here for nearly his entire lifetime, about th' price she paid for th' eggs or what th' apples cost, when she never got a peep from th' ol' man. He knew she was doin' her best, but th' young master is that nervous an' picky about things now, he's nigh on t' drivin' us all crazy."

"What can you tell me about that old hat hanging over the bar?"

"That's hung there since at least my great-granddad's time. I don't know why, but old Boniface was very proud of it."

"Well, if the food here is as delightful as the help, our lunch should be a real treat." Holmes dropped another coin on the table and in an instant both the second half crown and the waitress disappeared with a friendly wink.

The sandwiches were good and I enjoyed mine. Holmes barely touched his, his mind obviously not on the food. He stared at the old hat for the entire meal, then seeing that I had finished, drained his beer and got up to leave. Just as I turned toward the door, he gave a start. I turned quickly to see what had surprised him. I caught a glimpse of a shadow flitting across the wall behind the bar door that led deeper into the building. I instinctively took a step toward the apparition but Holmes caught me by my arm and steered me, instead, out the front door and over to our waiting dog-cart.

He urged me in and took up the reins, guiding the horse and cart out of the courtyard and back to the Castle. He didn't speak and the look on his face precluded my asking any questions. In silence he strode into the Castle as I handed the rig over to the stable boy. When I followed him, I found the door to the library firmly shut and at my query a familiar voice asked me to leave him alone. "I have to think, Watson," he said through the door and I heard nothing more.

Sherlock Holmes remained locked in the library all through dinner. Even when Lord Sessamy, confused by his guest's behavior and not reassured by my explanations, asked him if he was feeling all right, he received no reply. We left him there and finally retired. Lord Sessamy gave directions to the staff that if Holmes requested anything, anything at all, he was to be given whatever help the Castle could supply.

It was long after the breakfast buffet had been cleared away the next morning when Holmes finally opened the library door. He refused food. Instead he accepted a cup of coffee and declared that he had solved the riddle of the map.

"What is the solution?" asked the Baron eagerly. Holmes motioned us to be seated and filled his pipe from a pouch he brought out of his pocket. He indicated the hand-drawn map, spread out on the table.

"It has already been established that this is an old map, created by an amateur artist who was not trained as a cartographer. The map dates roughly from the early 1700s, as I established last night through a study of the paper and the ink. It covers the area around Dyrebury and Cliffdale Castle. Twenty-seven caves are marked on it. Landmarks like the "Forest", the "Lamb and Lion" and the "Bridge" are marked on the map. All these places are important points in the story of the Dyrebury Danger and Jarvis Sessamy. It was that story that was written in the early 1700s by the young author Berengaria. There is evidence that the map was drawn by young Berengaria. Berengaria's book was the only item missing after the violent death of Garrett Aydin, the librarian who wrote his brother that he might have enough money to invest in his brother's business and that he looks forward to the same happiness that would come to his brother as a married man.

"How could Mr. Aydin, a man who earned only a librarian's salary, look forward to coming into a great deal of money? He had no rich relations from whom he might inherit. Who was the mysterious woman Mr. Aydin mentioned to his brother, the woman who could be persuaded to marry him if his "discovery proves correct"? She is the woman who would accept him only if he comes into a large sum of money. Where would Garrett Aydin find such riches? If it is connected to the legend of the Dyrebury Danger, where has it been hidden so long? What was the final step of the search for the money that Berengaria missed and Mr. Aydin discovered? Most importantly, who killed the librarian and why?"

"Well, tell us, Mr. Holmes!" cried Lord Sessamy.

Sherlock Holmes shook his head. "I must do a bit of final investigation before all can be revealed," replied the detective. "I need an old suit of clothes and a pair of shabby boots. My face has been seen in Dyrebury, but now it is necessary to create a disguise to tie up the final last facts that will solve this case once and for all."

Bewildered, Lord Sessamy called Handy, whom Holmes swore to secrecy. In a few minutes the trusty butler supplied the necessary garments from his own cupboard. He even produced a disgraceful slouch hat. Owen Sessamy and I watched as a transformed Holmes, wearing the ill-fitting clothes, slipped away from the Castle toward Dyrebury, cutting across the fields and disappearing into the Forest that once sheltered Jarvis Sessamy.

We heard nothing more of him for the rest of the day. Under strict orders not to discuss his departure with anyone, Handy returned to his duties. Lord Sessamy and I, not having the luxury of required chores, remained in the library, pouring over the map and wondering about Holmes' movements and motives. We spoke in low tones, in order not to be overheard, and finally, bursting with curiosity and frustration, Lord Sessamy suggested that we take a gallop over the estate after lunch. I agreed and we spent a vigorous afternoon exploring the surrounding fields.

At sunset we returned to the Castle using the same route that had carried Jarvis Sessamy back home for the last time over two hundred years ago. There was no sign of Holmes. After dinner Lord Sessamy and I sat in silence over brandy and cigars in the library.

The clock sounded ten o'clock. I looked up to find Sherlock Holmes at the doorway. He had shed his disguise and stood clad in his own garments. He was holding an unlit dark lantern. Behind him Handy stood carrying our hats and coats. The butler stepped forward and offered them to us.

Holmes greeted us both in a cheerful manner.

"Good evening, gentlemen! It is past ten and most honest men have gone to bed. Would either of you like to accompany me to see the conclusion of this mystery of death and treasure?"

Lord Sessamy and I looked at each other. "Mr. Holmes!" the Baron cried. "Have you really solved the puzzle of how poor Mr. Aydin died?"

"I have every hope in bringing the entire affair to a head tonight, my lord. Here are your hats and coats. Thank you, Handy. Watson, have you your service revolver in your pocket? Good man! Here is the Baron's carriage ready for us and here is Constable Relyonn ready in the box. Forward, Constable!"

With a creaking of springs and a jangle of harness, the carriage rolled out of the Castle courtyard and down the drive toward Dyrebury with us three inside and the figure of a stolid Yorkshire policeman up high handling the reins.

"I made the constable's acquaintance this afternoon when he caught me lurking outside the back of the "Lamb and Lion"," Holmes remarked. "We had a long talk back at the station and came to a meeting of the minds. He was troubled by Garrett Aydin's death too, but the decision of "death by misadventure" from his superiors effectively closed his mouth. Now he has consented to help me test my theory based on the map, the book, and the letter."

"Where are we going, Holmes" I asked.

"We are on our way to the one spot that is the center of all the stories about the Dyrebury Danger, the reason Dyrebury is famous throughout the land and the one spot that is not on the old map; St. Galena's spring."

The horses drawing the carriage clip-clopped quietly through town, past darkened windows and closed businesses. All we could hear were the calls of a few night birds and the distant barking of

45

some farm dogs. The residences we passed were invisible in the darkness of the night with only an occasional streetlight to shed a glimmer on the cobblestones to indicate the street's existence. Rural communities like Dyrebury are accustomed to closing their doors earlier than the great cities, for farmers must rise early to care for their stock and properties. The moon was low in the black sky and few stars were visible. The only signs of life were lights gleaming behind the red curtains of the old coaching inn and the faint sounds of revelry that issued from within it, indicating that not all had yet gone to bed, despite the lateness of the hour.

Our pilgrimage's end was located halfway up a tall hill a half-mile from the last house outside Dyrebury on the far west side of the village. Behind a thick stand of trees was a little gully where the policeman left the carriage. We disembarked and, after Lord Sessamy introduced me to Constable Relyonn, we trudged around the rocks and brush of the hillside until we came to the front of the shrine. It was a pool of spring water surrounded by rocks and sheltered by an overhang of the cave behind it. Lord Sessamy murmured that the land on which the spring was located had been owned by an ancient family, now defunct. When the last owner died in his grandfather's time, the spring was acquired by the Sessamy family to keep control of the property within the district. Holmes lit the dark lantern and flashed its beam on the pool.

The circle of light from the dark lantern slid over the spring, barely the size of a large wash tub. Within, water bubbled up from beneath the surface, always in motion yet never overflowing the edge. There must have been a channel running away under the surface. Steps and an iron railing led down into the spring for the ease of the sick to bath their limbs. A few dead leaves floated on the surface. Holmes' light illuminated the stacks and piles of small stones and pebbles inside the cave left by centuries of pilgrims to show their faith and gratitude to St. Galena. On one side of the cave's mouth was placed a time-worn statue of the saint, bent over a suffering man as she offered him a drink from a chalice. Except for the burbling of the spring, all was silent.

Holmes pulled out his watch from his waistcoat pocket and held it up to the light from his lantern.

"Our travel here took longer than I calculated. I expect developments soon. Please find hiding place behind those boulders over there. We must be prepared to wait. Regrettably I don't believe it safe to smoke."

We took up our positions as directed and Sherlock Holmes slid the shutter closed on the lantern. That plunged us into the blackness of the surrounding night and left only the smell of hot metal behind.

Lord Sessamy and I were bursting with questions, but Holmes' statement effectively shut our mouths. The four of us huddled in the darkness. It was quiet except for the sound of our breathing. I couldn't check my watch, but we sat there long enough that I grew weary of the inactivity. I had just dared to stretch out my leg to relieve a cramp when we all heard scraping noises from the direction of the spring.

It was the sound of footsteps climbing up the hill, using the irregular limestone outcroppings as stairs to the pool. A bobbing lantern showed two figures labouring up toward us. They were the figures of a man and a woman. They reached the mouth of the cave by the water and the man dropped a shovel on the rocky ground. The woman placed the lantern next to the shovel and sat down on a large stone. He bent over her. His face was lit by the glow from the lantern. It was Linus Boniface.

We all strained to hear their conversation.

"It's a long climb up here," said the man. "You rest a while and then we'll go to work. My family has waited over two hundred years to claim their inheritance from Jarvis Sessamy and a few more minutes won't matter."

"It's no longer than the trip from the kitchen to the fifth floor of the Castle," replied the woman. I recognized her voice as that of Abigail the maid. "I've walked that often enough and for less reason than this. Oh, Linus, you have no idea how hard I've worked for this! Ever since Mr. Aydin took a shine to me and told me about his "great discovery" I've been trying to figure it out so you and I could get the treasure and finally be together!"

"You've been a clever girl and no mistake," said Linus Boniface. "What you put up with from that old man!"

"I had to encourage him in order to get his secret. It wasn't nice for me, you know. Every time he touched me I thought about you."

"I wish he had never put his hands on you. You know, when you lured him down to the library that night and he finally showed you the book that held the key, I was glad to smash in his head with that cosh. It gave me a lot of satisfaction to see him dying on the floor, with the blood running out, and know he'd never bother you again."

"I had him convinced that I'd marry him if he had enough money," said Abigail, with a low laugh. "Now I've spent a week reading that highwayman story and I know I've solved the puzzle. Just think, Linus, all that money your ancestor stole and was going to give to Bess Boniface! We'll dig up it up and be half-way to Edinburgh before sunrise. Oh, Linus, do you love me?"

The innkeeper grasped the housemaid with strong hands and kissed her passionately. "What a question to ask! Bring the lantern and just show me where to dig."

The deadly duo moved into the cave. We could hear the sounds of the piles of stones and pebbles clattering against each other as the two climbed over them to reach the inner depths if the cavern. Their light reflected off walls and the ceiling as they rounded a curve and disappeared within.

Sherlock Holmes broke the silence. "There you have your confession, Constable," he whispered.

"With plenty of witnesses to back it up in court," Relyonn growled. "I don't see why we can't just go in and grab them, Mr. Holmes."

"Have you ever seen a pair of rats backed into a corner with no way to escape? It is better this little drama be played out to the end. You will go home tonight with your murderers, Constable, and an iron-clad case to present to the judge. Now we must wait again."

It was just past midnight and the half-moon hung high in the sky behind a rack of black clouds. The wind picked up and we drew our coats about us as we huddled in the darkness. Dry leaves skittered across the rocks and got caught up in the stalks of dry grasses that fringed the spring. We could hear the sounds of digging from within the cave, for the walls seemed to have the power of amplifying noise. The soft thud of loose earth being thrown up with a shovel alternated with sudden clinks as the metal blade hit solid rock. A few minutes later the soft thuds would begin again, only to end when the limestone floor was exposed in a new place.

This exercise had occurred over and over again for better than two hours when we heard a loud shout and the shovel flew out of the cave and clanged against the rocks below. An instant later Abigail ran out, clutching the lantern, as Linus Boniface followed. She turned to face him by the large stone. By the light she carried we could see his face as he, clearly enraged, advanced toward the cowering woman. She tried to placate him with a trembling hand as she cried out.

"No, Linus! I was so sure! It must be in there! We just haven't dug in the right spot!" Her voice was cut off as his fingers closed around her throat.

"It's all rock! Solid rock to the middle of the Earth! For this I killed a man! You devil!"

Holmes reached him first, although we were all close behind. He tore the innkeeper away from the woman. The Constable managed to fix his handcuffs to Boniface's wrists but the wretch continued to struggle until Lord Sessamy thrust out a foot and tripped him up. Even prone he still writhed and shouted as the men secured his ankles with the Baron's necktie. I handed my revolver to the Baron, who held it on the innkeeper. I crouched over Abigail's limp body on the ground and shone the light from Holmes' bull's-eye lantern on her white face. Holmes left the others and came over to where I was tending to the woman.

"Is she badly hurt, Watson!"

"Bring me some of that water and quickly!"

Holmes dipped his handkerchief into the spring and handed it to me. I squeezed some liquid between her lips and bathed her neck where the bruises were forming. She gasped and trembled, then moaned and opened her eyes. Terrified, she looked up at us, and her expression changed to confusion.

"What happened? Where's Linus?" she whispered.

His shouting had stopped. Abigail struggled to sit up and I indicated his bound body. "He tried to kill you."

She gazed at her paramour. When she talked she could only croak out the words. "Don't hurt him, gentlemen! Don't hurt him! Oh, Linus, I'm sorry. I really thought the treasure was hidden here. I'm sorry! I am so sorry!" She burst into tears.

Constable Relyonn droned out the customary warning. Our prisoner snarled at us all then lapsed into a sullen silence. Lord Sessamy, Holmes and the policeman carried Boniface to the carriage. I determined that Abigail's injuries were not life-threatening and helped her to the coach. The constable and his two charges were deposited at the Dyrebury station where our statements were taken. Caught red-handed, Linus Boniface confessed to the murder, laying most of the blame on his lover. She, on the other hand, said that the idea was Boniface's. She admitted she had hidden Berengaria's book in the servants' quarters and had smuggled it out in her valise under our very eyes when she left the Castle in Boniface's hack.

The sun was just peeking above the Yorkshire hills when we three arrived back at the Castle. Handy opened the door and noted our disheveled appearances with a steady eye.

"Breakfast shall be ready in an hour, sir," he intoned to the Baron. "In the meanwhile I will have extra hot water taken up to your rooms."

Clean, fed and rested, we three met again in the Castle library that afternoon. Outside heavy grey clouds filled the sky and threatened a storm. The temperature had dropped, the wind blew steadily and we were grateful for the blaze in the fireplace. The lamps were lit and Handy had placed several additional candelabras on the table against the early darkness promised by the weather. We sat in armchairs before the fire, Holmes with his pipe and Lord Sessamy and I with cigars.

"Well, you have discovered the culprits and solved the murder, Mr. Holmes," said Owen Sessamy, "for which I thank you. Poor Mr. Aydin! I never realized he was ensnared in a romance with Abigail."

"Human nature, no matter how dedicated or controlled, will have its outlets, my lord," replied Holmes. "She is a perfidious woman. She went to great personal lengths to get the secret from Aydin. All the while the attraction between herself and Linus Boniface was of long standing. Both were ambitious and it was only lack of money that held them back from leaving Dyrebury and building a life together. I discovered as much in the alley behind the "Lamb and Lion" yesterday afternoon.

"When we were leaving the inn after our lunch I caught a glimpse of her through the doorway behind the bar. It was then that I realized that she had not gone to her sister's as she had told us. There was a connection between her and Linus Boniface. I rushed Watson out because I could not take a chance she would recognize us, and I later went back in disguise to discover more.

"She had Berengaria's book with her and was discussing it with Boniface. She declared that she could lead him to the treasure at once. Boniface said they had to wait until the inn closed after 10:30 to begin. He said his family had been searching for the Captain's share for generations. They considered it only fair that the descendants of Bess's child collect it. But Abigail figured wrong and the treasure wasn't buried in St. Galena's cave. I think even Garrett Aydin thought it was there."

Handy brought in a note on a silver salver. Lord Sessamy tore it open, read it and crumpled it up with a groan. He tossed the paper into the fire and turned to Holmes.

He sighed. "Well, the money is well and truly lost now. Every cave in the district, even the holy cave of the saint, has been searched and found wanting. That message was from my estate agent. I left word for him and a crew of men to drag the bottom of St. Galena's well this morning. It was the only place left to search. They found nothing. The treasure of the Dyrebury Danger shall forever by part of legend in the Yorkshire Dales."

We sat silently for several minutes, looking into the flames, until Holmes took the pipe from his lips and spoke.

"That is not necessarily true."

We looked at him in amazement. Lord Sessamy leaned forward.

"You don't mean to say that you know where the treasure is located!"

"I do," smiled Sherlock Holmes. "At least I know where Jarvis Sessamy hid it."

"Where is it, man?"

I echoed his question.

Holmes seemed to be waiting for us to ask. He leapt to his feet and grabbed a candlestick. "I take it that neither of you gentlemen are afraid of ghosts?"

"Holmes!"

"It's alright, Watson. I haven't changed my opinion on that subject and I know you haven't either. But we must brave the ominous depths of the Castle to solve this mystery and with a storm approaching the question might come up. It is time to pay a call on the other long-term inhabitant of Dyrebury Castle; the Grey Yeoman."

At the end of the corridor that housed the kitchens and storerooms of the Castle, we met Handy, already primed with sacks, a steel bar, and a shovel. He gripped a heavy ancient dresser that stood before a stone wall. With surprising ease, the dresser moved to one side. Holmes held up his light and pushed at the wall. It swung back to expose a secret chamber. A set of stones steps spiraled downwards. Holmes exchanged his candles for the dark lantern the butler carried and led the way.

"I never heard of this," exclaimed the Baron.

"I believe the secret died with Jarvis Sessamy," said Holmes. "I found it only after a lot of searching during the past few days. I have not spent all my time locked in the library."

The twisting steps led ever downwards for a long time. As the four of us descended the stone staircase the shifting flames of our candles and Holmes' light illuminated rime-streaked limestone walls. We came out into a narrow cold passageway far below the Castle. Over our heads was the vaulted ceiling of a corridor that stretched far ahead into darkness. We walked past the heavy barred doors of secret cells once used by the Baron's ancestors to imprison unfortunate captives from the Border Wars and other forgotten conflicts.

I heard the rustle of rats' feet and breathed in the dank, earthy air of an underground world neglected for hundreds of years. We brushed past spider webs and listened to the steady drip, drip of moisture oozing from the walls. I felt an oppressive feeling of great weight hanging over my head as we penetrated deeper under the Castle.

At long last we came to a jumbled pile of fallen masonry. Obviously it had fallen from the ceiling. After some hard labour we cleared a passageway to what lay beyond.

We climbed over the rocks and found ourselves in a huge square room. Two rows of massive Norman pillars stretched away to the dim opposite wall. With our lights we could see that many of the supports were broken and nearly two thirds of the arched roof they had supported had collapsed, the rubble filling the space before us. Faint light streamed in from above the broken ceiling and through the holes in the walls. It was still odiferous with the heavy odor of smoke from a massive fire five hundred years old.

Above our heads we could glimpse through the missing ceiling parts of a tall tower that reached up to ragged crenelations outlined against the darkening sky. There was a sudden clap of thunder and a lightning bolt streaked from one side of the battlement to the other. It illuminated burnt beams still sticking out from the stone walls, showing where floors had stood when the Castle was first built.

The ashes and rubble of the ancient conflagration covered the floor at our feet. A few signs of the rebuilding efforts of long ago moldered amidst the fallen beams and charred stones that had plunged down from the lofty heights to the tower's cellar floor five hundred years before.

"Behold the Grey Yeoman's lair," said Sherlock Holmes. "It has been feared for centuries as a place of supernatural activity. Shunned by all as the home of a mysterious apparition, this tower had developed its own legend. Jarvis Sessamy knew the legend and he knew the power of superstition that kept everyone away from this spot. He knew that the treasure of the Dyrebury Danger could remain hidden here for years and never be discovered, guarded by the trustworthy specter of the Grey Yeoman, loyal minion of the Baron of Dyrebury."

There were more rumblings from the massed grey clouds overhead. Holmes turned to the soot-covered walls of the chamber, holding his light close to the stones, obviously searching for the niche that must conceal Jarvis Sessamy's secret.

It was well-hidden. Behind a pile of fallen stones, wedged between two broken blocks, he pulled out an old metal strongbox. It was covered in rust and dirt, but one blow from the steel bar was enough to open it. The lid flew up. Within, a fortune of gold, silver and jewelry gleamed and sparkled as another lightning bolt shot across the sky far above. We marveled at the contents and began to fill the sacks Handy had brought with him. Suddenly a stone, from someplace far above, fell on the section of vaulted ceiling that still stood behind us. It brought down more blocks that crashed to the floor and threatened to bring down what remained of the room's roof. Was it the Grey Yeoman, faithful to his post, doing his best to protect that which a Sessamy had entrusted to his care so long ago? We didn't stop to ask. The pile of rocks we had to climb over would explain the earthquake long ago.

Back in the library, Lord Sessamy spilled out the treasure from the sacks to which it had been hastily transferred. Outside the storm had broken and heavy rivulets of rain ran down the stained glass windowpanes with noisy abandon. Inside we marveled at the crude hand-hammered coins bearing the names of ancient kings mixed with early machine-made coins stamped with the names of Charles I and James II. There were two necklaces fashioned of thick gold and inlaid with diamonds and emeralds. Several rings and three chains of precious metal in ancient designs shone in the light as we carefully polished each item picked out of the pile. Even Handy, who sat assiduously at work with his cleaning cloth looking for all the world as if he was merely caring for the Baron's table silver, could not keep himself from commenting on the shoals of wealth that passed through his fingers.

"Here's a gold piece marked with Oliver Cromwell's likeness," he marveled. "And here is another. I can make out Queen Bess's name on this silver piece and I do think this stone might be a ruby. However did you know where all this was hidden, Mr. Holmes, if I may ask?"

Holmes pulled out his pipe and filled it from his tobacco pouch. "Jarvis Sessamy was a wild, reckless young man. He didn't like rules but he liked to be in charge. He had a sharp sense of humour, as evidenced by his jibe at the fat merchant whose carriage he had torn apart. He told his men that he had hidden his share of the robberies in a cave. Yet every cave in the district has been searched and no treasure found. Nevertheless Jarvis Sessamy did not lie."

"How could that be possible?" asked our host.

"It is possible because the third son of your ancestor had a French mother. He didn't want anyone to discover his hiding place, but in a perverse sort of way he didn't want to lie to his companions. So he told them the truth. He hid his share in a cave. In French the word cave indicates a cellar or a vault."

"The cunning rascal!"

"Yes, he was cunning. Because of his cleverness, a good man is dead, two families have been dishonoured and a man and a woman face the gallows. And for what? For this so-called treasure, the ill-gotten gains of a rogue, a heap of coins and stones tainted by greed and violence, now to be picked by the Crown to end up enclosed behind glass and stared at by a curious public.

"So the last chapter of Berengaria's book can finally be written and the whole matter be laid to rest with Garrett Aydin. What's that, my lord? Brandy? Yes, let's raise a glass. To the pilgrims of St. Galena, all those who were helped and all those who were not and finally, to all those who had the misfortune to meet the Dyrebury Danger and contribute to this sparkling pile."

A few weeks later a letter arrived at 221b Baker Street in the early morning post. When my friend tore it open, two slips of paper fell out as he drew out the letter. I picked up the checks and looked at them in wonder.

"This is a lot of money, Holmes!"

Sherlock Holmes was reading the note. I noticed that it bore a crest at the top. "That is part of the finder's fee for the Dyrebury Danger treasure, Watson. My, my. Lord Sessamy writes that he has sent an equal share to Douglas Aydin, the librarian's brother in Australia. Mr. Handy's share allows him to take over the "Lamb and Lion". The balance will be used to benefit the citizens of Dyrebury and the surrounding district. He writes that he hopes by this action to make up for some of the troubles his ancestor visited upon the locals long ago. The trial of Linus Boniface and the woman Abigail will begin in a few weeks. We are invited to stay at the Castle during that time. There is one last thing Lord Sessamy wanted me to tell you."

"What is that?"

"He says that since the treasure was removed from the Castle no one has seen or heard anything of the Grey Yeoman. The lights have vanished, the cold spot is gone and the sounds from the tower have stopped."

"Owen Sessamy is a believer, Holmes."

"Í too have my beliefs, Watson, and one of them is that the workman is worthy of his hire. Let us take these checks around to our respective banks as soon as they open and then after you see your patients we can meet at one o'clock for something nutritious at Simpson's. There is a Chopin concert this afternoon at Albert Hall and I feel like celebrating. Just hand me the telephone and I'll make the reservations."

The Case of the Meandering Motorists

I was privileged to assist my friend Mr. Sherlock Holmes during twenty-three years of his remarkable career. As the years advanced and we both grew older our relationship altered. He was always independent, remaining in our original rooms at 221b Baker Street, eventually taking over the entire building and paying our landlady a princely sum for the convenience. Indeed, I wondered if he could have found a better home anywhere else in London. Mrs. Hudson waited on him hand and foot, put up with the strong reek of his chemical experiments and admitted the steady stream of troubled clients that rang her bell at all hours seeking the help of the famous detective. Although she rolled her eyes and complained *sotto voce* about his eccentricities, I believed her spirit would have been crushed if he had ever chosen another flat and moved away before his formal retirement took him to the hills of Sussex.

As the years passed and my personal circumstances caused us to spend less time together, I became more like a habit to him, like his pipe and his scrapbooks. I served as a sounding board for his theories and reflections, while also assisting as his trusted companion on some occasions when Holmes' investigations left the confines of 221b Baker Street. Many times we spent our hours together in the sitting room, relaxed in the worn armchairs, feet thrust toward the fire as he spoke over his current case, or, rarely, reminisced about old ones. Other times I was whisked out the door as soon as I appeared, to climb into a waiting hansom and clatter through the cobblestoned streets of London before I really knew what Holmes had planned for me to do.

Usually I was called to Baker Street, but sometimes Holmes came to me, either at my home or to the offices I maintained as my surgery. It was such a visit I received late one afternoon on a crisp September Friday afternoon during the last decade of the century. My final patient had just left and I was tiding my consulting room, putting my cleaned instruments away into the glass-fronted cabinets, when the door opened and Sherlock Holmes and Inspector Stanley Hopkins of Scotland Yard entered.

I had not seen Holmes in some weeks. He had been out of England, working a case in Italy involving a little boy who had disappeared with a traveling puppet show. The English newspapers had followed the progress of the case, which came to a satisfactory conclusion with the return of the little boy to his father. I shook hands warmly with both men and urged them to enter. Holmes looked thinner than usual, and I noticed that his hair seemed a little greyer at the temples. He smiled at me and seated himself in the chair behind my consulting desk. I greeted Hopkins, an old friend from Scotland Yard, and we turned to Holmes. He had spread out a large map of England over my blotter.

I stood behind him and peered at the map. It was folded to display a large section of the Midlands and the south-east area. Traced in red ink from Birmingham to West London was a twisting, convoluted line, running through miles of country roads from the great manufacturing city south toward Bath and then eastward to London.

"You may well look puzzled, Watson," Holmes laughed. He pointed to the wavy, contorted red line. "This is the route of one of the most unusual road races ever staged in Great Britain. Sir Harvey Harris, who owns several steel mills in Birmingham, has developed an experimental gasoline motor car. He spent a lot of time and money on it, employing the best engineering minds of the Midlands. He was proud of his "Fast Leap". But he found a fly buzzing about his head just as he was ready to unveil it to the public, an annoying fly that would not go away and let him enjoy his triumph.

"Egbert Shelby is a former mechanic in one of Harris' factories, a worker with a dream. He laboured on his own time, studied the literature, built his own parts, and tinkered for years on his own automobile invention. He rolled out his "Shelby Sled" one day before Harris announced his accomplishment. The public took up his side, preferring to champion the little inventor, working in his back garden, over the rich and powerful Sir Harvey Harris, with his hired minds and muscles.

"A feud quickly developed in the newspapers. The entire mess has culminated in a road race, from Birmingham to London, and may the best motor win. The *Birmingham Voice* offered a prize of 2,000 pounds to the winner. This writhing course, designed to test the machines' endurance involving every variation of road condition available in England, is supposed to prove which is the better invention.

"The rules of the race as set forth by the *Birmingham Voice* stated that each motorcar owner was allowed one assistant to help with maintenance and relief driving. Sir Harvey Harris chose Kit Travelore, the second son of General Travelore, the hero of Point Ramble. After leaving Oxford early, the boy had devoted himself to mechanics and become quite an expert on internal combustion engines.

"Shelby asked his son, Miles, who helped him in building the "Shelby Sled", to assist him."

"I read about the race in the morning paper." I mused. "It began Monday morning, from in front of the Birmingham Botanical Gardens, and is due to finish at the London Botanical Gardens in Regents Park on Saturday, which is tomorrow."

"That's right, Dr. Watson," said Stanley Hopkins. He indicated a point on the map where the red line ended in the nearby London park. "I have been assigned to be at the finish line. Each leg of the race has been divided into fifty-mile sections, with a resting place reserved each night at a local inn or hotel. They will stay at Walker-on-Thames tonight, which is fifty miles from Regent's Park. Sir Harvey Harris and Mr. Shelby are expected to complete the race tomorrow. The race results depend upon the time spent to complete each leg, plus extra points given for crossing the finish line first."

"But, Inspector, what has this to do with you? I see no crime here."

"On Wednesday the fifty-mile race section ended at the "Pilgrim's Rest" Inn near Standhill Abbey, the ancestral home of the Duke of Treadlow. That night a dinner was given with the contestants as guests of honor by the Duke and Duchess. The Duke has investments in one of Sir Harvey's factories. The guest list included several local dignitaries. Thursday morning, after the vehicles left on the next leg of their trip, an alarm was raised. Two important jewelry pieces, a diamond and gold necklace worn the night before by the Duchess and the famous Mitgleid rope of pearls owned by her mother-in-law, the Dowager Duchess, were missing. The Duke demanded Scotland Yard be called in at once. Detective Sergeant Proudfoot and I left for Standhill Abbey by the next train. I met Mr. Holmes on the station platform, just returning from Italy, and invited him to accompany us."

"What was found?"

Holmes took over the story. "We arrived at mid-morning. The Abbey is situated on an estate of over 20,000 acres, with extensive gardens, woods, several working farms, a small village and a large lake. The main building was constructed on the ruins of an ancient Catholic abbey destroyed by Viking invaders long before Henry VIII had the same thought. The modern construction shows its Tudor bones, along with early Norman and later Georgian traces, and stands at the top of the highest hill in the district. Hence it was given the name Standhill. The main road runs past at the bottom of the hill and was part of the race course.

"The entrance, flanked by a pair of granite pillars topped with the Treadlow eagles, splotched and stained with centuries of lichen and mosses, led through nearly a mile of old-growth forest to the massive stone porch of the ancient pile owned by the Treadlow family. A broad sweep of crushed gravel brought our carriage to the wide, shallow steps. A silent, dignified butler stood ready to admit us as we approached the iron strap-hinged double doors that opened to the vast garde-room, now used as an entrance-hall.

"We were ushered past an intricately carved oaken staircase into the presence of the Duke and Duchess of Treadlow. He is a tall, broad man, his Norman heritage plain on his face and demeanor. She is a slight, richly-dressed woman, well-known for her head of lustrous copper hair. The Dowager Duchess remained upstairs in her bedroom, unwilling to sully herself with any contact with the police. The Duke did the majority of the talking.

"After the dinner Wednesday evening the jewels had been locked in a drawer in the Duke's walnut armoire in his dressing room on the second floor, down the hall from the oaken stairs. That was the normal practice after parties; it saved the servants a special trip down to the wine cellar where the safe is kept. The next morning the two custom-made cases would have been transferred downstairs to the basement safe, situated in a special stone room, well-fortified by steel gates and the latest in locks. The valet entered the dressing room early Thursday morning and found the drawer had been forced with a narrow metal tool like a narrow chisel. There were no footprints on the carpets or stairways but that was not surprising, since the weather had been dry for the past two weeks. The immediate windows, including those of the dressing room, the Duke's bedroom and the window at the end of the hallway outside his doors, were securely fastened and showed no sign of tampering. These physical facts I determined for myself, upon examination of the crime scene.

"The gravel of the driveway sweep was normally kept neat and even by twice-daily raking. It had been cleaned and rolled very early that morning, as scheduled, and was useless for indicating any sign of the thief or thieves.

"I spent the day with Hopkins, interviewing the occupants of the Abbey, including the family, the twenty-five house servants, the fourteen outside servants and eight of the twelve guests that were available from the local population. The Duke and Duchess were co-operative, but you have never been royally snubbed until you have tried to question the Dowager Duchess of Treadlow about a criminal case. The interview took place in her boudoir, a great favor, to be sure.

"She did tell us that Sir Harvey Harris talked a lot during dinner, giving them an elaborate, highly detailed account of the race, starting at the gates of the Birmingham Botanical Gardens and including every breakdown, repair and delay of the trip. The captive audience included the family, the vicar, the local magistrate, the doctor, and the largest landowner in the district besides the Duke, along with their wives.

"The four guests we couldn't interview were Sir Harvey, Kit Travelore, and Egbert Shelby and his son Miles. You remember that Travelore and young Shelby served as members of the motorcars' crews.

"It was determined by higher-ups at Scotland Yard that during the early investigation Stanley Hopkins was not to interrupt the race but to wait and question Sir Harvey and Mr. Shelby at Regents Park after the winner is declared.

"We couldn't complete all the interviews that day so we put up at the "Pilgrim's Rest". After we saw the last of the witnesses this afternoon, Hopkins and I took the afternoon train home. A thorough search of the Abbey and its extensive grounds is still being conducted under the guidance of Sergeant Proudfoot."

"What had you discovered, Holmes?" I asked.

"Nothing unusual happened during the festivities. After the meal was over and the locals and the contestants left, the Duchess' maid removed her diamond and gold necklace and placed it in its custom-made case. The rope of pearls was put into a similar case and both were locked in a drawer in the Duke's dressing room by his valet.

"Both servants slept in the servants' wing that night, as they usually did. They had strong alibis. The Duke's head housemaid had a bad toothache and was up and down all night, prowling the servants' quarters for relief. Her story was backed by that of the housekeeper, who was treating her. The ladies' maid never left her room. The valet shares his room with the under-butler. He had a history of sleepwalking in the past, so the under-butler routinely locks the door and sleeps with the key under his pillow. He swears the valet could never have left the room. All the servants with any possible contact with the jewels have worked for the Duke's family for years and have no criminal records.

"There was one odd occurrence. Bootner, the valet, said that on his way up to his room in the servants' quarters after locking up the jewel-cases, he thought he saw a shadow on the wall as he rounded the landing right above the Duke's floor. It was below and behind him, in the corridor outside the Duke's rooms. He retraced his steps and examined the entire hallway but saw and heard nothing more. After a minute or so he decided he must have been mistaken and went up to his bed.

"Stanley Hopkins and I spoke to the other guests. They were the vicar, Dr. Goodpastures, the local magistrate, Col. Lawson, the physician Dr. Steele, and Sir Richard Landers, who owns the second –largest estate in the county. We also talked to their wives. On the train ride back to London today we compared notes. We gleaned a wealth of information on the subjects of county gossip and local politics, but nothing about the burglary. The contestants wanted to get an early start, so the party broke up by ten. All the guests had left before eleven o'clock, saying goodbye in the driveway as they were put into their carriages.

"Indications are that the theft is not an inside job. The outside door to the pantry storeroom had been forced. There was also a new break in the hedge in the direction of the main road."

Stanley Hopkins shook his head. "Sir Harvey and Mr. Shelby, since they were guests of the Duke and Duchess that night, need to be interviewed also, along with their crews. That is why Mr. Holmes and I are meeting them right after the race tomorrow."

"I took the liberty of suggesting to Inspector Hopkins that you come along, Watson." Holmes began folding up the map. "I thought you might enjoy the diversion."

I accepted eagerly. A time was set for me to be met by Inspector Hopkins Saturday and the two men left. I locked up my surgery and headed home through the waning light of the streets. As I walked past the buildings that lined my usual path through the labyrinth of London, I noticed the traffic around me. The streets were filled with the ordinary carriages, drays, hansom cabs and growlers that daily crawled through the capital city. I saw horses that were well-cared for and old hacks that barely could pull the loads they were lashed to trudge past me in an unceasing tide. Then the sounds of horses' hooves and the rumble of steel-shod wooden wheels were interrupted by the putt-putt of an internal combustion engine and the smell of oil.

I looked around. One of the new-fangled automobiles, its polished mahogany bodywork gleaming in the gaslight and with its front seat occupants resplendent in white dusters and round-lens goggles, was chugging up the street. I recognized Lord

Spedwell, the MP, and his chauffeur as they headed to the Houses of Parliament for a night session. One thing was true, I thought to myself. Motoring was a rich man's game, with toys so expensive that they would never be able to be afforded by regular citizens. The most that might be expected by John Bull would be public transit in the form of large, awkward omnibuses. I looked forward to the opportunity to examine closely these dashing new inventions while Holmes and Hopkins talked to the two contestants.

Saturday I held surgery as usual in the morning and returned home for lunch. I perused the latest edition of the paper with my meal. The Treadlow robbery was the headline, with news that the two jewel cases taken from the Duke's dressing room had been found in a copse of trees near the main road as a result of the search of the grounds. The case designed to carry the diamond and gold necklace was empty, but the other still contained the Mitgleid rope of pearls.

What could be the meaning of such a find? I wondered. The diamond necklace was worth 24, 000 pounds, according to the paper. But the rope of perfectly matched Oriental pearls handed down in the Mitgleid family since the time of Charles I was reported to be priceless and could be sold on the Continent for twice that amount. Why had such a valuable item been left behind?

The rope of pearls was historically important. Yet the pearls were never taken out of their case. If they were not to be stolen, why was the case taken at all? As I mulled over those baffling questions, the maid announced the arrival of Stanley Hopkins' cab. I joined him in the growler and we swung past Baker Street to pick up Holmes on our way to Regents Park and the London Botanical Gardens.

In the cab with the great detective, I was bursting with questions, but Holmes turned them back with a raised eyebrow. "Must I remind you, Watson, that it is a capital mistake to theorize before you have all the data? Thanks to young Hopkins here, I've been receiving regular reports from Standhill Abbey since yesterday. I sent Wiggins, my Baker Street irregular lieutenant, to the telegraph office asking for particular information from several sources. I received two answers and I expect the third to arrive momentarily. Wiggins is waiting back in Mrs. Hudson's kitchen, making deep inroads on yesterday's cold steak and kidney pie, ready to deliver the final message to me at the race's finish line. Meanwhile, I see the crowds are gathering. We must be near the Botanical Gardens entrance."

Indeed, the press of the crowds hurrying to see the end of the celebrated race was growing and the cab was finding the way increasingly impossible. Finally we dismounted from the growler and pushed our way to the imposing Administration building. Grandstands had been erected before its front door to mark the finish line and to hold invited dignitaries and the press. We passed through the doors and were met inside by the Director of the London Botanical Gardens, Sir William Jardin. He was a short man in his middle years, formally garbed, with a brown pompadour and a monocle stuck in his right eye.

"Indeed, it is an honour to meet such a famous neighbor as you, Mr. Holmes. Baker Street is so near it is a wonder we haven't met before this. And Dr. Watson! I have followed your stories with great interest. Inspector Hopkins, I don't quite understand what you need from me. The officers of the

71

Metropolitan Police are doing a fine job with the crowds. Even the members of the press, including newsmen from all over the British Isles and abroad, have behaved well. I see no reason for the presence of the C. I. D."

"Mr. Holmes and I just need a few minutes with the two contestants, Sir Harvey Harris and Mr. Shelby, after the race is over. It is in connection with the theft of the Treadlow diamond necklace."

"Oh, yes. I did hear something about a jewel robbery earlier in the week from my wife, but I have been so busy preparing for today I didn't pay it any attention. The latest word from the racers is that their scores are equal and the final decision will be decided by the automobile that gets over the finish line first. I have reserved seats in the grandstand for you all, just behind myself and Lord Spedwell. Lord Spedwell is presenting the prize, you know. Look at the time! This way, please, gentlemen."

We walked out of the Administration Building into a mob of people. As far as the eye could see the crowds spread out to the horizon, surrounding the Botanical greenhouses and other buildings like a human sea. Thousands of men, women and children were thronging across the Park grounds, jostling for space to see the finish. Many were laden with picnic baskets, umbrellas and folding chairs. Muffin men were selling hot treats, and ginger beer sellers ranged about, doing a brisk business. I even recognized some bookies working the crowds, money changing hands discreetly.

The street before the grandstand was marked with a red line painted on the cobblestone surface. A flapping Finish Line sign hung over it. A double line of police kept the crowd back from the course. The London Automobile Club had hired a brass band and stationed it opposite the grandstand, where it was playing popular tunes from the music theatres of the West End. Holmes, Hopkins and I had just taken our seats on the packed risers when a cheer broke out. Lord Spedwell had arrived and was being escorted to his place next to the Botanical Gardens Director.

Soon there was a shout from someone in a high window of the Administration Building behind us. The motorcars were approaching!

I recalled from the map Sherlock Holmes had showed me in my office that the race course ran once around Regent's Park on the Outer Circle then led into the Inner Circle, where it ended in front of the Administration Building. Now, with thousands of others, I watched eagerly as two dark spots in the distance slowly resolved themselves into a pair of motorcars, trailing clouds of dust and smoke as they circumvented the Gardens beyond the crowds. The people fell silent as they followed the sight of the vehicles as they puffed around the track. When the machines drove behind the Administration Building a roar went up and there was a surge toward the grandstand. A few moments later the sound of the motorcars grew louder and the dusty, travel-worn automobiles turned into the home stretch.

Everyone in the stands, including myself, got on their feet. The larger vehicle, obviously the invention of Sir Harvey Harris, was in the lead. It had a high wooden body set on four pneumonic tyres, with Sir Harvey and another man occupying the front seat. The afternoon sun glinted on the goggles of the driver who clutched the steering wheel as the other man waved to the crowd.

Just behind them chugged the Shelby automobile. It was of lighter build, really just an old buggy body set on wire bicycle wheels, being guided with a tiller by one of two muffled figures seated in it. It was covered in a thick layer of dust, obviously thrown up by the machine in front of it. Suddenly there was a loud report and Sir Harvey's vehicle began throwing out great black clouds of smoke. Slowly it rolled to a stop, just yards short of the finish line. The little motorcar slipped past it and chugged across the line, braking to a stop just past the grandstand.

The crowd yelled and the police struggled to hold the excited people back from engulfing the two machines. It was several minutes before order was restored and the two Shelbys, father and son, stood beside Lord Spedwell. Sir Harvey Harris and his crewman, Kit Travelore, sullenly stationed themselves nearby.

The black smoke had ceased pouring out of the "Fast Leap", and a cordon of officers surrounded it, protecting it from the crowd. A similar party of men encircled the "Shelby Sled" as an elbowing mass of photographers attempted to take pictures of the winner.

Mr. Jardin began his speech. He was followed by Lord Spedwell, who spoke on behalf of the London Automobile Club. The London representative of the *Birmingham Voice* pronounced the "Shelby Sled" the winner and Lord Spedwell presented Egbert Shelby with a check.

Mr. Shelby replied briefly to the speeches and the ceremony was over in a few minutes. With the excitement over the thousands of people gathered to witness the end of the race dispersed quickly. It was nearly time for tea.

Now it was the turn of the gentlemen of the press. There were more pictures taken and both Mr. Shelby and Sir Harvey submitted to answering shouted questions. Finally the crowd thinned and the men were able to direct their attention to their machines.

With the members of the press and the photographers gone, Mr. Jardin and Lord Spedwell quickly departed.

As we left the stands and approached the four, young Wiggins, Holmes' little lieutenant of the Baker Street Irregulars, the band of urchins who served as the detective's eyes and ears around London, ran up. He gave a yellow telegram form to Holmes, who tossed him a coin he caught in his grimy hand. The boy was gone by the time my friend had read its contents and put the paper in his pocket. When Hopkins and I reached Holmes he was standing next to the two vehicles, which had been rolled to a patch of lawn beside the grandstands. I pulled my attention away from the two automobiles to focus on the four meandering motorists who had just completed the famous race.

Young Miles Shelby stood by the "Shelby Sled", his hands in his pockets. Kit Travelore, son of the famous General, with the chest and the limbs of a Hercules, had his hands deep in the engine of Sir Harvey's automobile, a frown on his slab-like face.

Sir Harvey was of medium height with a head of brown hair, large ears, prominent front teeth and an air of entitlement that draped him like a cloak.

"I don't understand it," Sir Harvey was saying, hovering by Travelore's side, his attention on the engine of his motorcar. "There was no reason for that backfire or all that smoke."

Egbert Shelby was short, with rounded shoulders, straw-coloured hair, a long wrinkled neck and freckles spotted all over his face and hands. He folded the prize check and tucked it into the pocket of his duster.

"Mine was just the superior vehicle, Sir Harvey. Not bragging, just a fact."

Sir Harvey Harris swelled up with indignation and opened his mouth to speak.

Shelby was faster. "Before you tell me again, in excruciating detail, how the finest engineers of the Midlands worked months on creating your "Fast Leap" in all its perfection and cost, let me remind you again who won this race. This money is very welcome, but I have decided that my real reward for coming in first is that I will never have to listen to one more word about you, your vehicle, and your factories and how sure you were of the results of today's race. In short, Sir Harvey, please go away. I know I am not considered a gentleman in your circle, but I can assure you that with your arrogance, your insensitivity and your self-centered talk, you would not be considered a gentleman in mine."

Sir Harvey's face turned bright red and he looked as if he was going to have a stroke. Stanley Hopkins intervened. "I am Inspector Hopkins from Scotland Yard. I need to ask you all some questions about the dinner given to you by the Duke and Duchess of Treadlow at Standhill Abbey Wednesday night."

Sir Harvey turned his anger on this fresh target. "What are you blabbering about? What does that evening have to do with Scotland Yard? In case you don't know, I am a personal friend of the Duke, not to mention the Home Secretary, and I protest being harassed in this fashion by some police flunky!"

"Sir Harvey! My name is Sherlock Holmes and this is my friend Dr. Watson. I can assure you that this concerns a serious theft, and your cooperation will be greatly appreciated."

"I heard something about a jewelry theft, a few days ago, but I didn't know it happened at the Duke's. I have no objection to questions, Mr. Holmes, and neither does my son," said Egbert Shelby. "We will gladly help in Scotland Yard's investigation."

Sir Harvey grimaced. "Well, I'm going to have to consult with my solicitor, Inspector. I don't believe that incident had anything to do with me."

"Where is young Travelore?" I asked. At the announcement of Holmes' name, the fourth man had turned away from our group.

"There he goes, across the lawns. He grabbed something from the boot of Sir Harvey's motor and left." Miles Shelby pointed to the duster-clad figure moving away with the dwindling crowd.

"After him, men! He's the thief!" Holmes shouted. Hopkins and my friend ran after the retreating figure across the trampled grass of the Gardens. Two constables from the group guarding the automobiles joined in, their truncheons bobbing wildly at their belts as they stumbled after Travelore. I joined in the chase, leaving a bewildered Sir Harvey and the Shelbys gazing after us.

Travelore glanced behind and saw us. His quick trot turned into a run. While he ran, he seemed to shove some bulky items into his coat pockets. I gauged the distance and the terrain. I saw he was headed toward the Broad Walk that bisected Regents Park on the east. It was thick with retreating members of the great crowd gathered to witness the race's end. I veered off from the other men dodging through the scattered revelers.

I had not exerted myself like this since the days of Charles Augustus Milverton and the desperate dash across the moors during the case I later wrote up as "The Hound of the Baskervilles". I felt the passage of the years since those days in the strain on my lungs and the pull on my leg muscles. Yet I knew that if he reached that crowd, he could melt away into the millions that made up the population of London and never be seen again.

I managed to cut the distance between us. As he rounded a clump of bushes I called upon my Rugby experience, found a last burst of energy and tackled him. We crashed to the ground and rolled until we came up against another bush. Strong hands reached down and pulled him up. I regained my feet to see Kit Travelore in the clutches of Inspector Stanley Hopkins.

Sherlock Holmes steadied me. "Watson! Watson! Indeed, I shall never get your limits! Why, you've not lost a bit of your old form! The same blithe old boy as ever!"

I was winded by the run and bruised by the fall, but Holmes' words warmed my soul. He seldom gave compliments and I treasured his words.

"Just helping, Holmes."

"And a good job, too," said Stanley Hopkins. The two policemen ran up, soon followed by Sir Harvey Harris and both of the Shelbys. One of the policemen clicked a pair of handcuffs on Travelore's wrists. "Another minute and he would have left the

Park and been gone. What do you have to say for yourself, young man?"

Travelore held up his manacled hands. "Why am I under arrest? The race was over and I was just leaving."

"You were leaving with the Duchess of Treadlow's necklace. Search his pockets, Hopkins," said Holmes.

A make-shift contraption made up of tubes and wires, about the size of a small book, was retrieved from one pocket. I looked at it in wonder.

"What in the world is that?"

Sir Harvey and the Shelbys, father and son, joined us. "Let me see that," said Miles Shelby. Hopkins handed it to him and the young man turned it over in his hands.

"I recognize this piece as a smoke bomb. If these wires were hooked up to the automobile accelerator, the explosion would have cut access to the petrol line. There would be an explosion with smoke and the engine would stop"."

Sherlock Holmes pulled a large round tin out of Travelore's other coat pocket. A continued search yielded nothing else. Holmes examined the flat, round container.

"Whatever Travelore may have done to make Sir Harvey's machine lose the race, there is no sign of a necklace, Holmes," I said. "Just that tin of grease. Travelore acted as mechanic for Sir Harvey's motorcar. It would be natural for him to have a tin of grease in his pocket. He would use it for maintenance of the vehicle."

Holmes smiled and held out the tin. "Read what is printed on the label, Watson."

"Voyage Axle Grease for Carriages."

"Precisely, Watson. This is grease for the lubrication of carriage wheels. Motorcars use an internal system for greasing their wheels. This tin's contents are useless for an automobile."

"Then why would Travelore carry it about?"

"That is a very good question, my friend. Do you remember the one unusual fact of this case? Didn't it strike you as odd that while two necklaces were stolen, one was left behind at the scene?"

"Yes, it did."

"Both the gold and diamond necklace and the rope of pearls were taken because they were in identical locked cases. Only when the thief broke open the cases did he know which necklace to steal. The determining factor was the means of transport. The pearl necklace wasn't taken because it couldn't be smuggled away by the thief."

"But the pearl necklace was worth twice what the gold and diamond one was!" said Hopkins.

"The very act of hiding the rope of pearls from inquisitive eyes would have destroyed its value." Holmes took the tin and pried open the lid. Inside was a dark pool of thick grease, glistening in the light. "Watson, give me your handkerchief, if you please."

I pulled out my handkerchief and watched in fascination as Holmes' thin, sensitive fingers dug into the tin's contents. After a few moments we gasped as he pulled forth a long, blobby, slimy object from the grease. He ran it through his fingers and handed it to me. It was heavy and slick, dripping black drops onto the grass. I wrapped it in the cloth and tried to wipe off some of the oily covering. I nearly dropped it in shock as my efforts produced a glimpse of gold and a flash of diamonds. I was holding the Duchess of Treadlow's gold and diamond necklace!

Sherlock Holmes calmly wiped his fingers on his own handkerchief. At the sight of the recovered jewelry, Kit Travelore struggled against the two policemen who held him, but his efforts were futile. Inspector Hopkins gave commands and the prisoner was taken away to Scotland Yard. Hopkins took possession of the necklace and ruined his own handkerchief polishing off the last of the grease.

"There must be quite a story behind how you figured out who was the thief, Mr. Holmes," he said. "I will need the information for my report."

"Come to Baker Street this evening and I'll explain," Holmes replied. "Meanwhile, hand over your soiled handkerchief to Hopkins, Watson. Undoubtedly he needs to include it as evidence in his report. In its present state it's of no use to you."

By eight o'clock that evening, Stanley Hopkins was settled in my old armchair at 221b Baker Street. I sat on the sofa and Sherlock Holmes lounged in his own armchair except when, during his explanation, he rose to pace back and forth across the carpet. Brandy was served and our guest was encouraged to smoke. Stanley Hopkins and I had cigars while Holmes lit his old clay pipe and smiled at us both.

"I will start at the beginning and answer any questions you may have at the end. When we arrived at Standhill Abbey I examined the scene of the crime before we talked to any of the Abbey's inhabitants. As I said, Watson, it was clearly an outside job. The storeroom door was forced, the outer means of access at the upper floor was securely locked and the alibis of the servants, the guests and the family were iron-clad.

"Yet the thief needed intimate knowledge of the Abbey in order to know where the jewels were kept after a party. My attention centered on the meandering motorists. I questioned the Duke about them.

"Mr. Egbert Shelby and his son Miles had never been to Standhill Abbey. That is not surprising considering their social circumstances. Kit Travelore's father, the General, had visited a few times with his wife, as a social lion collected by the Duchess. Sir Harvey Harris, on the other hand, owned successful factories that the Duke had invested in, and between social and business interests, practically had the run of the place. He would be the most familiar with the Abbey's routines."

Hopkins looked at Holmes. "Are you saying Sir Harvey was involved in all this? You pulled that tin of grease out of young Travelore's pocket yourself."

"Kit Travelore had no *first-hand* knowledge of the routines of Standhill Abbey, gentlemen. However, remarks given by the Dowager Duchess of Treadlow and Mr. Shelby indicated that Sir Harvey likes to talk. And talk. And talk.

"Imagine Kit Travelore, sitting beside Sir Harvey day after day during the race, listening as his employer continually chattered for hours, bragging about his factories, his accomplishments and his connections, including the famous and very rich Duke of Treadlow and his ancient family. I'm sure that the entire layout of Standhill Abbey and details about every daily habit were repeatedly laid out during the early days of the race.

"The telegrams I sent out inquired into the financial status of Sir Harvey, Mr. Shelby, Miles Shelby and Kit Travelore. Egbert Shelby sunk his life's savings into creating the "Shelby Sled". He had to deny his son's request to attend medical school because every spare penny went into the machine. So the Shelbys, father and son, had use for 24,000 pounds, the worth of the necklace. But the 2,000 pounds of prize money was enough to send young Miles to medical school.

"Sir Harvey had spent a lot of money developing his "Fast Leap" but he was better able to afford it. His motorcar was an expensive hobby. He had many chances to steal the necklace during his previous visits to the Abbey, but no reason to take it.

"Kit Travelore, on the other hand, had left Oxford under a cloud. It seems there were questions raised about certain gambling clubs of which he was a member.

Holmes pulled the yellow telegram form he had received that afternoon out of his pocket. "It pays to have discreet friends on Fleet Street.

"The General had managed to keep the scandal out of the papers, but Travelore was forced to leave his staircase and face life with only an inadequate (he thought) allowance. The entire route and the stopping places each night were published in the papers even before the race began. The dinner party at Standhill Abbey had been announced by the press long before the motorcars started from the Birmingham Botanical Gardens. The General's son must have had the idea about the necklace before the race began because he cobbled up that smoke bomb and brought along the tin of grease. After Travelore was taken away I examined the tools in the "Fast Leap" boot. I found a metal screwdriver with signs of furniture varnish on its tip. Kit Travelore was the second son, with no hope of inheritance. 24,000 pounds would have been very handy indeed.

"The final proof was when he ran. I must say, my dear Watson, I am greatly impressed with the agility you displayed this afternoon. It was quite like the old days. Now, Inspector, let me offer you another glass of this fine old brandy. The *vino* of Italy has its points, but nothing equals a glass of wine at home in the company of old friends."

The Case of the Lost Lad

It was February in Baker Street and no one had knocked on our door in nearly a week. The newspapers were full of nothing but politics and weather reports. Sherlock Holmes had kept busy during those days by researching the physical effects of the musical scale on the common house-fly, although where he had obtained a supply of house-flies in the depths of winter was beyond me. We heard the ring of the bell below and in a few moments Mrs. Hudson brought in a calling card on a salver. I sat up from my position on the sofa, where I had been trying to concentrate on a yellow-backed novel. Holmes put aside his violin on which he had been plunking odd notes and picked up the bit of cardboard.

"Edged in black, Watson," said he, "with the name Mrs. Laurie Vogelbauer engraved with a Cheshire address. Well, it must be a serious case indeed that would bring a young widow so far from home to consult with a London detective. Send her up, Mrs. Hudson."

He threw a handkerchief over the glass jar of flies that stood on the windowsill, and exchanged his purple dressing gown for a frock coat. I straightened my tie and looked at him inquiringly.

"How do you know she is a young widow, Holmes, and with a serious case?"

"A calling card edged in black indicates the death of a close relative," he replied, "and the use of the first name Laurie indicates she is young. An older woman would have used the formal designations Laura or Laurel as an indication of her dignity. She has the title Mrs. on her card, indicating a marriage, but it does not bear a man's name, showing he is no more. Men named Lawrence sometimes are called Laurie, but never on a formal calling card. Also, the card is a woman's card, shown by the delicate font selected. Her husband's death would explain the black border. Therefore, she is a young widow with what she considers a serious problem, evident by her willingness to bear the travails of a journey to London in such weather as February brings the patient Londoner."

A few minutes later Mrs. Laurie Vogelbauer was seated on the sitting room sofa, telling us about her situation and in so doing confirming all of Holmes' deductions.

She appeared to be in her later twenties, of medium height, dressed in deep mourning, the black hair under her widow's cap and veil touched with a few premature grey hairs. Her face was pale and drawn. Her fingers, thin like the rest of her, rested on her lap, clutching a black reticule. Her dark eyes, however, gazed at Holmes steadily, and there was no hesitation in the direct manner in which she addressed the detective. She had a very slight accent.

"My brother and I are the children of Antonio Bass, the Italian tenor, who made such a success at the Royal Opera Theatre back in the '70s," she began.

"Our mother is English and insisted that my brother be educated at Durham. She made a home for us there during his college years. My father continued to travel and work during that time. Unfortunately neither Robert nor I inherited his musical talents. Robert became a solicitor. He bought into a practice in the village of Tilston in Cheshire and settled there. Then our mother rejoined our father. I was my brother's housekeeper until he married, and then I met Edward Vogelbauer. We fell in love, Edward was hired as a clerk by the East India Company and we were sent out to New Delhi shortly after the wedding.

"We made a home in India and the two of us were very happy. A year later our son was born. I named him Lohengrin in honour of my father's greatest role and we called him Lonnie. He looked just like my husband. Four years ago our father died in Milan and our mother moved to Tilston in order to be near my brother's family.

"Just over a month ago, when Lonnie was five, William was promoted to chief clerk and given six months leave back to England before he took up his new duties. A week later we sailed on the *Lyric* bound for Liverpool. We were passing Weymouth on January 28, two weeks ago. That night a vicious storm blew up and our ship was cast up on the Chesil Banks.

"That treacherous sandbank broke the *Lyric* into pieces and everyone was thrown into the sea. We were in sight of Weymouth and heroic efforts were made at rescue. I was saved, but my husband drowned and my son was torn from my arms by the force of the waves."

Her eyes filled with tears but her voice did not falter. "My husband's body was found on the beach the next day. I was taken to hospital where I lay insensible for three days. Lonnie's body was never recovered.

"My brother came down from Tilston and brought us back home. I barely managed to get through the burial service at St.

Mary's. Afterwards I collapsed and my recovery has been slow. It is only in the past couple of days that I have been able to move about at all. My brother was against my coming down to London to consult you, but I wouldn't give in. He insisted that my mother accompany me, but I left her back at the hotel. I came here alone by hansom cab."

Holmes had been listening with his eyes fixed on his fingers steepled before him, sunk into his armchair. Now he lifted his eyes and looked at our visitor.

"We extend our sympathies, Mrs. Vogelbauer. What is it you request of me?"

"I want you to find my son."

"You said your son was dead."

"I wish to lay flowers at his grave."

"You just said your son's body was never recovered."

"While I was in hospital my brother made inquiries. No one of Lonnie's description was found on the beaches around Weymouth. But since I recovered, I have been thinking. The storm came from out in the Atlantic. What if he was swept eastward away from the scene of the shipwreck? Someone could have found him down the coast. He might have been buried in some small hamlet's cemetery and never identified."

"That is possible."

"I wish you to find him, Mr. Holmes. Or, failing that, to find out what happened to him."

"If his body was swept out to sea, it will be impossible to find him."

"I do not ask the impossible. I merely want to know if he has a grave anywhere along the Dorset shore. He was my son, sir. I ask as a mother."

"Much time has passed."

"I know you are an honourable man. If you take my case, you will do your best. If you fail, I will accept the fact that Lonnie is lost forever and I will place a memorial to him in St. Mary's Church in Tilston."

I had never seen a woman so steadfast in her purpose. Clearly, she was not going to accept anything less than the famous Sherlock Holmes agreeing to help her. He stood and held out his hand.

"I make no promise of success, but I will take your case, madam, and I will keep you informed of what progress is made."

"That is all I ask, Mr. Holmes. My mother and I are staying at the Pilchard Hotel by the Embankment." She pulled a photograph out of her reticule. "This was the only personal item my brother was able to recover after the wreck. Please take care of it."

It was a water-soaked photograph of three people. One figure was Mrs. Vogelbauer, looking younger and healthier, seated beside a man who had to be her husband. A boy stood by her knee. Edward Vogelbauer was older, dressed in a white tropical suit, with light hair and a luxurious walrus mustache.

Lonnie Vogelbauer had his father's coloring and was dressed in the sailor suit currently fashionable for young boys. At once it was evident why his father sported such a hirsute upper lip.

Young Vogelbauer was given by Nature an elongated upper lip over a wide mouth. It was quite odd-looking, almost a disfigurement, and I could understand why his father sought to hide such a physical feature. A few minutes later I ushered Mrs. Vogelbauer out and returned to the sitting room.

Holmes was studying the photograph closely. After a few minutes he put it down and dragged out bundles of newspapers from under his chemical table. He began throwing old issues around the room, searching for those of two weeks prior.

He retired to his armchair with an untidy stack and settled down to read newspaper reports about the wreck of the *Lyric*. His brain busy on the case, I knew he would be no company for the rest of the evening. I retired to my own bedroom, but I found it hard to get to sleep. The image of Laurie Vogelbauer speaking so earnestly to Holmes would not leave my mind. For her to ask my friend to find a dead child, lost for weeks! Had Sherlock Holmes finally accepted a case that was impossible to solve? Was it kind of him to give hope to the lad's mother? I felt terrible for her losses, but I couldn't see how it was possible for Holmes to locate the grave of a child lost at sea. Finally I must have slept, for when I opened my eyes I saw weak, watery winter sunlight through my window and it was morning.

I arose late, and breakfast followed me quickly into our sitting room. I found Holmes at his desk, consulting several almanacs and his own indexes, all the while scribbling on a large sheet of foolscap. The floor was a sea of discarded old newspapers and when I bent to pick up some I saw they each contained an account of the *Lyric* disaster.

I sat down to eat and was half-way through my soft-boiled egg when Sherlock Holmes dropped the sheet of foolscap on the breakfast table and poured himself a cup of coffee.

I lifted it off the toast rack and examined it. I was surprised to find the paper covered with several columns of figures, the lines headed with words like "sea current" and "tide levels". I tried to make sense of the numbers but found the entire sheet incomprehensible.

"What is this, Holmes?" I asked as I handed it back to him. "You have done a lot of figuring, but to what purpose I cannot fathom."

"Quite out of your depth, hey, Watson?" he chuckled. "I have spent the time since last night working on Mrs. Vogelbauer's case. I now fancy that I know as much as I would have had I been on the spot during the storm. Those figures you see before you were generated by the information I gleaned from several newspapers, including the **Times**, **The Dorset Sentinel**, my almanac and old copies of **The Shipping News**. I believe I have determined the exact spot where the body of Lonnie Vogelbauer would have washed up on the Dorset coast."

"And where is that?"

"Lulworth Cove, a pebble-covered beach less than a mile from Durdle Door and one-half mile south of West Lulworth. It is a goodly distance from Weymouth, but I have gone over my calculations carefully. I have that appointment with Scotland Yard tomorrow morning that I cannot avoid, but our afternoon will be free. Our first stop, Watson, will be at the Old Trinity Church of West Lulworth. There I am sure we will find the answers to end Mrs. Vogelbauer's sorrowful quest."

The next day we left London from Waterloo Station on the two o'clock train with tickets for Weymouth. A hired horse and trap took us from the city down a well-traveled road eastward. The Dorset coast benefitted from the temperate winds that blew in from the Gulf Stream and the fogs and chill rains of London were nowhere in evidence. Occasionally, if the road took us close enough to the cliffs, we could hear the sounding surf and smell the salt air. We passed a series of dairy farms and clumps of woodland as we traveled. After nearly twelve miles Holmes and I saw the tower of Old Trinity and the surrounding roofs of West Lulworth rise up as we approached.

By now it was late afternoon and the light was failing. We drove directly to Old Trinity Church, with its square Roman tower and Portland stone walls. It didn't look that old to me but Holmes informed me that the original Old Trinity had been torn down in 1869 and this replacement building was constructed in a new location.

We found the vicar on the front steps with a broom, sweeping the entrance steps. He introduced himself as Rev. Starr and apologized for the broom.

"Normally the sexton does this, but he's come down with the grippe and is confined to his own bed. So I have been trying to take his place ever since, not altogether successfully, I fear." He opened the front door and led us into the chancel.

Rev. Starr was a young man, going prematurely bald and dressed in the customary black. Holmes asked to view the church burial accounts and the cleric led us to the records room, pointing out some of the more noteworthy features of the church on the way.

In the records room Sherlock Holmes gave a more detailed account of our mission. Rev. Starr frowned. "I took up this post just a week ago. I don't recall any talk about finding a body on the beach after that storm. However, there may be a note of it on the proper page of the ledger." He lit a lamp, for by now the winter dark was drawing in, pulled a thick book off a high shelf and opened it out on the table in the center of the room.

"Here are last year's notes. Well, it seems it was a quiet year. No one died until July, when Toby Shell died at the age of 87. After that it was quiet again until December 10th. I see that the old vicar, Mr. Sands, officiated at the funeral and burial of Mrs. Welkes. She was the wife of the local magistrate."

Holmes frowned. "There have been no burials this past month? What about the surrounding towns?"

"Our sexton keeps up with the local news pretty well, since his wife cleans in all the churches and chapels around here for miles. He's told me a lot of the gossip she has collected, in order to bring me up to date on the community. I don't remember any mention of a drowned child found on any of the local beaches."

Holmes looked rather abashed. I felt badly for my friend. Obviously the boy's body hadn't been swept down the coast at all, but out to sea. Sherlock Holmes was rarely wrong in his observations and deductions and for his sake I felt this failure keenly. What a blow this information must be to his pride!

Holmes and I left Rev. Starr on the front steps of Old Trinity Church and, on the recommendation of the vicar, turned the head of the horse to the Cliff House Hotel. Holmes was silent throughout our drive. The Cliff House Hotel was a modern pile, not yet thirty years old, perched on an outcropping overlooking the sea. We left the trap with the stable boy and entered the lobby. My friend asked for two rooms and signed the guest register. Mr. Gull, the hotel manager, looked at our names as he handed us our keys.

"Mr. Sherlock Holmes and Dr. Watson of London! What an honour for Cliff House! I have followed the accounts of your adventures avidly. I suppose you are down here to investigate the sea monster."

"What sea monster?" I asked.

Mr. Gull was a short, dapperly dressed man whose head jerked and bobbed in bird-like fashion as he spoke. He handed me a copy of the local newspaper. "People have been talking about the sightings for days, but it was only today that an official story appeared in the paper. Read for yourself. They even have an artist's rendering."

Comfortable in the solid belief that if something was printed in the newspaper it must be true, the hotel manager turned to another customer. Holmes and I took chairs in a corner of the lobby and perused the front page. The "artist's rendering" was a highly imaginative drawing of a squat, many-armed creature with an enormous head creeping up over the sand from the ocean toward two terrified children cowering by some boulders. It's huge, slavering mouth was open and its many sharp teeth gleamed against the black interior. Several arms were stretched out, as if clutching for the boy and girl, there were only slits for a nose and two bulging eyes glared at the prey with an inhuman intent fearsome to behold.

The story that accompanied this amazing illustration was detailed and if true, terrifying. Two children, a brother and sister, had run into their parents' public house, the *Whale and Minnow*, on the outskirts of nearby Littlebeach at six o'clock at night five days before. They were crying and shaking. It took nearly an hour for the parents and their patrons to calm the children down and extract their story.

The boy, who was seven, said that he and his sister, who was five, had been walking home on the beach from Skylar's Woods, east of Littlebeach, when they saw something struggling in the water. Although the light was failing, the child declared that he saw a monster with many arms and a gaping maw stagger out of the surf and head for them. Its skin was dark streaked with white. He stooped and grabbed up some stones from the beach and flung them at the beast. It cried out and advanced upon them. The children screamed and ran. As they scrambled up the path that led over the chalk bluff to Littlebeach, they both swore that they felt the monster's cold, clammy breath on their necks and heard it's gurgling, slobbering cry just before they reached the top and escaped.

It was quite dark by the time the children had sobbed out their tale and no one felt like rushing out to search the beach for the monster. Indeed, the patrons showed a strong inclination to linger, ordering more beer and casting many glances out of the pub's windows as they drank. Finally, as the hour arrived that forced the *Whale and Minnow* to close its doors they began to leave in groups, talking loudly as they hurried away through the night. The pub owner and his wife both checked the locks and bolts of all the doors and windows before taking the shaken children up to bed.

The next morning the children still clung to their story, but the adults, encouraged by the new day and the absence of any further signs of the monster, shrugged off the alarm and chided the boy and girl for causing such a disturbance the night before. Soon it took on the aspects of a joke, although the children refused to leave the house and insisted that the sea creature existed.

A few days passed. Then the day before our arrival at West Lulworth Constable Gil Reed of the Dorset Constabulary filed an official report that he saw something strange in Skylar's Woods as he passed through on his way from Reefside to Littlebeach. The officer reported to his superiors that he caught a glimpse of "a body" slithering through the underbrush of the Woods away from the path on which Reed was riding his bicycle. He noted that the most prominent features of the encounter were the sight of a wide, sloppy mouth and the babbling sound he heard as the "thing" disappeared into the dusk.

"What a remarkable story!" I explained as I studied the illustration. "What do you think of it, Holmes?"

"The description would fit tales of the mythical monsters called Grindylows the old people tell to frighten the children when they misbehave," drawled my friend. "But this has its own unique features. This article intrigues me. I think we will make a stop at Littlebeach on our way back to Weymouth tomorrow."

"You can't believe this twaddle!" I exclaimed. "Such an animal is impossible! You yourself have told me repeatedly that once one eliminates the impossible, whatever remains, however improbable, must be the truth."

"That's it!" Holmes turned to me, his face suddenly alert. "Watson, you are indeed invaluable to me. You have hit on the very thing I neglected to do, an action so basic that for failing to do it I should be forced to turn in my magnifying glass and never be allowed to take another case as long as I live. Thank you, Watson. I am going up to my room."

"What about dinner?" I cried in astonishment.

"I don't need food for my body, Watson. I need food for my brain and you have just given me much to chew over." He jumped up and left the lobby.

Puzzled, I walked into the dining room. We had not eaten all day and I was famished. I had no idea what I had said, but whatever it was had certainly galvanized Holmes into action. The rest of the evening was quiet. I took a corner table, but when two American ladies asked to join me I could not refuse. They were sisters, the Misses Silaco from New York City, USA, on a tour of English humane societies. After I introduced myself as a doctor, I was treated to a long treatise on the anti-vivisection movement, both here and in the United States. The food and wine were only adequate and I when I reached my room later, there was no sign of Holmes, although there was a strong smell of tobacco in the hallway.

When Holmes joined me at breakfast the next morning we were greeted by Mr. Gull with the news that the Danish big game hunter, Stolt Drabsmanden, had been found in Bournemouth, just having given a lecture on his adventures in Africa to the Philosophical Society of that city. The Dorset Constabulary requested that he come to Littlebeach as a consultant on the case. He was due to arrive at the Littlebeach police station at 10 o'clock that very morning. After breakfast we went spinning back on the road that led to Littlebeach and ultimately to Weymouth. Holmes was silent as the horse and trap with our bags in the back passed the farmhouses and strips of trees that stood off in the fields around us. Finally he turned to me and spoke.

"I found the account of the "sea monster" very interesting."

"Surely you don't believe in such a thing!" I exclaimed.

"Don't think of it as a story of a monster, Watson. Think of it as a story of an unusual occurrence. If you look at it dispassionately, the entire account then takes on a different aspect. By the way, did you know that in China there is a giant salamander, over five feet long, that has a wide mouth and lives in water? You will find a full account of its discovery in the *Journal of Exploration* of the British Royal Society, issued three years ago. Here is Littlebeach and the police station is just down this street. I am very interested in what Stolt Drabsmanden has to say about the creature."

Littlebeach was a tiny group of stone buildings perched on top of a cliff overlooking the sea. The police station was near the cliff's edge, at the bottom of the High Street, and several officials stood outside, along with a new arrival, the great Danish big game hunter.

Drabsmanden stood at least a head taller than the Dorsetshiremen, dressed in an Arctic whaling overcoat with a furred hood and carrying an elephant gun, the likes of which I had not seen since my days of Army service in India. His leathery face was solemn and his faded blue eyes squinted into the distance, towards a stand of trees that had to be Skylar's Woods. He was addressing the group of men in a thick Danish accent as we drove up and stopped the trap.

"Then it is agreed. We will start at beach and track animal into woods. Its trail is sure to be wide and slimy. After we find lair, it will be simple thing to dispatch it. Then I ship carcass to Antwerp and have it mounted, ready for Royal Natural Museum. Any questions?"

"Don't you think you are a little premature in planning to shoot the creature on sight, Mr. Drabsmanden? Wouldn't it be better to try and capture it alive?" Holmes called from the trap. Drabsmanden turned at the unexpected interruption.

"You have advantage over me, sir."

"My name is Sherlock Holmes. This is my friend Dr. Watson."

"Well, Mynheer Holmes, I have spent greater part of thirty years in wild places discovering unknown animals and primitive peoples. I think I much more experienced on safari than you. Now you will excuse us, these officers and I find dangerous sea monster now."

The crowd of men moved off toward a stairway that led down to the beach. Holmes shook his head. "I didn't expect Stolt Drabsmanden to listen to me, Watson," he said. "He has a reputation in scientific circles of shooting first without determining the nature of the hunted animal and dragging back his prizes in wholesale lots. One thing is clear. We must find his quarry first."

He turned the trap around and whipped up the horse. In a few minutes we had left Littlebeach and were approaching Skylar's Woods from the north. A graded path led us to its outskirts, where we left the trap and plunged into the growth of timber. There were acres of trees stretching out before us on all sides. Branches and twigs tore at our coats as we zigzagged through the bushes and thickets that filled the spaces between the trees. Deep shadows and dappled light bedazzled our eyes as we progressed through the forest. Dried leaves and bracken crunched under our feet. Holmes led the way, examining the forest floor and looking up at the overhead canopy. Somehow he found an almost invisible path that took us deep into the woods. As we rounded a stand of oak I blinked in surprise. Centered in a little clearing was a tiny clapboard cabin with a thatched roof. There were signs of a straggly vegetable garden on one side, with dried cabbage stalks near the paling fence and wooden tomato stands leaning against the hut's grey walls.

"Holmes, how did you know this place was here?"

"I deduced its existence."

"Then who is inside?"

"That will be revealed by good, old-fashioned detective work. I shall walk up and inquire. Meanwhile, stay out here and keep a lookout. That trigger-happy Dane is still searching for his sea monster in the woods, with his organized lynching party. They are bound to make a lot of noise. Warn me as soon as you hear them."

Sherlock Holmes knocked on the door. It opened to show a tiny old woman standing on the threshold, leaning on a crooked stick. Her left ankle was wrapped in a thick bandage. She had pure white hair twisted into a long braid that coiled twice around her head and wore a black dress covered by a worn apron. She looked at Holmes with sharp green eyes.

Sherlock Holmes pulled the Vogelbauer family photograph from out of his pocket and handed it to her. She stared at it wordlessly and then motioned him to enter.

I was left alone in the garden. I stood silently, my ears straining for any sounds from the forest around me, while I thought over the actions of this case.

Sherlock Holmes had been shaken by his failure to find the boy's body. He had seen something in that newspaper story that I had missed. My repeating back to him his own dictum about eliminating the impossible had obviously struck a chord. Somehow all that had led us to this clearing and this little hut. What was happening inside between the old woman and Holmes? Could she know anything about the sea monster? Could she be harboring it? Where did it come from? Could it have been cast up out of the watery ocean depths by the same storm that sank the *Lyric*?

Then I heard a rustling of the underbrush from the east. A moment later there was a babble of voices. Obviously a large crowd of men were approaching the clearing. I pounded on the door of the cabin. "Holmes! Holmes! They're coming!"

The door flew open and Sherlock Holmes stepped out, clutching in his arms a large bundle wrapped in a brown blanket. Behind him I caught a glimpse of the face of the old woman, her eyes wide and frightened as she fumbled to close the door behind him. Holmes strode across the clearing and back on the trail that led to our horse and trap. I scurried behind him as the voices became louder. The hunter and his police escort were rapidly getting closer.

We retraced our path back to the forest's edge as quickly as we could. I slipped on slick leaf litter and tripped over protruding roots as we struggled through the underbrush. All along the way we heard crashing in the distance as the search party followed us. At the trap Holmes motioned me to mount to the seat and then he placed the bundle into my arms. I had barely grasped the blanket when he leaped in and with a word and a snap of the whip, had the trap headed toward Weymouth. We galloped for two miles until he pulled up the horse and we settled into a trot.

"It is six miles to Weymouth, Watson," he said. "Please fold back the blanket. That poor creature needs some fresh air."

Hesitantly I did as I was bid. I didn't know what I expected to see, a many-armed sea monster or a giant Chinese salamander, but it surely wasn't the startled face of Lonnie Vogelbauer that I found looking up at me from the depths of the thick cloth. We stared at each other for a moment, and then he opened that unusual mouth and said something in a foreign tongue that I recognized. His words were in Hindi!

"That explains the strange noises the "sea monster" made that the children and the policeman heard," said Holmes. "Remember, the child was born and raised in India, with native servants." He smiled at the boy. "This is Dr. Watson, son. Say hello properly."

"Hello, Dr. Watson," the young boy responded. "I am very glad to meet you. Mrs. Waverly said you and Mr. Holmes are taking me to my mother."

"That is correct, Lonnie," I replied. "Who taught you Hindi?"

"I learned Hindi from my amah and English from my parents. We were coming to England in a big ship but there was a storm. Mrs. Waverly found me in the water and gave me soup. It was good."

"That is enough, Master Vogelbauer," said Holmes. "Close your eyes now and take a little rest. Soon we will be in Weymouth and your mother will be very happy to see you."

Obediently the young boy turned his head and snuggled into the blanket. I held him securely and turned a questioning eye to Sherlock Holmes.

"You quoted my own dictum to me, Watson," Holmes said. He clucked at the horse and smiled. "'After eliminating the impossible, whatever remains, however improbable, must be the truth.' But I had not done my basic work; I had not eliminated the impossible. After listening to Mrs. Vogelbauer's story I had accepted her conclusion that her son had drowned. All my calculations and actions were based on the actions of a stormy sea on a dead body. When my deductions proved wrong and the child's body wasn't found, I considered that he had been lost at sea. Then we arrived at the hotel and read that newspaper article. Your timely remark reminding me of my failing sent me on another train of thought.

"I had to approach the question from an entirely new direction. Working from the new theory that the boy survived, I considered what would have happened after the storm. He most likely would have been thrown up on one of the numerous beaches between Weymouth and West Lulworth, but the fact that his recovery was never reported seemed sinister.

"We have both noticed that young Vogelbauer has an unusual appearance, one that strangers might even consider ugly. Two young children, seeing something totally unfamiliar and trying to describe it to adults, could easily exaggerate what they saw and create an unbelievable story. Even a policeman, a trained observer, could file a distorted report of a "sea monster" only glimpsed through thick underbrush in a darkling forest.

"I considered the chances that a missing child and a mysterious "sea monster" could show up in the same area at the same time and found them very low. I eliminated the impossible and decided the child was more likely to be real than the monster.

"His last sighting had been in Skylar's Woods. The wreck had been two weeks ago. It was doubtful that a six-year old boy could survive on his own for that long a time, so it was apparent that someone was taking care of him. When I found that person I would find the child. Since the sightings had all been of the child alone, I deduced that he wasn't being held prisoner.

"Therefore I decided that there was a dwelling in the woods where Master Vogelbauer was being cared for, even given exercise, but the occupant was for some reason unable to report his presence to the authorities. An elderly person, unable to get out easily, seemed the best answer to that question. It was at that point in my reasoning that I felt confident enough to lay out a search plan for the woods, in order to find the child.

"The calling in of Stolt Drabsmanden, the famous big game hunter, by the police this morning was a complication. His trigger-happy methods presented a real danger to the boy. It was imperative that we find him first. I knew there had to be a shelter in that wood and that the boy would be inside.

"Mrs. Waverly was the person caring for the child. She and I had a chance to talk before you gave the alarm. She had found him on the beach just after the storm. She dressed his wounds from the wreck, fed him and let him rest up, but the day she was planning on taking him to Littlebeach, she twisted her ankle badly and was unable to walk. That is why no one knew where he was. She has only infrequent visitors because she has spent her life gathering arcane lore about the herbs and healing roots of the forest and the locals avoid her, believing her to be a witch.

"A few days ago the boy felt well enough to walk as far as the beach, but he fell in the water and came back dripping wet and with some cuts and bruises. He told her some children had thrown stones at him. She kept him in for a couple of days. The next time he went out he was surprised in the woods by a man on a bicycle. The child was shaken by all that he has been through, which is not a surprise, and he ran back to Mrs. Waverly, terrified by the encounter. He hadn't been out of her sight since. It took some convincing for him to agree to come with us."

I looked down at the unfamiliar burden in my arms. The boy was asleep. The scratches and abrasions he had suffered from the wreck of the *Lyric* had healed, but there was evidence of fresh injuries from the stones that had been thrown at him by the boy from the *Whale and Minnow*. I held him a little tighter. What emotional wounds this child must have borne! To literally be thrown out into the world from his mother's loving arms, to struggle to live with only a stranger to care for him, and then to bear up against the violence shown him by frightened, ignorant people! Little Lonnie Vogelbauer, I decided, was one of the bravest people I had ever met.

We stopped briefly in Overcombe so Holmes could send a telegram to Mrs. Vogelbauer, telling her of the recovery of her son and asking her to come to Weymouth by the next train. He left young Lonnie and me at a café near the train station while he drove off to return the rented trap and horse. I took a table inside and managed a swift examination of the boy, finding no serious injuries. Then I ordered us both lunch and watched in amusement as young Vogelbauer consumed two fish-paste sandwiches and innumerable cream buns, washing it all down with a large glass of fresh milk.

Sherlock Holmes rejoined us with our bags and, urged by the boy, actually ate a cream bun with his cup of coffee. His gentle questioning brought out information about Lonnie's life in India with his parents and his experiences after the wreck of the *Lyric*. Finally we led him to the station, where the latest train from Waterloo soon pulled in and the anxious form of Mrs. Vogelbauer appeared on the platform.

Young Vogelbauer ran into her arms. Their reunion was touching. Holmes and I stood back, unwilling to intrude.

Holmes looked thoughtful. Then he spoke. "Do you hear the music, Watson?"

I looked at him in surprise. "I hear no music, Holmes. I can hear the idling train, the sound of traffic on the street and some voices behind us, but not music. What do you mean?"

"When she first came to our rooms, Mrs. Vogelbauer told us that she did not inherit her father's great talent. Rest assured, my friend, right now her heart is singing."

I looked at the two figures embracing each other on the now-deserted platform. I realized that I could hear the music, too.

The Case of the Hunted Hound

It was late November and the sight outside our windows at 221b Baker Street was bleary and drear. A pea-souper of a fog had descended on London. The wind had died away and for two days the city had sat draped in a thick yellow veil of icy water vapor and soot. It made the cobblestones in the streets slick and grimy and coated the buildings in a cold greasy slime. It was taking one's life in one's hands to venture out on the wet, slippery streets. The unnatural fog forced the gas lamps lining Baker Street to waver and burn fruitlessly during the sunless days and blur into near invisibility during the ever-lengthening nights. Even the gaslight that burned in our sitting room had to work against the wisps of atmosphere that slipped in through the cracks around the windows and the door as it flavored our lungs with coal smoke and damp. Our fireplace glowed fitfully instead of burning with its usual cheery blaze. Sherlock Holmes and I pulled our armchairs nearer to the hearth in an effort to extract any heat at all from the mound of sea-coal Mrs. Hudson had kindled there.

This morning we sat before the fire, Holmes in his dressing gown and I in my smoking jacket, as we opened the post with gloved hands to ward off the chill of the room. Holmes' Bunsen burner was kept lit under a kettle of hot water and I had busied myself in making pot after pot of strong tea rather than distress Mrs. Hudson, who was coping with her own domestic problems below stairs. I helped myself liberally to the warming beverage in a futile effort to keep warm the inner man. Holmes had spent the time since breakfast puffing on his old clay, adding another layer of stuffiness to the air, as he carefully read every word of the several newspapers to which he subscribed. Finally he stood up and flung the last aside.

"Nothing! Nothing at all!" He strode to the sideboard and poured out a stiff whiskey although it was only eleven forty-five o'clock in the morning. He turned to me, bundled up in my refuge by the fire.

"How can I make use of my finely-honed talents, Watson, when the best criminals lie doggo in their lairs, penned in by this infernal weather? This pea-souper of a fog has brought major crime to a standstill. Certainly there are newspaper reports of pickpockets and thieves snatching things from people forced out into this thick, frigid mist, but nothing interesting, nothing bizarre. The papers carry little but accounts of injuries caused by men and horses slipping on the treacherous streets along with gloomy weather reports. How is a consulting detective to earn his bread and cheese if the very air itself prevents clients from reaching his door? Confound this dratted fog!"

"Man cannot control the weather, Holmes," I said mildly.

"No, he cannot, but he might stop contributing to the conditions that aggravate it. You, Doctor, of all men are aware of the tons of soot and dirt that rain down through the atmosphere on London from the thousands, nay, millions of chimneys and smokestacks that fill the Thames valley from whence this vapor originates.

"Excuse me, Watson," he said when he saw my face. "You must forgive this diatribe. My nerves are at the snapping point from lack of stimulation. I need a case today, if ever I needed one before. I have not had a problem to solve for nearly two weeks and I have been confined to these four walls for too long. I am anxious for any outlet to keep my brain from stagnation."

I nodded in agreement. My friend needed, above all else, to have something with which to occupy his great brain, to be able to mull over a mystery, to engage his mental powers in decoding an impossible cipher or researching an esoteric problem. Lacking stimuli, he was prone to endlessly pace the floor or lie motionless and silent on our sofa. Watching him for the past days had put my nerves on edge, ever vigilant as I was over his moods and physical state. Now I leaned forward and plucked from the rug a forgotten telegram that had fallen out of the pile of newspapers he had been reading.

"Perhaps this is something, Holmes," I said as I offered it to him.

Sherlock Holmes took it in his thin, nervous fingers and ripped it open. A moment later I was startled to hear a peal of laughter ring out. Chuckling, he dropped back into his chair and handed me the yellow form.

"Here is the answer to a prayer, Watson. Not a big case, not an important case, but a case nonetheless. I will take it just for the relief of working again, no matter what the facts prove to be."

I read it aloud.

"I say, I hate to bother you, I truly do, but you see my dog is missing and he must be found before my wife gets home. I know it doesn't sound like much, no missing jewels or mangled corpse on the library floor, but I really am a desperate man. I will call at 221b Baker Street at noontime today. This is urgent, you see, because my marriage depends on my wife not finding out the dog is missing. I will call at noontime. Don't forget this is urgent. Bingo Little. "

"What can this mean, Holmes?"

"I have no idea, but if a dog is missing, a dog must be found. What a message! Can a man be so afraid of his wife and yet find the courage to consult me without her? It is nearly noon. I look forward to meeting this Bingo Little."

Just then the bell rang down below and in a minute Mrs. Hudson ushered in our new client. He was a handsome young man, dressed in the latest Savile Row fashion, and carried a top hat in his hand. He looked from Holmes to me, his face a bit vacuous and well-meaning, but with evident confusion showing as to what he thought his next move should be.

"Which one of you chaps is Mr. Sherlock Holmes?"

"My name is Sherlock Holmes, Mr. Little. This is my friend and associate, Dr. Watson. Please hang up your coat and take a seat by the fire. Then you may tell us about your problem."

"Oh, I say, thank you." Bingo Little removed his overcoat, shiny from the droplets of greasy fog outside, dropped into Holmes' armchair and smiled at us uncertainly. Holmes pulled up the old wooden chair and wedged in between us so that the meager warmth of the coal-fire had an equal chance to spread to our feet. Mr. Little's shoes, I noticed, were clad in spats.

"You are the detective chappie, aren't you? I mean, the man in the papers who solves all those mysterious mysteries, what? I can never figure out how you do it. Solve the mysteries, I mean. Bits of tobacco ash and old hats must litter every crime scene. Read about you in the press, you see. Jolly old press, so knowledgeable about race results and how to wear one's socks. Anyway, I'm in trouble. After he disappeared I didn't know who else to consult. I have a friend, Bertie Wooster, who has a man, Jeeves, who is an absolute whiz at problems like this, but Bertie went off to the French Riviera and took Jeeves with him and while Bertie did tell me where they were staying I have forgotten the address."

Sherlock Holmes smiled at this odd speech.

"I am that "detective chappie", Mr. Little. Please tell me of your problem. Besides the facts that you are newly married, hold membership in the Drones Club, and like your hats perfectly fitted, I can determine little else."

Mr. Little started and dropped his topper, which rolled toward the fire. I rescued it from the threatening embers and handed it back.

"I say, are you some kind of wizard? You must be a roar at dinner parties. Call me Bingo. Everything you said is spot-on. How did you know all that?"

"Your telegram mentioned your wife, Mr. Little, in such a way that for such a young man you must have been married for only a short time. The dew is still on the rose, and you are going to great lengths to conceal from her this adventure of yours, thus showing me that the honeymoon period of your relationship is still active and you are unwilling to disappoint her. She still sees you as her knight in shining armour and you do not want her to discover your human feet of clay."

Mr. Little pulled his smartly shod feet back from the fire and said, "You read me like a book, Mr. Holmes. How did you know about my membership in the Drones?"

"In the course of my work I have made a small study of the various customs and mores of the prominent London clubs. Your suit lapels are covered in breadcrumbs. The throwing of bread rolls at table is a notable feature of the Drones. As for your taste in hats, I saw the sticker with Bodmin's name emblazoned thereon inside yours. Nothing more needs to be said."

Our client's face was slack in astonishment. "I say, you are the cat's whiskers, Mr. Holmes! Please, call me Bingo. Wait until I tell Bertie about you! Are you sure you never ran into his man Jeeves? Do you eat a lot of fish?"

Holmes waved off that line of questioning and urged Bingo Little to tell us his tale. In a few minutes we had it all, and it promised to be as remarkable a case as Mr. Sherlock Holmes had ever handled.

"I am newly-married, Mr. Holmes, and to a wonderful girl. She is Rosie M. Banks, authoress of *Only a Factory Girl*, *Mervyn Kane, Clubman*, *'Twas Once in May* and other works. We hit it off from the start like a couple of lovebirds. But now I am within a toucher of being in very serious trouble in the home."

"Pray continue, Mr. Little."

"I know you are not a married man, Mr. Holmes, but please understand that in a marriage circumstances can arise which will cause the female lovebird to get above herself and start throwing her weight about. If my one and only gets on me what it appears inevitable that she must get on me, it will keep her in conversation for the rest of our married lives. She is a sweet little thing, one of the best, but women are women and I think there can be no doubt that she will continue to make passing allusions to this affair right up to the golden wedding day."

"An affair?" I asked.

"Nothing like that, Dr. Watson," said our client. "It began like this. My old partner in sickness and in health just finished another novel, entitled *Life Among the Coffee Cups*, and three days ago, just before the fog descended, she took off on a book tour that sent her though the Northern Counties, the Lake district and sections of Scotland. She was scheduled to be gone a week. As we bade goodbye to each other in Euston Station she appeared concerned and said she was worried about me being all alone while she was gone and that she thought I needed some companionship.

"You see, she was taking our latest housemaid along to see to her wardrobe and hair, and just the day before our cook had received a sudden summons home to Lyme Regis because her niece was stricken with housemaid's knee. I would be left alone in the flat. Since our marriage I had managed to become a dab hand at grilling on the balcony and last summer my tossed salads were considered quite the bees' knees among the younger set on the Cote D'Azur. Also my club has an adequate chef and an excellent wine cellar. She wasn't worried about my meals; she was worried about the empty hours I would have to endure until she returned to the old homestead.

"I assured her that I could find all the companionship in the world among my fellow Drones, but that just made her frown even more. "Huddled up in the Drones library is not my idea of companionship, Bingo, darling," she replied. It wasn't mine, either; I had been thinking of the card room, but at this point I let her get her thought out. "I think you need fresh air and exercise and a new interest to occupy you until I get back. So, I have arranged a little surprise that will be waiting for you at home after lunch."

"The mention of fresh air and exercise seemed to me to have sinister connotations, but as much as I teased and kissed her, she refused to tell me what the surprise was. Soon the train puffed out of the station, my wife waving her handkerchief at me from her First Class window, and I slunk back to the Drones for an apprehensive lunch.

"After a quiet meal, made possible because many of the members had been called back to the estates of their various aunts and uncles to account for their movements since last Quarter Day, I finished my meal by flinging my bread roll at Oofy Prosser, our one member who is both a millionaire and has no living relatives, and went home. Our love nest is a modern flat on the second floor of a nifty little building just off Park Lane. I had barely taken off my coat and settled in the living room with a fresh pack of cards to practice my trick shuffle that I planned on dazzling the boys with at Catsmeat Potter-Pirbright's birthday party next week when the doorbell rang.

"When I opened the door I found two burly men standing in the hall, holding a large wooden crate with a brown paper bundle on top. They didn't stop to introduce themselves, but staggered in and deposited the crate on the foyer tiles.

"Sign here, mate," said the burlier of the two men. He thrust a clipboard at me. The other man proffered a stubby pencil.

"What am I signing for?" I inquired as I scribbled my autograph.

"Do I look like a man who would peek into another man's crate?" asked the first man. He scowled at me and took back the clipboard. I considered him for a moment. He didn't look like a man who would peek into another man's crate. With his broken nose and his enormous biceps, he looked like a man who would rip you limb from limb for looking at him cross-eyed, but not like one who would peek into another man's crate. The other man snatched back his pencil and frowned at me in a fine imitation of his friend.

"No," I answered. "How do I get this open?"

"The second man pulled a crowbar from his belt and held it out with a sneer. I thanked him with a smile and applied the bar to the crate.

"An instant later I was flat on the floor with a great slobbering hound, all gleaming sharp white teeth, rough scarlet tongue and glowing red eyes astride my supine body. Dimly I heard terrified shouts and the distant sound of a slamming door.

"My head was abuzz. A continuous growling came from the beast and he nuzzled and licked around my throat and face as if he were cleaning a large patch of skin to be ready for surgery. His weight pressed me down like guilt on a new sinner and the very blackness of his coat filled my sight like the darkness of Egypt. I reached up in a hopeless effort to push him away and my fingers encountered a leather collar around his neck. A tag hung from the buckle and I managed to read it. It was inscribed "Cuddles."

"Off, Cuddles!" I shouted. To my amazement he scrabbled away. By the time I had gotten off the floor and managed to pour myself a restoring snifter from the drinks table, Cuddles had taken possession of the couch in the living room and was chewing on a throw cushion in a morose manner."

"Please give me a description of the dog," said Holmes. I pulled out my notebook from my smoking jacket pocket and took up my pen.

"Well, it was a six-foot couch and he filled it pretty well," replied Mr. Little. "His coat was black, and he had enormous gleaming teeth and blood-red eyes. The interior of his mouth was also red, he had dripping flews and his massive tongue hung outside every time he opened his mouth. He looked like a cross between a mastiff and a bloodhound, with some Irish wolfhound and a lot of North American Grizzly bear thrown in. He turned his head and stared at me like I was the next thing on the menu and howled as if his tummy hurt. In short, Mr. Holmes, he looked like the hound from Hell. Did I mention his glowing red eyes?"

"Yes, you did."

"Well, I didn't want to leave out such a salient feature. I noticed an envelope on the floor by the crate, doubtless dropped by the deliverymen in their haste to leave the two of us alone. I managed to move over and pick it up, while Cuddles kept an eye on me as if I were a burglar trying to pull a fast one on his shift. The note was from my wife. Here it is."

Holmes took the note and handed it to me. I read it aloud.

"Here, Bingo, darling, is a little something to keep you company while I am gone. Please walk him twice a day and remember to give him food and water. I have included a supply of Donaldson's Dog Joy and other needed items to make him comfortable. I expect to find you both the best of friends when I return. Love, your very Own."

"As you can imagine, Mr. Holmes, this put a different complexion on things. I could no longer think of this beastly invasion as a calculated attempt on my life by person or persons unknown, but instead had to accept the brute as a gift from my loving wife. What's more, she clearly intended that we bond and that I spend my time caring for it, worrying about its diet and making sure it gets enough fresh air and exercise. I gulped down the rest of the brandy and eyed man's best friend in a thoughtful manner.

"Several questions arose. Did it have a leash? Did it come with dog dishes for food and water? Did we have any Donaldson's Dog Joy? Did we have enough Donaldson's Dog Joy? Where would it sleep? If it didn't like where I put its bed, where would I sleep?

"It seemed comfortable enough on the couch, so I decided to check the enclosed bundle. Sure enough, there was a complete set of dog dishes, two leashes, various combs and brushes, squeaker toys and a bag of dog food. Regretfully, I didn't find a packet of animal tranquilizers, but everything else was there. I had decided early on in our acquaintanceship that I never wanted to see Cuddles unhappy if it was humanly possible to prevent that. Accordingly, I carried the bundle's contents to the kitchen. I briefly considered ducking out the service entrance and spending the rest of the week at the Drones, but Mrs. Bingo had absently-minded locked that door and taken the key with her to Scotland.

"I readied some food and water for the animal and swung open the kitchen door to see where he was. He was still on the couch, now starting in on the second cushion. I chirruped at him in what I hoped he would take as a friendly manner and he raised his head. It was like Grendel checking out Beowulf for the first time.

"Here, Cuddles. Here, boy. Yummies."

"With a smooth, muscular motion he left the couch and headed right for me. I managed to gain the top of the kitchen table just as he came through the door. He ignored my quivering carcass, however, and went straight to the dishes of Donaldson's Dog Joy and the water.

"One of the favorable features of the apartments in our building had been the roomy kitchens, well stocked with cupboards and countertops and furnished with the latest of modern appliances. I was dismayed, therefore, to suddenly find myself in a tiny room largely filled with Dog. I scrambled off the table and slipped into the living room. He heeded not my passing.

"I needed some air. I opened the French doors to the balcony and stepped out into the afternoon light. My old ball and chain was most probably halfway to Chester by now and I was faced with the prospect of seven days alone with Cuddles. All my friends were out of town. Even Oofy Prosser had told me at lunch that he on his way to catch the boat-train to Monaco. I decided to bite the bullet. I would go back inside and do my best to make friends with Cuddles. It was either that or pack a bag to emigrate somewhere far, far away, and I didn't know where my wife kept the extra suitcases.

"I returned to the living room and found Cuddles back on the couch. Clearly he had taken it for his own. I remembered that he had moved when I told him to get off me and to come for his dinner, and a faint hope arose in my heart. Perhaps he was trained to follow commands! Accordingly I said, "Sit, Cuddles!" and he Sat. Up.

"In a few minutes I had learned his entire repertoire. He sat up, lay down, rolled over, offered his paw and even stood still while I attached a leash to his collar. With a happy cry of "Walkies!" we left the apartment and went out for a brisk run."

"Then you did make friends with your wife's gift, Mr. Little. I fail to see a problem here." said Sherlock Holmes.

"Please, call me Bingo. After that first trip, during which I took him by the Drones to show him off to McGarry, the barman, we were confined to the old homestead because of this awful fog. During the night it slipped over the house like an oilcloth cover on a parrot's cage. The squeaker toys helped to pass the time, particularly one shaped like a goat, but still the hours dragged. Cuddles had to get his exercise by running up and down the hallways, which caused comment by the neighbors, and I developed a nice case of cabin fever. Yesterday morning I gave Cuddles the last of the Donaldson's Dog Joy and was faced with the prospect of a hungry Cuddles by dinnertime. We were getting along famously by then but every once in a while, especially before meals, I had caught a gleam in Cuddles' eye when he looked at me much as would a French gourmet contemplating a lobster dinner after a week of dieting ordered by his doctor. I had vowed to keep Cuddles happy and I didn't believe either his happiness or mine would come from an empty dinner bowl.

"That evening I offered him fruit and bread, all the kitchen had to offer. To be fair, I was forced to dine from the same menu. He ate, but that look was getting stronger in his eye. This morning, when I awoke, I found he had gotten up in the night and assuaged his hunger by devouring my best pair of Italian leather shoes. He had finished off the meal by chewing on my new Ascot topper, which I had worn only once.

"The only things left in the cupboard were several bottles of wine, both red and white. For lack of anything else, I poured out a bowlful of Beaune to blunt his hunger and determined to brave the fog in search of food. While he was occupied, I pulled on my hat and coat and left.

"My expedition through the murky, dun-coloured streets was successful and I returned with an economy-sized bag of Donaldson's Dog Joy and some staples for myself, like steak and beer. Imagine my shock, Mr. Holmes, when I entered my flat to discover the living room couch empty, the French doors smashed, the balcony floor littered with shards of glass, and Cuddles nowhere to be found. I can only conclude that he had become unhappy with his current accommodations and had left for brighter shores. That is when I sent you that message from the nearest telegraph office and made my way to Baker Street through all this choking fog."

"When is Mrs. Little due to return?" asked Sherlock Holmes.

"In four days, on Thursday," our client replied.

"That should be enough time," said Holmes. "London only has about five million residents and someone must have seen such a large dog as Cuddles. Watson, I think this is a job for the Baker Street irregulars."

"The what?" exclaimed Mr. Little.

"They are a band of street Arabs who aid Holmes in his investigations sometimes," I explained. "They go everywhere, see everything and are Holmes' eyes and ears in the city."

"Never heard of them," said Bingo Little.

"I've written about them a couple of times," I said.

"I must have skipped those stories," he replied.

Holmes went to his desk and wrote furiously for several minutes. Then he rang for Mrs. Hudson, handed her a fistful of telegram forms, directed her to have them sent immediately and shed his dressing gown for his hat and coat.

"You have mobilized the irregulars," I said.

"Very good, Watson," he drawled. "I told them to fan out across the city and seek this animal. Such a large beast cannot slink through the streets of metropolitan London in this day and age without someone noticing it. I instructed them to report each sighting to Wiggins, who will report to me. I expect to get results within hours."

"But what about the fog?" I asked.

"Yes, there is fog. Well, it cannot last forever and when it fades away everything will become clear. Possess your soul in patience, Watson. I shall accompany Mr. Little home where he will await developments and I will inspect the premises. I doubt the animal left a note, but there may be some other indication of its intentions."

The afternoon passed and the fog grew darker and thicker. After Holmes returned from his expedition into the murk, he occupied himself at his chemistry table. He said only that Bingo Little had hired a glazier for the French doors and planned on throwing out the couch cushions. I tried to immerse myself in one of my yellow-backed novels but the thought of that black beast roaming amid the unsuspecting population of London gave me a feeling of suspense as thick as the vapors outside our windows. By late afternoon I was jumping at every ring of the doorbell, but each ring only announced the arrival of another telegram from the gang of children Holmes employed.

The first one read

"Large dark shape reported to have spent ten minutes splashing in basin at Trafalgar Square. Disappeared into mist when approached. Wiggins"

An hour later we got another one.

"Hulking black beast startled the Guard at Buckingham Palace. Escaped to the east in the fog. The Queen is safe. Wiggins"

Hours passed until a third telegram was delivered.

"Strange movements marked outside the Bank of England. Police theory is it indicates the planning of a massive robbery. Have stationed an entire squad of officers around building. Only clues are numerous footprints of a gigantic hound found on front steps. Wiggins"

There was nothing more that evening. In the morning another telegram came up with the curried chicken and the eggs.

"Howling heard outside the walls of the Tower of London last night. Thick mist and darkness obscured all. First thought to be the ghost of Anne Boleyn's dog. Later level of noise convinced those hearing it to be the combined moaning of spirits of all those held prisoner and tortured at Tower since construction. Madame Blavatsky sent for. Wiggins"

Then silence fell. The green and ochre murk outside grew more dense. No more telegrams were delivered to 221b Baker Street for the rest of that day or that night. Late the next morning another yellow form arrived.

"Funeral procession disrupted in Highgate Cemetery by mysterious huge dark shape running through crowd. Witnesses were unable to describe it because of thick fog. Pallbearers dropped the coffin and dispersed with cries of "Dracula has returned!" Wiggins"

That afternoon, just before tea, a last message was received. It read

"Patrons at Criterion Bar reported enormous black monster spotted in Piccadilly Circus, looking in at them through the glass doors. No further description possible because of fog. Sight was so hideous one half of crowd swore on the spot to drink nothing but milk in future, while other half insisted on being led to Criterion's lower regions for safety and being locked in wine cellars. Fiend then disappeared into the fog. Wiggins"

No more telegrams from the Baker Street irregulars arrived at 221b. After reading the last report, Sherlock Holmes spent hours on a divan made of pillows in the corner of the sitting room, smoking his pipe and pouring over a folded sheet of paper. Periodically he made marks on it then sent Mrs. Hudson out for more tobacco. In order to breathe, I was forced to stick my head out a window every once in a while, despite the encroaching tendrils of mist that slipped past me to twist and curl through the room and finally blend with the smoke from Holmes' pipe. The atmosphere became intolerable. Finally I retreated to bed.

On the morning of the fourth day, mere hours before the scheduled return of Mrs. Little, her husband made his way through the persistent pea-souper atmosphere of our room to the sofa. A strong breeze was lifting the fog outside and I threw open a window in an effort to clear the air. Holmes thanked Bingo Little for coming in response to his telegram and announced he had not yet found Cuddles.

Mr. Little was despondent at the news.

"I'm jolly sorry to hear that, Mr. Holmes. How I wish Jeeves were here. I have seen that man perform miracles solving problems much more convoluted than simply that of a missing dog. What a brain! All Bertie's friends think the world of Jeeves. If only I could remember that address in the South of France!"

Sherlock Holmes stood up, stiff and austere, and handed Mr. Little his hat. "If you believe my services are inadequate..."he began.

"No, no, Mr. Holmes! Please, don't think that! I am sure you're straining every nerve and putting your entire coconut into my case. I've never had much brain power, you see, and I really admire the birds with the goods that can just look at a crossword or a newspaper acrostic and blurt out the answers like water from a pipe. Please continue your investigation. My better half arrives today at 5:30 and I am booked to meet her at the station. What will she say if I don't have Cuddles in tow? My life will not bear living without your help."

"Very well, Mr. Little. I will remain on the case. Please get up off your knees."

"Oh, thank you, thank you both. Call me Bingo. Is there anything I can do to help?"

"I do have one request."

"Name it, Mr. Holmes, and it will be yours, up to half my kingdom."

"I see the fog has lifted. I think the next step is to have lunch at your club. Both Dr. Watson and I have been cooped up here too long and could do with a change of scenery."

"Certainly, Mr. Holmes. And you too, Dr. Watson. Call me Bingo. I'll be glad to treat you to lunch. I think you will enjoy it. The Drones have a fine wine cellar, the chef is a good sort and the bread is always fresh. Some of the members have come back from their relatives' places in the country and we'll find such jolly fellows there."

Holmes and I got our coats and hats and in a short time we found ourselves walking into the famous Drones Club. Mr. Little spotted Bailey Cavendish, the Club manager, who was hovering in the entrance hall. The man hurried over to our client and touched his sleeve discreetly.

"Excuse me, Mr. Little. We have a problem here. Do you happen to know Mr. Wooster's address in France?"

"No, I don't. Why do you need Bertie's address?"

"Well, it isn't really for him. Mr. Freddy Widgeon suggested that Mr. Wooster's man Jeeves would be of great assistance during our current troubles. But if you can't help us…"

"Wait a minute, wait a minute! If it's little grey cells you need, I have just the ticket standing right here. This is Mr. Sherlock Holmes, the great detective, well-known as the sharpest knife in the drawer. He happens to be doing a little something for me right now. I'm sure he would be happy to listen to your problem. Would you bend your brain to this, Mr. Holmes?"

"Of course. Is there somewhere we can speak privately?"

This seemed like a good idea, since the foyer where we stood seemed to be the location of a rugby match and the noise from the bar, where men stood three deep clamoring for refreshment, was deafening. Cavendish led us through the dining room, where boisterous members were flinging rolls at each other as if they were trying to knock over bottles at a fun fair, and into a small office. He closed the door and motioned us to chairs.

"Normally this is something that would be taken up by the Committee, but every blessed member has been detained in the country by their aunts and they all are currently forbidden to come down to London upon threat of disinheritance. As for the problem I mentioned, to make a long story short, I believe the Drones Club is haunted!"

Bingo Little gave a great start. "You mean like ghosts? Spirits? Wraiths, shades, organized ectoplasm? Conan Doyle's special friends?"

"Exactly."

Bingo Little needed clarification.

"You are talking about those who have gone to their reward, departed this life, and are currently pushing up daisies?"

"Yes, I mean travelers to the Great Beyond, who have gone to their eternal rest, entered the next world and now inhabit the Happy Hunting Grounds."

"Mr. Cavendish, what gives you that idea?" said Sherlock Holmes. He nudged me and I began taking notes.

"I do think it is only a couple of ghosts, sir. It is not like one cannot walk down the corridor without tripping over a winding sheet or eat a meal without faint hollow voices disturbing one's enjoyment of the *Coc au Vin*. But there have been strong signs since yesterday and the incidents are getting worse."

"Tell me about the incidents."

"You must understand that until today, when the fog began to lift and many members were able to return to London, the Club has been very quiet. Last night's dinner special was *tripe a la Baltimore*. It was just out of the oven and was left to finish on the table in the kitchen. The chef turned his attention to fixing the salad and when he turned around, the entire dish was gone!"

"You mean the food had been eaten?"

"Exactly! Tripe, shrimp, mussels, seasonings, every splash of gravy had vanished. All there was left was the large stoneware baking dish that had held it all."

"The chef saw nothing?"

"He claimed he didn't, but I must admit he is French and drinks while he cooks. That is not all. Later that evening I noticed a chair out of place in the smoking room, and when I moved it back I found a pipe on the carpet, badly chewed."

"It is not unusual to find a pipe with teeth marks on the stem," said Holmes.

"This pipe had teeth marks on the bowl, sir. It had an unusually large bowl, carved out of African ironwood. It belonged to Mr. Freddy Widgeon, sir, and he had been detained out of town by police authorities for a week. Something about a policeman's helmet. He just got in today. He said it was not in that condition when he last saw it."

"What else?"

"Three newspapers, both morning and evening editions, including the comic pages, were discovered chewed to a sodden pulp in the library, an overcoat belonging to Mr. Prosser, left behind when he debarked for Monaco, was found ripped to shreds in the cloakroom, and, most sinister of all, the club kitten is missing."

"Nothing else?"

"Only the sounds in the night."

"What sounds in the night?"

"Irregular sounds, sir, from the ballroom. As if people were dancing."

"Any music?"

"No, sir. McGarry, the barman, only heard scuffling noises last night. He told me this morning and I went up to investigate. There were marks in the dust."

"Well, I've never heard of a floating apparition leaving marks in the dust before. Perhaps your ghost has a more earthly origin, Mr. Cavendish. Who else knows of these incidents?"

"Just myself, McGarry and Mr. Freddie Widgeon. I thought it best not to panic the staff or the members by spreading such news around. I asked Mr. Widgeon about the pipe, you see, and he advised me to get hold of Mr. Wooster's man Jeeves."

"I think we can carry on without Jeeves," said Sherlock Holmes. "Since the ballroom was the site of the latest occurrence, let us begin there."

Bingo Little was still uncertain. "Wait a minute, Cavendish," he said. "When you say ghosts, you are talking about the dearly departed, someone who has gone the way of all flesh, and is most sincerely dead?"

"Yes, sir. I'm talking about someone from the hereafter, who has left this vale of tears, met his Maker, been fitted for a set of wings and collected his room key to that Grand Hotel in the Sky."

"Ah. Just making sure, Cavendish."

The Club manager led the way upstairs on the Grand Staircase. He explained that the basement of the Drones building held the kitchens, pantries, wine cellar and swimming bath of the club, along with changing rooms for the bathers. The ground floor was the one we had just left, with the foyer, the bar, the dining room, the small office, the library, the writing room, the smoking room, the billiard room and two card rooms. The first floor was divided into small bedrooms. They could be reserved for use by club members if they found themselves stuck in London between trains or when certain authorities or relatives might be searching for them. Above that was the ballroom, decorated in the style of Louis the Fifteen, and topping out the structure was a veritable labyrinth of attic rooms, stuffed with the flotsam and jetsam of things that frequently collect as a Club goes through life.

"I believe that an attic should be stocked with only those things that will prove useful," said Sherlock Holmes as we climbed past the bedrooms.

"An admirable sentiment, Mr. Holmes," replied Cavendish, "but impractical in a community situation such as the Drones. Suppose that Lord Ferryside, an old member and Club benefactor, comes back from his travels in the Canadian wilderness and gifts the Drones with a giant hairy moose head, complete with a full set of antlers, and all of it mounted on a wide slab of Sequoia wood. It would be far too hideous a monstrosity to hang anywhere in the public rooms, yet the…the…"

"Old fathead," said Bingo Little.

"Well, yes, the member will expect it to be exhibited in a prominent place when he comes down next spring to see his dentist. We just chuck it up in the attic, along with the other monstrosities, and whip it along to the library when he telegrams to reserve a room the next time he is on his way. There is a special peg there reserved for gifts from the members, along with a shelf for ugly vases and statues adorned with clocks in their stomachs and such. After he leaves the *object d'horror* is put back in the attic. The system has worked like a charm for years."

"What if the donor appears unexpectedly?" I asked.

"Then he is delayed at the bar, not a difficult thing to accomplish, and the item is quietly carried down the back stairs and put into place. Ah, this is the ballroom."

Cavendish opened a pair of tall carved doors and turned on the electric lights. I blinked at the sight within. The long, wide room was lined with mirrors. Each sheet of reflecting glass was bracketed with marble columns. Each column was adorned with a golden electric sconce. Between the mirrors were sets of golden curtains draped over floor to ceiling windows. Against the wall at our left were stacked dozens of gilt chairs, under draped white cloth, while at the far end stood a stage fitted out for an orchestra. The ceiling was painted with famous scenes from the history of the Roman Empire. From plaster medallions covered with gilt hung four elaborate crystal and gold chandeliers. A waxed hardwood floor stretched out before us, throwing back a dull gleam from the brilliant lights above.

"Do you have many dances here?" asked Holmes.

"Frankly, sir, we do not. The members seem unwilling to put in the effort to organize formal balls or cotillions. This room is used mostly by the members for roller-skating."

"Good times," murmured Bingo Little. He dreamily extended his arms and shuffled his feet out onto the dance floor, obviously remembering past glories. Sherlock Holmes' voice snapped him out of his reverie and brought him quickly back to heel.

"Mr. Little! Please do not disturb the evidence. Watson, keep him and Mr. Cavendish by the doors." Holmes pulled out his magnifying glass and began to examine the room. He started with the stacks of chairs then spent a lot of time looking at the floorboards. When he finished that he shifted his attention to the mirrors and curtains. He ended up on the faraway stage, searching the carpet underneath the musicians' chairs and music stands. Twice he picked up something from the floor and placed it in an old envelope and tucked the envelope into his pocketbook. Finally he walked back to our little group, returning his glass to his coat pocket and dusting the knees of his trousers.

Just at that moment a distinct series of loud thuds were heard overhead. We all looked up at the ceiling. The effects of the thuds' vibrations were obvious. The chandeliers overhead swayed while the numerous cut-glass crystals that adorned the gold frames of each tinkled against each other. The thuds seemed to have come from a portion of the floor above that was covered with a painted scene of Rome's founding.

"It's the ghosts!" gasped Mr. Cavendish.

Holmes moved toward the hall doors.

"Mr. Little, Mr. Cavendish, please stay here. Watson, come with me." He led the way up the last flight of stairs.

The door at the top of the steps opened into a weird scene worthy of a Bram Stoker novel. Dimly-lit rooms led off to other rooms, each filled with ghostly white forms. It took me a moment to recognize the massive irregular shapes as various piles of furniture and miscellaneous objects, all covered with old linen sheets. We walked through chambers of silent white forms, the scenes lit only by weak November light coming through dusty windows. Tiny motes hung in the air and some of the sheets were an inch thick in grey dust. We threaded our way through the labyrinth, dodging sharp edges and peering into cobwebbed corners, until we reached the doorway of the last room. It, too, was filled with massive dim forms. Set in the far wall was a large Gothic window, its smeared stained glass panes depicting a fox hunt. Before it was a heavily-carved table with thin elegant legs ending in carved hairy paws clutching ebony balls showing under the ubiquitous white cover, lumpy like the rest. As we approached I heard a moan and the white sheet began to rise up.

I watched in horror as the white shape grew larger, filling the window and looming over Holmes as he stood between the table and me. The vision was backlit by the window's light, and that fact only served to increase the awful effect. My spine prickled in fear and I longed for my revolver or a stout walking stick or even a silver cross to hold out toward that apparition to stop its progress. The moaning grew louder and the specter swayed forward toward my friend. I grabbed at his shoulder.

"Holmes, watch out!"

The white shapeless mass, a figure out of a nightmare, loomed over us both. I had seen and endured much during my service in Her Majesty's Service, but no Afghan campaign or jazail bullet had ever put such a terror into my soul as that terrible sight in the gloomy half-darkness of that cramped and spooky room.

Sherlock Holmes reached out and pulled the sheet off the apparition before us.

That action revealed a huge black animal with gleaming blood-red eyes standing on the table before the window. It was enormous, with long black legs and a miss-shapened head that resembled a bad cross of mastiff and bloodhound and something else, like no dog's head I had ever seen. Spittle dripped from its loose, sagging lips as it opened its enormous jaws and howled at us.

"Heel, Cuddles!" At Holmes' command the animal jumped down and landed loudly on the boards in front of us. The whole building seemed to shake. His mouth was open and his long scarlet tongue lolled out between rows of sharp white teeth as he looked from my friend to me. Holmes pulled a leash out of his pocket and clipped it to Cuddles' collar.

The dog looked back at the table. I followed his glance, and saw a small orange kitten huddled on the spot where Cuddles had stood. I picked it up and followed Holmes and Cuddles as they made their way back to the others.

"Cuddles! Here, boy! Here, boy! Oh, Cuddles, I have been so worried!" Bingo Little fell upon the dog's neck like the old father greeting his prodigal son. Bailey Cavendish accepted the orange kitten but took care to stand back from the master and dog reunion. It did take up a lot of space. Joyous Cuddles' fast-moving bushy tail, nearly four feet long, whipped back and forth, threatening to knock down anyone who came within reach.

After several minutes of Cuddles, his front paws on Little's shoulders, laving his face and neck with its enormous red tongue and growling in his ear, our client managed to calm his pet and lead us down into the dining room. The room quickly cleared at the sight of us and Holmes, Little and I were shown to a center table. Mr. Cavendish disappeared into the kitchen with the cat and presently a delicious lunch was sent out. Cuddles was presented with his own large platter of sliced roast beef. Bingo Little handed Sherlock Holmes a folded check and could hardly eat for all the questions he had for my friend. Finally Holmes put down his knife and fork and addressed our client.

"After I examined your flat and found nothing that had not been included in your story, I relied upon the efforts of the Baker Street irregulars. It would have been futile for one man or even two to try to canvass the entire Greater London area looking for one dog. The many eyes of the irregulars, however, can cover the city easily." He pulled out the telegrams he received from his pocketbook. "I kept track of the reports Wiggins sent me on a map of London." He showed us a small folded map with a meandering line drawn on certain streets that described a rough spiral. "As you see, the first sighting was at Trafalgar Square. Then there was a disturbance at Buckingham Palace. The animal was frightened off and headed east. The police were called to surround the bank of England in the City when gigantic footprints of an enormous hound were discovered on its front steps. Obviously this was our quarry. Cuddles got as far as the Tower, where it's heartbroken howling kept the guards and neighbors awake all night. Lost and confused in the fog and, I am sure, missing you, Mr. Little, the dog headed northwest. He disrupted a funeral at Highgate Cemetery that turned his steps toward the southwest. He was seen in Piccadilly at the Criterion Bar, which is near the Drones. Mr. Little had mentioned that when he and Cuddles took their walk he had shown off his new pet to the barman at the club. Among many other things, Cuddles is part bloodhound. I therefore deduced that when the sightings stopped, the animal had remembered that walk and managed to reach what he would consider a safe haven, i.e. his master's club.

"I requested that you, Mr. Little, bring us to the Drones for lunch. As soon as we entered Mr. Cavendish announced that he

137

believed the building was haunted. I connected the two problems and realized that Cuddles was the active agent. I asked to see the last place the disturbances had occurred. In the ballroom I found hairs from both a black dog and an orange cat." He extracted the envelope from his pocketbook and showed us the contents. It was a blended wad of animal hair, some coarse and black, the rest fluffy and orange.

"The most logical place for a large animal such as Cuddles to hide in an occupied London club would be the least-traveled part of the building, the attics. The club kitten had obviously joined forces with him. The scuffling the barman had heard last night were the sounds of the two animals gamboling about in the ballroom. The thuds we heard from the rooms above pinpointed his location. Since I do not believe in Hounds from Hell dancing in ballrooms, I searched the attics for Cuddles. It was child's play to uncover the dog's hiding place. And just in time for lunch."

Bingo Little' jaw hung open as he listened to my friend's explanation. His eyes traveled from Holmes, seated at the table, to Cuddles, crouched protectively over the platter on the floor, which he had licked clean.

"That is wonderful, Mr. Holmes," he said. "Jeeves couldn't have done any better. It is amazing how you wove it all together. Please, call me Bingo."

Mr. Cavendish approached our party. "Mr. Little, there is a lady asking for you at the front desk. You know the Club's policy about females. You will have to go out to the foyer to see her."

"A lady asking for me here? I can't imagine who it could be. Excuse me, gentlemen, I must toddle off and see about this." He rose and gathered up Cuddles' leash.

Since our meal was over, Holmes and I followed him out to the entrance. There we saw a stylishly-dressed woman, with brown eyes and a lissome figure, carrying an over-sized handbag and wearing a brown traveling suit and matching hat. Bingo Little gave a start.

"That is no lady, that is my wife! Rosie, what are you doing here?"

She greeted her husband affectionately with a kiss on the cheek. "I had the chance to catch an earlier train, darling. I took a cab from the station back to our flat. When I found it empty I figured you would be here and so I came by. I have something to show you."

"I must show you my surprise first, darling." Bingo Little tugged on the leash and Cuddles stepped out from behind him. Mrs. Bingo gasped and retreated behind the coat rack. Her face went white and her knuckles pale where she gripped her handbag.

"What in the name of all that is holy is that?"

"Why, darling, it's Cuddles."

"Who is Cuddles?"

"This dog."

"It's a dog? Are you sure?"

"Yes. His name is Cuddles."

"Where on earth did you find him?"

"You sent him to me the day you left on your trip."

"I did no such thing."

"Don't be silly. Of course you did."

"Why would you harbor such an insane thought?"

"I signed for him."

"Bingo, darling, I love you dearly, but after all this is sorted out you must have your head examined at the earliest opportunity. I never sent you that beast."

"He was delivered with a note, written by you."

Mrs. Bingo frowned.

"Is that animal safe?"

"He's on a leash and just had lunch. He's as safe as he ever is. What is it, my love?"

Mrs. Bingo stepped out from behind the coat rack and opened her large handbag. Out popped the head of a tiny black and white dog, notable for a pair of large long-haired pointed ears and two intelligent black eyes. A silky tail curled over its back. Cuddles shifted his weight and gazed at the little dog with interest. His massive tongue ran over his chops. I thought what a good thing it was that he had just finished that large platter of roast beef.

"This is Ruggles," announced Mrs. Bingo.

"Who is Ruggles?" asked Bingo Little.

"This is Ruggles. He is the dog I sent you."

"No, he's not."

"Yes, he is."

"No, dearest, he is not. I would have remembered. This is the dog you sent me."

"I didn't send you that monster. I sent Ruggles. When I got back to our building today he was with Carlton, the doorman."

"Dearest, I can tell the difference between Cuddles and something that looks like a squeaker toy. Why do you think you sent me that dust ball?"

"I went to the pet shop the day before I left on my book-signing tour. I wanted you to have a companion, a little friend we could take on walks and keep me company while I wrote. I chose Ruggles, who is a Papillon, and gave instructions for his delivery to our flat to the clerk."

Sherlock Holmes had a suggestion. "It is a capitol mistake to theorize without having all the data. Why not call the pet shop and ask them about this?"

Mrs. Bingo stepped into the telephone booth in the foyer and made a quick call. She came out shaking her head.

"The pet shop made a mistake. I went to the front desk to have the clerk fill out the order. I told him I wanted Ruggles, but he must have misunderstood and wrote down Cuddles. The two dogs were sent to the wrong addresses. Ruggles was shipped back to the store and the shop sent him to us this morning. Since you

141

were not home Carlton the doorman signed for him and kept him until I arrived."

"The fatheads! Well, we'll just keep both dogs."

Ruggles ducked down into the handbag. I saw its sides quiver. Cuddles licked his chops again. Mrs. Bingo shook her head. "We can't. That beast has already been sold. A man from Devonshire or Cornwall or someplace is going to pick it up tomorrow and take it back with him on the train."

"But Cuddles and I get along so well!"

"Nevertheless, darling, it must be returned. The pet shop is sending a delivery van right now. It will be here in a few minutes."

Bingo Little's face was a study in sorrow. He leaned over and scratched behind Cuddles' ears. "I'm sorry, old man," he choked. "I shall never forget you. Be a good dog. Take care of yourself." He dejectedly shuffled out the front door to the pavement. We all followed and stood by the steps. Shortly thereafter an unmarked delivery van appeared and the driver stepped out.

Little and the driver, who seemed very familiar with Cuddles, put him into a large steel crate in the back. The animal whimpered as they clicked shut the padlock. Our client said a few more words of farewell to his pet, which was endeavoring to lick his face through the bars, and the driver shut the doors. Little joined us as the driver pulled into traffic. We heard a mournful howl as the van disappeared around the next corner.

"Now what?" he sighed.

Mrs. Bingo was brisk. "I noticed that we needed to buy some new throw cushions for the couch," she said cheerfully. "After than you can take Ruggles and me to tea."

Bingo Little shook hands with us. "Thank you for all your help, gentlemen," he said. "Please, call me Bingo. I will never forget this week. I'll have quite the story for Bertie and Jeeves next time I see them. Goodbye."

He turned to his wife and took her elbow. "By the way, darling," he said, "what was the name of that pet shop?"

Mrs. Bingo was busy arranging Ruggles so he could peer out of the handbag and see his surroundings. "I found it in Fullham Road. The name on the door was Ross and Mangles."

Holmes smiled and looked up in the sky. "The fog has quite retreated, Watson," he said. "I propose we walk back to Baker Street. You and I have had an interesting time and a good lunch, and I think we can both agree that we are glad we shall never see that hound again."

The Case of the Bewildered Bootblack

"I deduce that we are about to entertain visitors, Watson," Mr. Sherlock Holmes remarked one morning in early spring. I was finishing the last of my breakfast while Holmes stood at the window of our shared sitting room gazing down into a busy Baker Street.

"You see someone in the street coming this way."

"That is correct. You do know my methods."

"Who is it?"

"It is my lieutenant Wiggins of the irregular Baker Street forces and a young friend. I would put the stranger's age as about ten. He lives with his mother who keeps him in clean, mended clothing, and he has one sibling. A sister, judging from the new hair ribbon peeking out of his pocket and obviously bought as a gift. He earns his living as a bootblack. His father is an able-bodied seaman in her Majesty's service. That is evident from the cut-down shirt made from a sailor's kit that he wears. The thrifty mother makes over her husband's clothes to fit the boy. He brought his problem to Wiggins and Wiggins has brought him here to consult me."

The doorbell rang. Holmes stepped to the head of the stairs. "Send them up, Mrs. Hudson," he called before our landlady could begin her usual objections in admitting any of Holmes' street Arabs. The Baker Street irregulars might have been "sharp as needles" that "went everywhere and overheard everything" but they were not known for high levels of personal cleanliness.

A few moments later Wiggins and his companion were ensconced on the sofa, tucking into the last of the toast and fruit left from our breakfast. I took my usual seat by the fireplace with my notebook and pen. Holmes stood before the boys, his hands clasped behind his back and his grey eyes fixed on the pair.

"Wiggins, I can see this call is your doing. Report, please."

The youth sat up straight and looked from his friend to the detective. "Mr. Holmes, this is Jeremiah Hopwell. We call him Jerry for short. He lives on my street with his mum and little sister. He came to me last night with his story and I promised to bring him to you. I told him you could figure out how he could collect his reward from the lady. Jerry, tell Mr. Holmes and Dr. Watson here what happened in that alley."

Jerry Hopwell leaned down and patted the shoeshine box that had told Holmes his occupation. It must have given him reassurance, for he straightened up and replied in a clear, steady voice. He was tow-headed and slender and his fingers were stained by the polish he used on his customers' footwear.

"I lives with me mum and me sister Jenny by Wiggins' place, like he said. Me dad's in the Navy, stationed on the *HMS Golden Ball* out in the Indian Ocean. He's been gone for over a year but he's due back next Christmas. His allotment doesn't go far, so Mum does sewing and I shines shoes. Jenny's just a baby so she stays with Mum.

"I works as a bootblack, you sees. I got a corner where I gives shoe shines, but about four o'clock every other day I gots a regular

145

route in an insurance building near St. Paul's. The manager lets me go from office to office offering to shine shoes for the gentlemen who works there. I pays him a percentage of my tips, but it's worth it. Then I picks up some bread or whatever Mum needs from the stores and goes home.

"Two days ago I'm walking by a blind alley just past the Monument on my way home when I sees a lady struggling with a bruiser just inside. He's pulling at a handbag she carries and she's holding on to it for dear life. I steps into the alley and she sees me. "Help me, boy!" she says. "Don't let him get my bag! Stop him and I'll give you a reward! I promise!"

"He's a lot bigger than me, but I takes up my bootblack brush and throws it at his head. He lets her go and turns toward me with an ugly look on his face. I'm getting ready to run when two of my regular customers comes up behind me on their way home. The bruiser doesn't fancy the odds, I guess, and he suddenly bolts past us without a word. The lady falls to the ground and my customers helps her up. She's upset, but she still has her bag. They helps her to a cab and she calls out the address, 333 Castle Square, but she never pays any attention to me in the bustle. I writes down what she says so I won't forget it. Here."

He handed Sherlock Holmes a dirty scrap of paper. Holmes accepted it solemnly.

"I'm due home then, but yesterday I looks up the lady's address on a telegraph office map, before the manager chases me away. After work I takes a 'bus to her home and a fine, handsome building it is. All white, with shiny windows and iron bars protecting flower pots running along the first story and a front porch with columns. There's a set of scrubbed white steps up to

146

the big front door and a doorknocker there fit for Buck House itself.

"I manages to lift it up and it sounds like a tree falling when it hit the door. A big, fat bloke dressed like a toff opens the door and looks down at me.

"What do you want?" says His Nibs.

"I wants to see the lady," says me.

"What about?" he says with a sneer.

"Well, I don't like his tone, so I says "None of your concern; it's between me and the lady." And he says "Go away," and starts to close the door. Just then there's a stir in the hall behind him and I hears the lady's voice. She says "Has our carriage come, Shields?" The fat bloke turns his head and says "No, Madame, it's just a dirty little beggar. I've sent him away." I figures this is my only chance to see her, so I pipes up and say "Lady, lady, it's me, the boy from the alley!" I see her look over the fat bloke's shoulder and I know she recognizes me, but just then another toff steps up beside her and says "What is going on, Virginia?" Her face changes and she says "It's just a boy who's knocked on the door, Randolph." He pushes forward and frowns at me and says "Go away, boy, don't hang about here. Shields, get rid of him." With that, the fat bloke steps out and closes the door behind himself. He grabs my arm, marches me down to the pavement and pushes me about six feet into the street.

"Don't come back here, boy, and don't let me see your face again. There's always a copper around when one is needed, and if you come back I'll introduce you to a couple." With that he marches up the steps again and goes inside. I stands outside for a minute or so, but there's no chance to get in that way, so I slips around the corner into the mews and counts out the back areas until I comes to the right house's gate.

"I peeks over the brick wall but all I see is a couple of tall guys smoking outside the back door. I see the fat bloke talking to them and holding his hand out to about my height so I figures he's warning them to be on the lookout for me. A big stable door behind me opens and a fancy carriage pulled by a pair of greys comes out and it trots down the alley and turns into the street. I remembers what she says about waiting for a carriage so I figures that's hers and now she's gone. I can't think of anything else I can do so I gives it up after a while and go back to St. Paul's. I finds Wiggins and tells him my story. We agrees to meet today and he brings me here. He says you can help me get my reward. She did promise to give me something. I sure hopes you can help, Mister Holmes. The lady did promise and me mum could use anything I could get."

Holmes had listened to young Hopwell's story with interest. Now he smiled. "I agree with you, Jerry. A promise is a promise and not something to be ignored. This case does deserve investigation. I will send word by Wiggins as to when I need you. Meanwhile, here is the price of two shoe-shines, one for me and one for Dr. Watson, to be done at a later date. Take him back, Wiggins, and watch out for my message. Farewell, Jerry. Thank you for bringing such an unusual problem to my attention."

A minute later the two boys burst out of the front door onto Baker Street and ran down the street. Sherlock Holmes sat at his desk and reached out for a map of London and his well-worn copy of *Debrett's*. He spread out the scrap of paper Jerry gave him and opened the book. He consulted the materials and in a few minutes gathered everything up and piled it on his desk. He leaned back.

"I wasn't joking when I said this was an unusual problem, Watson. It appears to touch the upper levels of both society and government. There are hidden depths that must be explored in order to shed light on the behavior of Sir Randolph Wells' wife. Tracing her through the address she gave the cab driver was simplicity itself."

"Is that the American Virginia Crown, society beauty and wife of the Sir Randolph Wells who is the Member of Parliament spoken of as the future Secretary of the Home Office?"

"Indeed, Watson, and a man who has based his political career on his integrity and honesty. In nearly every public speech Randolph Wells has made during the past three years, he has included the phrase "my word is my bond". He neither smokes or drinks or has any other known vices, and is rumoured to be nick-named "Old Rectitude" by his House colleagues. He is the second son of Lord William Wells, the City financier who died just before the Robbins-Sparrow bank scandal broke. Nothing was proven against him, of course, but Randolph's brother Joseph, who inherited the title, lives on the meager rents of what's left of his father's estate and is said to have become a broken, grey-haired old man, though he is barely forty. Sir Randolph works hard to uphold his sterling reputation, possibly as a reaction to his father's own life story. He does have one flaw, however, which proves he is human after all. He is visibly jealous about his wife.

"Virginia Crown met Randolph Wells at a ball three years ago, before his father's death, and they were married a scant five months later. Her father is Donald Crown, the Pennsylvania coal-

149

king. There have been no children from the marriage, but Lady Wells has made a name for herself as a great beauty in high social circles. She is said to be beautiful and kind, but to have no close friends. Apparently she proves my adage that women are secretive. So what is Lady Wells, wife of the notable MP, doing in an alley alone at the edge between the City and Whitechapel struggling with a brute over a handbag?"

"What are you going to do, Holmes?"

"I am going to investigate her behavior, Watson. Secretive women are usually secretive for a reason." Holmes picked up a newspaper from the stack delivered that morning. I was surprised to see him consult the society pages. He smiled and threw down the paper as he rose to his feet

"You need some fresh air, Doctor," he said. "I propose a walk to the Lothard Arcade. If we start now we will get there just in time."

"Just in time for what?" I inquired.

Holmes said nothing more, but led the way out into the sunny street.

The Lothard Arcade was a newly-built row of shops on one of Mayfair's most exclusive boulevards. In front of its fine façade we were treated to the sight of a carriage pulled by a fine pair of greys pull up to the kerb. The coat of arms of the Wells family was painted on the door. A tall lady with brunette hair, clad in a blue walking dress and a fashionable bonnet, and with a carved ruby brooch pinned to her high collar, opened the door. Holmes stepped up and extended a hand to help her step out to the pavement.

She gave him a careless glance as she accepted his offered help. I was impressed by her beauty. She had a fresh American air about her. Large brown eyes looked out from under rounded brows. Her nose was perfectly formed and her lips and chin complemented her high cheek bones. Her figure was slim and graceful. But I noted a caution in her look as she surveyed the pavement while she dismounted from the carriage, as if she expected trouble in some form. A moment later she murmured her thanks to Holmes and turned to the entrance. But Sherlock Holmes didn't let go of her hand. Instead he whispered something into her ear which made her stop and stare at him. Her face became alarmed. She shook her head and tried to walk on. But Holmes spoke more insistently, leaning in close to her ear. Finally she whispered back, nodded and he released her hand. Lady Wells strode into the Arcade without a backwards glance.

"Lady Wells is attending a meeting to plan a charity event here, Watson," said Holmes. "I have just made an appointment to see her at her home this afternoon. With an American the direct approach is usually the best. We have some time to walk the Arcade before we pick up young Hopwell at St. Paul's."

By two o'clock Holmes and I had collected young Jeremiah Hopwell and arrived at 333 Castle Square, near Hyde Park. We climbed out of the hired four-wheeler and climbed the scrubbed steps to the front door with its impressive doorknocker. The portal was opened at our knock by young Hopwell's "fat bloke", who silently ushered us into a fine hall and through it to a sitting room on the left.

It was decorated as a lady's sitting room, all overstuffed furniture and pink-and-white chintz. A magnificent Jacobean mantelpiece rose over a brightly-polished fender and the room had multiple Persian carpets on the hardwood floor. The walls were lined with silken cloth. Little tables filled with books and delicate knick-knacks were arranged tastefully next to a spinet and bench. Lady Wells rose from an armchair by the window as we entered. Holmes introduced us. We were not offered seats.

She spoke in a cold manner to my friend. "You name is well-known to me, Mr. Sherlock Holmes. Believe me, it is only your brother's name, which my husband has mentioned to me, that has allowed you to enter my home at your request. What is your business with me?"

Sherlock Holmes was respectful but firm. "I have come to you in an effort to right a wrong done to a child. Have you ever seen this boy?" Holmes urged young Hopwell forward. "Cast you mind back a few days to an encounter in an alley near the Monument, with a brute who tried to steal you handbag. Now do you recognize this boy? You pleaded with him for help and promised him a reward."

She cast her wide brown eyes down to Jerry Hopwell's face and I saw her expression soften. But when she raised her eyes to Sherlock Holmes, her visage changed. I saw wonder first, then fear. Just as she opened her lips to reply, another voice was heard from the doorway. She shifted her gaze in that direction and her face went white.

"Virginia, who are these gentlemen? Why are they in my house?"

We all turned. An impeccably dressed Sir Randolph Wells stood on the threshold. He was thin, above medium height, and his aristocratic features, in particular his long, sharp nose and hooded black eyes, were in great contrast to his prematurely balding head. He was dressed in a dark suit, suitable for the House of Commons, with a wingtip collar and a subdued ascot. He shot a keen, questioning glance at his wife. Her eyes dropped. He addressed Holmes.

"What is your name and what business do you have in my house, sir?"

"My name is Sherlock Holmes. My business is personal, Sir Randolph."

"Personal? Personal! My dear, do you know any of these people?"

Lady Wells looked away. Now her eyes betrayed nothing and her face was expressionless. "No, Randolph," she answered quietly.

"Then you cannot have personal business with my wife, sir. You carry no letters of introduction with you, I see, and I have no overdue bills. I have never met you, so you cannot have any personal business with me. Therefore you have no business in this house. Shields!"

The butler appeared.

"Shields, these strangers have no business in this house. Please escort them out and make certain they never enter again. Good morning, gentlemen."

With that we were herded from the room and out into the sunshine. I may have fancied it but I think Shields gave little Hopwell an extra hard push out the door as we left. We climbed back into the four-wheeler which had brought us there and headed back to the City.

Sherlock Holmes sat stoically. He stared straight ahead and rested his hands on his knees. I was embarrassed for him. To be treated in such a rude fashion by Sir Randolph Wells and in front of such an audience! My cheeks burned. I wished there was something I could say that would help him, but I could think of nothing. Jerry Hopwell was also silent. He looked from Holmes to me and I shook my head.

When we reached St. Paul's I left the boy on the pavement by the statue of Queen Anne that stood before the great cathedral. I directed the cabby to take us back to Baker Street. It wasn't until we stopped in front of 221b that Holmes stirred.

"Did you notice her brooch, Watson?" he asked as I paid off the driver.

"It was a ruby," I replied.

"It was a carved ruby, Watson. I got a clear look at it when I spoke to her at the Arcade. I think the entire key to this case is centered on that brooch."

Upstairs Holmes went directly to his bedroom and shut the door. I mounted the stairs to my own bedroom and it was several minutes later before I came down and entered the sitting room.

To my surprise it was occupied by a female stranger. A lanky, shabbily-dressed flower seller was seated on the sofa. An old-fashioned poke bonnet covered straight grey hair, which was arranged in a low bun on her thin neck, and a worn fringed shawl was draped over her faded brown-figured dress. Voluminous skirts swirled around a battered pair of old high-topped cloth shoes and nearly covered the tattered woven basket on the floor that still contained a few faded flower petals and stems. A black veil hung down over her face from the edge of the bonnet and her gnarled fingers were covered in black knit gloves.

"I am sorry," I said upon seeing the old woman. "I didn't know anyone was here. Are you waiting for Mr. Holmes?"

"Yes, sir," she replied. Her voice was raspy, a smoker's voice. Her fingers picked at her skirt and smoothed down a bit of ribbon on her bodice.

"He is sure to be out presently," said I. I picked up a newspaper and sat in my chair. Several minutes passed as I rattled the pages and she remained on the sofa, fidgeting with her handkerchief. Finally she gave out a harsh cough, which would not stop, and I rose to my feet.

"That is a bad cough, madam. Would you like some water?"

"Yes, please," she choked. I poured out a glass from the pitcher on the sideboard and placed it in her hand.

"Thank you, Watson," said Sherlock Holmes, as he raised his veil and took a sip.

I was staggered. "Holmes! Really, you are a wizard! What a getup! I suppose this has to do with young Hopwell's case."

"Indeed, my friend. I am pleased to find that my simple efforts at disguise have proven to be so effective. Now that I have passed the Watson test, I can proceed."

He stood and shook out the skirts of his dress. "A pause to collect the marguerites from the vase on the downstairs' hall table and I am off. The flowers will add veracity to my disguise. No, Watson, you are not to follow me. The surveillance of that private home is better done by only one person. I will return quite late. Do not wait up." With that remarkable statement Holmes tripped down the stairs and stepped out the front door into the London sunshine.

It was after supper and dark when I returned from my club to our flat. There had been no sign of Sherlock Holmes or the old flower woman, said Mrs. Hudson, and so I retired to my room. In the morning I came down to the sitting room to find Holmes standing by the window again, wrapped in his old grey dressing gown, holding something small in his hand and examining it closely with his magnifying glass. When he saw me, he folded the item into his handkerchief and thrust it into his pocket.

"It is Saturday, Watson, and Mrs. Hudson has just brought up the breakfast tray. Please help yourself to the eggs and bacon or this excellent curried chicken. I expect visitors within the hour that will bring a resolution, one way or another, to the pretty problem brought us by young Jeremiah Hopwell."

Not another word would he speak, but left the remains of his own breakfast to smoke his pipe while I made a hearty meal. The dishes had been removed well before the doorbell rang and our young client appeared.

"I see you brought your shoe-shine kit with you, Jerry," said Holmes.

"I carrys it everywhere, Mr. Holmes."

"Look at Dr. Watson's boots. In your professional opinion, do they need a shine?"

"Oh, yes, sir."

"I have paid for two shines and I think it is time to collect. There is plenty of time before our next guest arrives. Stick out your foot, Watson. When Jerry is finished with yours, he can polish mine."

Young Hopwell fell to work, and soon I was the possessor of a pair of fine shiny boots. Holmes was next and the child was putting on the finishing touches when the bell to the front door rang.

"Now, Jerry, pack up your gear and run downstairs. Mrs. Hudson will give you something to eat in the kitchen. Wait quietly until I call you back. No questions, now, but go." The boy trotted down the steps while the doorbell rang again. There was a pause while the bell rang a third time, then we heard the street door open and close and footsteps climbed up to our sitting room.

I was not surprised to see Lady Wells on our threshold. She was wearing a dark blue travelling cloak over a grey walking dress and a black hat with a concealing veil. Holmes motioned her to take the sofa. In her gloved hand she clutched one of his business cards which she held out to him.

"You write a persuasive message, Mr. Holmes. As you see, I have come here at your request."

Holmes took the card and handed it to me. I read the words written on the back. "I know your secret. It involves a person from Barcelona. If you want help, I can give it. Come alone to 221b Baker Street at 11 o'clock this morning."

The lady lifted her veil and faced us both with blazing eyes, quite a different woman from the frightened wife of our first meeting. "I will not ask how you come to know my past history, Mr. Holmes. Your reputation does precede you. Tell me, sir, can you and your friend keep my secret? I am convinced that if news of it reaches my husband, it will cause a great scandal that may even affect the British Government. I was younger then, and very foolish, but I have vowed that my Randolph should not suffer for my mistakes. That is why I have let things go as far as they have."

"You are being blackmailed." It was a statement of fact, not a question, from Sherlock Holmes. "It would be best if you told me everything."

"Yes, it would. I cannot bear this burden alone any longer. Of all the people in England, including my husband, you may be the only one who can help me. Four years ago, while on the Grand Tour with my mother, before I met Randolph, I was attracted to our guide, a Spaniard named Senor Artemio del Fisgar. He was dark and suave and dashing. He knew all about art and literature, especially romantic Spanish poetry, and I thought he was the most fascinating man in the world. We exchanged notes unbeknownst to my mother, and I allowed myself to listen to his impossible dreams. There were moments between us, just moments, several times, but in the end I decided to leave him at Calais. I demanded that he return my letters and he brought me a packet, which I destroyed immediately. He promised it contained all of them and I believed him. I met Randolph and found a good life in England. But three months ago he showed up when Randolph was away, and showed me two of the notes he had kept back. Singularly each was innocuous, but together they seemed to tell a much darker tale, a tale of things that never happened. He threatened to send them to my husband. I delayed him with what money I had with me, but he returned in a week. His demands grew. Finally he said that if I could raise a certain sum, a very large sum, he would hand over the notes and disappear from my life forever. I determined to get the money by turning some of my jewels into paste.

"I found a jeweler in the City that could do the job, and I secretly took my ruby brooch, my emerald bracelet and my diamond choker to him. The choker and the bracelet I owned before my marriage, but the brooch had been a gift from Randolph. I was hesitant about taking it, but I had nothing else that would have been valuable enough to raise the sum needed except my wedding ring and the few pieces handed down from Randolph's family. The jeweler did wonderful work. A few days ago I went alone and picked up the originals and the duplicates. I couldn't tell them apart. Only the fact that the real jewels were placed in their original cases allowed me to keep them straight."

"You placed the two sets of cases in your handbag and started to walk back to where you could find a cab. In an alley by the Monument you were accosted by a thief who tried to steal your bag."

"That is correct, Mr. Holmes. I thought I had no hope of keeping the jewels safe from that man until the little bootblack appeared and distracted him. Naturally I didn't want to tell my story to the police, so I left as soon as possible, with the help of those two gentlemen. Back home I sent word to Artemio that I had his payment. We arranged that he would come in a few days to pick up the jewels and give me the notes. Imagine my shock and fear when you demanded a meeting using your brother's name. When you and your companions showed up in my sitting room and my husband found you there I thought all was lost. I believed you had found out about the duplicate jewels and were about to tell Randolph before I could recover the last two letters.

"Last night was the hour agreed upon between Artemio and me. Randolph left for the House and I gave the servants an early evening off, to clear the way for my blackmailer. I let Artemio in by the back door, he gave me the notes, which I read and destroyed, I handed over the original jewels and he left. I thought the entire affair was finished until I opened your letter delivered to me in this morning's post. Oh, Mr. Holmes, you know my secret. Please tell me my ordeal is over and my dear husband will never know my foolish mistake. Think of the damage to his career if it becomes known his wife was blackmailed. It will call into question every public decision he makes in the future."

Lady Wells' voice trembled, her eyes bored into Holmes' eyes and her hands clasped in supplication before her. Never had I ever seen such a scene played out in our sitting room. My friend frowned and sat back in his chair.

"I know I must make allowances for youthful blunders, Lady Wells, but by trying to handle your troubles by yourself you have unnecessarily caused more problems. Madame, when first approached, you should have gone to your husband and confessed everything."

"I know, Mr. Holmes, but my husband is such an upright man, one so dedicated to honesty in both his public and private life...I couldn't do it. I couldn't admit I was weak and be a failure in his

160

eyes. He has such a fine spirit and he is a good man. I can't bear to disappoint him in any way."

"Now that you are satisfied that all the notes are destroyed, what shall you do?"

"I thought that my life could return to what it was before, but I realize now that there are aspects of my past that might reappear to threaten my marriage again. Artemio pledged that he would never return, but he is a scoundrel. When the money he gains from the sale of the jewels runs out, he will come back, and what shall I do then?"

"If I might advise you…"

"Oh, please do, Mr. Holmes!"

"If you wish, I will undertake to recover your jewels from the blackmailing Spaniard and insure that he never troubles you again. But for me to agree to do that, you must promise to confide in your husband, the one man above all others who is pledged to protect you."

"Oh, Mr. Holmes! You are hard, hard. But I can see no other recourse. Yes, I promise. I will tell him everything tonight. But my jewels are gone. Artemio told me he was leaving on the first ship to Amsterdam, where he could easily convert the stones into cash."

"Nevertheless, go home and talk to your husband. Do you believe he loves you? Well then, trust him with your secret. Whatever results from your conversation will be better than your present uncertainty. I have one more request of you. You promised a reward to the little bootblack that helped you in that alley. Do you intend to keep that promise?"

"I do. If you could undertake to deliver it to him, I would be grateful." She pulled out a banknote from her handbag and handed it to Holmes. He glanced at it and smiled.

"I will be in touch with you in a few days, Lady Wells. Godspeed."

After we escorted Lady Wells to her carriage, Holmes called young Hopwell out of the kitchen. He appeared, covered in biscuit crumbs, and my friend handed him his reward.

"Cor! Wait until me Mum sees this! You kept your promise, Mr. Holmes. Thank you."

"You are very welcome, Jerry. I am sure you know how important it is to keep a promise. Now, it is time you went back to St. Paul's. I have called a cab for you and paid the driver. Tuck that carefully into your pocket and please give your mother my compliments."

The young boy left rejoicing and Holmes and I returned to our arm-chairs in the sitting room. I looked on in wonder as he settled into his chair and picked up a blackletter book.

"Holmes, you promised Lady Wells that you would track down del Fisgar and recover those jewels. Yet here you sit, not lifting a finger, while that villain has half-a-day's head start to the gem markets of the Continent."

Sherlock Holmes smiled again and reached into his dressing gown pocket. On the low table before us he spilled out his handkerchief's contents. Before my bedazzled eyes fell a carved ruby brooch, an emerald bracelet and a diamond choker.

"Holmes! You had these treasures in your pocket the entire time Lady Wells was here!"

"Have a cigar, Watson, and I will tell you the complete story of the blackmail dealings of one Senor Artemio del Fisgar against Sir Randolph Wells and his wife."

"Both of them?"

"Yes. I was called in to see Sir Randolph in his office two weeks ago by a high Government official. The problem was deemed so secret I couldn't tell you anything about the case at the time. Sir Randolph had received a demand for classified information concerning domestic security. As a prime candidate for the Home Secretary post he was in possession of such papers. If he refused to turn the files over, stories would be released to the newspapers about actions in his wife's life before their marriage. He reported the demand to the Prime Minister and I was called in.

"It took me only a few days to uncover del Fisgar and his connection to Virginia Crown. I also discovered that he was blackmailing her as well as Sir Randolph. I wasn't sure how she was raising the money he wanted until little Hopwell told us his story. I managed a meeting at the Lothard Arcade. During our whispered conversation I got a good look at her brooch. I saw that it was paste, although Sir Randolph had casually mentioned during one of our meetings that he had given it to her as a gift two years ago."

"If you had met Sir Randolph earlier, what was that charade played out in Lady Wells' sitting room? He threw us out, claiming that you were a complete stranger."

"That was Sir Randolph's idea and for Lady Wells' benefit. Sir Randolph didn't want her telling del Fisgar that Sir Randolph and I knew each other, in case the black mailer had seen me with Lady Wells when we met at the Arcade. His timetable demanded that he collect the secret files and then the jewels on the same night, before he embarked for Amsterdam. Both actions were scheduled for last night.

"Lady Wells, all unknowing, played her part in our scheme perfectly. She agreed to hand over the jewels at ten o'clock last night. She gave the servants an early night off. I learned the details of her acts from the footmen and maids who paused to buy flowers from me in the guise of the old flower seller. Flanked by hidden witnesses and authorized by his superior, Sir Randolph met with the rogue in his office in the House and handed over a copy of the files at nine thirty. Sir Randolph and the witnesses followed del Fisgar in a second cab as the villain made his way to Castle Square. I waited in the shadows in the back as the assignation time grew near. Del Fisgar entered 333 Castle Square through the back door, opened by Lady Wells herself.

"After a short while he emerged the way he had come, and there was a pretty little scene as he became entangled in my flower basket as he tried to escape down the mews. Sir Randolph and I had a fruitful conversation with him in the back garden. Sir Randolph heard the entire story of del Fisgar's plot against Lady Wells, and the important files were recovered, along with the jewels. One of Shield's helpful policemen was summoned and

Artemio del Fisgar was taken away by the sergeant, the witnesses and Sir Randolph."

"What will be the charge?"

"I fancy there will be no charge, at least on the public docket, Watson. Possession of the secret files is enough to get him special treatment from Whitehall. No one in authority wishes either case of blackmail to be exposed in the press. Senor Artemio del Fisgar may just quietly disappear to another country in one of those spy exchanges that happen between governments on occasion. I imagine his last glimpse of England will be from Blackfriars Bridge some dark night, as he boards a ship that will take him away. There is a particular embassy that may find itself welcoming new attachés in the next few weeks, the former ones having been called home under dark clouds of failure."

"Why didn't Sir Randolph take possession of the jewelry?"

"By Sir Randolph's order, I am to conclude my case concerning Lady Wells and her little bootblack savior. By requiring her to confess all to him before restoring the gems, he hopes she will learn to trust her husband in the future. Her reticence has been an obstacle in their marriage. So, in two days' time I will see the lady again and restore her jewels to her.

"Now the hour is late, Watson, and I wish to see my bed before the sun does."

It was two days later that I found Holmes standing in the window's sunshine again, his magnifying glass again in one hand and a familiar ruby brooch in the other, studying it with great attention. He handed the gem and the glass to me and bade me look at the carving on the piece.

165

"Notice that the lines are not sharp-edged, as they should be, but gently rounded. It is one sign of a paste gem. Others include over-heaviness in weight and a brilliant sparkle not native to the original stone. The choker and the bracelet are over there. Lady Wells acquiesced to my request to retain the fakes for my museum. The great soprano Renata Chanteur sings Verdi tonight at Albert Hall and I have been given two tickets to excellent seats. You will join me, of course."

The Case of the Kerchief Clue

I have written elsewhere that my friend Mr. Sherlock Holmes, when involved in a complicated investigation, frequently ignored his health during the days and weeks that he spent on a case. More than once I had been called to a hotel room in a distant land to find him physically exhausted while dozens of congratulatory telegrams covered every level surface and dignitaries and newsmen clamored for his attention. One day such circumstances forced me to take him from the plaudits of a continent over his handling of the industrial sabotage directed toward the Trois Chattes Petite mitten factory and bring him back to England, sick and huddled in a shawl, his face thin and white.. I settled him into a large, sunny bedroom over the surgery of an old friend, Dr. Galen Barnes, in Fletcherford, Cambridgeshire and conferred with my medical friend.

Barnes was a knowledgeable and capable man who had befriended me during our college days. He agreed to my course of treatment and put the entire house at our disposal. It was a bachelor establishment, except for the cook, who slept out. The air was fresh, the food was good, and several attractive walks were easily accessible from Dr. Barnes's back door.

Galen Barnes had a busy practice and Holmes and I were left much to ourselves. By the middle of the second week Holmes had grown well enough to go on short walks in the woods behind our lodgings. One afternoon, after tea, Holmes sat with me on the long wooden bench outside the front door of the brick house. He quietly puffed on a long churchwarden borrowed from our host and soaked up the rays of the sun as it slowly sank toward the western horizon. Inside Dr. Barnes remained in his study, deep in a treatise on infectious disease.

The doctor's house stood on the top of a hill. Fletcherford spread out before us like a checkered counterpane on a bed. The river that gave the community its name wound through the spreading cluster of buildings from west to east. We saw a vista of fields and buildings with thatched and clay tiled roofs spotted among trees, their leaves turning gold and scarlet from an early touch of frost. The ancient town's twisting streets were lined with more oaks and beeches, the autumnal tints adding sparks of color to the bucolic sight. A centuries-old church, its Norman tower a grey shaft of irregularly set stone, crowned the rise opposite. A strip of woods bordered a large field beyond the church. The sky spread out overhead like a fine Chinese bowl overturned. We heard birdsong.

For half an hour we sat in companionable silence. At last Holmes stirred and pointed with the stem of the pipe to a lone man approaching the house on horseback.

"That farm labourer wants the doctor," he drawled.

"How can you tell he is a farm labourer?" I asked.

"That is not a horse bred for riding or to pull a carriage. Look at its size and its feathery hocks. That man is riding a Shire, an animal meant to pull a plow or convey heavy loads. Observe the harness, clearly made to attach to a farm wagon. There is no saddle, yet the rider keeps his seat on the horse's broad back with practiced ease. What is more, his clothing easily betrays his occupation. Those are the shoes and coat of a man accustomed to the byre, not the drawing room. There is haste in his mission, as you can see by the slight lather on the horse. Here he is, Watson. Ho, man! Whom do you seek?"

The messenger pulled up his steed at the garden wall. "I've sommat for Dr. Barnes!" he shouted.

Behind us a window slid up and the doctor thrust out his head. "Is that you, Simon? Who needs me?"

"Constable Chartreux sent this." The man held out a folded sheet of paper, which I ran down and retrieved from him. I handed it in to Barnes through the window and waited as he opened it and read the contents. He handed it back to me and addressed the man waiting by the garden wall.

"Tell the constable that I will be there in twenty minutes." The rider touched his hat and galloped back the way he had come. Our host rang the bell and changed from his house slippers into a pair of shoes. The butler came in and his master gave instructions for his carriage to be brought around to the front.

"I am afraid you will have to excuse me, Watson," Barnes said through the window, as he shrugged into his coat. "That note, as you can see, calls me to the "Ingbong Bell" a public house on the other side of Fletcherford beyond the church. A little kitchen maid disappeared from there two nights ago and some of the men of the district have been searching for her. Now it seems that they have recovered her body from a disused well and the constable has asked me in to consult in the matter. I shan't be more than an hour or two. I hope this incident will not upset Mr. Holmes."

I murmured a response and resumed my seat by my invalid friend. He had put aside his pipe and had followed the exchanges with a show of lazy interest. Now he picked up the note that I dropped on the seat beside me and cast an eye over its contents.

"Just that, a summons to the "Ingbong Bell" to examine the remains," he said. "I…"

"Don't even think about involving yourself in this case, Holmes," I said forcefully. "You have only been out of bed a few days. In fact, I was just about to suggest that you lie down before dinnertime, to conserve your strength."

Sherlock Holmes let the paper flutter to the ground at his feet. "You are correct, friend Watson," he replied. "Very well. I dare say that Dr. Barnes will be able to fill us in on all the details when he returns." Without uttering another word Holmes allowed me to escort him upstairs to his room as our host drove through the front gate and clattered down the hill towards town.

The lamps had been lit and we were wondering if we should sit down to eat when Galen Barnes walked in the back door after leaving his horse with the stable boy.

"I have kept you waiting long enough, gentlemen," he said as he hung up his hat. "Please go in to the dining room and I will be with you in a moment."

We had just been served the soup when our host, hastily washed and brushed, took his seat at the head of the table.

With my sharp medical eye upon him, Sherlock Holmes made a great show of merely casual interest when Barnes mentioned, during the joint, about his errand to the "Ingbong Bell". "We don't have much excitement around here, Mr. Holmes. Fletcherford is much quieter than London. When the news first broke of little Kitty Cymric's disappearance, I thought it best not to say anything to you."

"You don't need any new excitement," I said. Holmes smiled.

"Well, friend Watson, the cat is out of the bag now. Watson will tell you, Dr. Barnes, once I get the scent there's no keeping this old hound out of the hunt." I knew then my cause was lost. I decided to be grateful for the days of rest Holmes had already had and accept the inevitable.

"You may as well tell all," I sighed, "or there will be no living with him."

The plates were taken away and cheese and fruit were placed on the table. Dr. Barnes offered cigars and port before he began to recall the events of his visit to the old public house.

"The "Ingbong Bell" was built on the foundation stones of a small Catholic abbey torn down by Henry VIII's order. The abbey was noted for the clarity of its bell, which was cast in the field nearby. St. Bartholomew's was built as Church of England. It got the bell for its tower during Elizabeth's time, but the name went to the public house.

"For the past twenty years the landlord has been Nathan Nebelung. He has two sons, who help him with the business. His wife, a local girl named Cora, minds the kitchen, and their daughter is barmaid. Mrs. Nebelung is the sister of Fletcherford's most successful merchant, the haberdasher Birman Manx. The Nebelungs also employ a young kitchen maid at the "Bell". The maid was Kitty Cymric, an orphan girl of fourteen summers, who had been there for nearly a year.

"From all reports, the girl was ordered about and worked long hours, but she had a sweet and accommodating nature. Kathleen Nebelung, the daughter, and her Manx cousin were particularly fond of her. The two girls made a kind of pet of her. Then two weeks ago Kitty and Kathleen had a falling out. Kitty grew quiet. While she did her work as faithfully as before, she took to disappearing during odd hours and refusing to tell anyone where she had been. Finally, two nights ago, she walked out of the kitchen after the last batch of dishes were washed and never came back.

"They missed her the next morning. At first Nebelung thought she had run away. But a search of her room showed at all her possessions, including her Sunday dress and a little hoard of coins, totaling 1 shilling, thruppence, had been left behind. That was when the alarm was given. The area was searched and today her body was found at the bottom of an old well forgotten in the woods at the edge of the abbey grounds.

"The remains had been taken to a shed in the mews behind the pub. Chartreux met me at the door. The shed had no windows and the only light came from the lantern he held up and the open doors. The body, clad in her work dress, stockings and shoes, was laid out on planks set on two trestles in the center of the room.

"She had died of a broken neck, doubtlessly from the fall. The well had been dry. There was evidence of a wooden cover, which had long since rotted away. In fact, knowledge of the well had been lost to the local residents. It must have served the old abbey. After the abbey's destruction it been hidden by a stand of trees and brush that grew up around it. Thomas Stout's dog had been barking at the trees. When Stout went to see the reason he nearly fell into it himself."

"There were no other marks on her?" asked Sherlock Holmes.

"I found nothing suspicious. Her dress was snagged by thorns from a wild rosebush that grew at the edge of the well. There was a bruise on her forehead consistent with what she would have received by falling down the shaft. It must have knocked her unconscious. The broken neck was plain enough. The only other mark was one on her forearm. I couldn't match it to anything caused by her fall. It almost looked like a set of fingers. But Mrs. Nebelung said she had slapped her arm the night she disappeared for some minor kitchen infraction. In fact, that's why they thought she had run away. I told Constable Chartreux I had a pair of London gentlemen staying with me and he allowed me to bring back the depositions he took from the witnesses who saw her that last night."

"Thank you. I will read them later. So you found nothing else on the body?"

"The only odd thing was what I discovered clutched in her right hand. It was a cloth wadded up into a tight ball. I unfolded it and found a lady's kerchief, with the initial K on it. I showed it to the Nebelungs. They had never seen it before. I thought that odd, so I asked Chartreux if I could bring it along for you to see. He agreed to let you look at the thing, although he believes Kitty's death was just an accident. She must have fallen down the well while walking in the moonlight that night. The coroner is away and the inquest has been planned for his return next week."

Sherlock Holmes took the proffered kerchief and smoothed it out on the table. "Observe, Watson. This handkerchief is made of fine linen and edged with lace. The letter K is hand-embroidered in pink silk floss. This scrap of finery didn't belong to little Kitty Cymric. This is not the kerchief of a kitchen worker. The question becomes how did the kitchen maid come into possession of such a prize?"

"Perhaps she bought it," said I.

"Such a thing would cost her three weeks' wages. Remember the little stash of coins found in her room. Kitty was a saver, not a spender."

"She found it, then."

"That would be unlikely. It is still stiff with the commercial starch new handkerchiefs are treated with during the manufacturing process. This scrap of cloth has never been washed. There are no marks or stains on it. Who would throw away such a nice kerchief? No, she didn't find it in a dustbin or along the road."

"A gift, then," Barnes suggested.

"Given to her by whom? There are no reports of a suitor. The people closest to her have never seen it before. Human nature would demand that a young servant would display such a prize to her friends."

"Then she must have stolen it," I said.

"Ah, there is that possibility," replied Sherlock Holmes. "Was she known as a thief?"

"No," said Dr. Barnes. "Her employers spoke highly of her honesty. She once confessed to the breaking of a platter that Mrs. Nebelung had forgotten she owned and would never have known was missing."

Holmes folded the handkerchief. "It is too late to continue the investigation this evening. I propose that we call it a night and resume our quest after breakfast tomorrow. Where is the body?"

"Constable Chartreux ordered a watch over the girl in the shed overnight while a coffin is readied for her funeral tomorrow afternoon. Due to the condition of the body it is thought prudent not to wait any longer than that. She will be interred in St. Bartholomew's churchyard at three."

"Then we have several things to do before the service, gentlemen. I would point out one fact to the constable, Dr. Barnes. On the night of the accident there was no moon. Good night. I will see you at breakfast."

We arrived at the "Ingbong Bell" the next morning. The public house stood with a small courtyard in front of it in a street at the far edge of town. There were stables and sheds in a narrow mews behind it. Beyond that was a section of the woods and a fallow field. The brick and timber "Bell" was three stories tall with a line of dormers sticking out of the long thatched roof. Multi-paned windows flanked either side of a low entrance door in the center. The courtyard was paved with flagstones laid down before Shakespeare was born. Dr. Barnes guided the carriage into the mews at the rear of the "Bell" where the stables and storage sheds were situated. The doctor pulled up in front of an outbuilding with a bicycle propped up by the door. He was greeted by a burly man in a police uniform. Our host introduced us to Constable Chartreux, a tall Cambridgeshire native with a large brown mustache. Sherlock Holmes wasted little time in conversation but moved to examine the body of the unfortunate girl. He motioned for Chartreux to pull back the sheet covering the still form.

"I am particularly interested in the bruises on her arm," he said. "In which hand did you find the kerchief, Dr. Barnes?"

"In the right hand," replied the doctor.

"Then we may take as supposition that she was right-handed. Yes, the right palm and arm are slightly larger than the left. The hand has been exercised more; therefore the muscles are more developed." He drew back the sleeve of her dress. "Ah, here are the bruises mentioned. Look at this, Watson, through my magnifying glass. The marks curve around the arm, the thumb on top and four fingers on the bottom. Now, friend Watson, hold out your arm. I slap you thus, as might a housewife if a child reaches for the sugar bowl. Observe that all the fingers strike you on the top of your forearm. None curl around the arm. It doesn't matter from which angle the blow is made. The result is the same. The only way to explain these bruises is that the arm was gripped, and gripped hard, and held for a time."

"That is amazing, Holmes!" I said.

"The bruises also show that the attacker was also right-handed, male and quite strong. Look at the size of the finger marks. They were made by a man's hand. The color of the bruises indicate the strength used. Someone wanted her to open her fingers and release the kerchief."

Dr. Barnes and Constable Chartreux watched in fascination at Holmes' demonstration. When he was finished, Chartreux pulled up the sheet. Just then we were interrupted by a knock on the open door and the appearance of a young lady. Dr. Barnes introduced her as Kathleen Nebelung, daughter of the innkeeper and little Kitty Cymric's former friend.

She was a young woman of eighteen years, chocolate-box pretty, with rosy cheeks, blonde hair and blue eyes somewhat bedewed with tears. Her plumb figure was dressed in a green cotton gown and a little black bow rode the waves of her piled-up locks as her sign of mourning. A gold locket on a chain nestled on her bosom just below her smooth throat. She wore no rings, as befit a young woman who was required to squire tankards of beer to thirsty customers each day, and she stood in the doorway twisting a corner of her apron with her fingers.

Sherlock Holmes questioned her gently, asking about Kitty's early days in the pub and the way the friendship grew between the kitchen maid and the innkeeper's daughter. In a short while he had gained Miss Nebelung's trust and she relaxed under his eye.

"I understand that a week before Kitty disappeared you and she had a falling-out," said the detective. "Please tell me about that."

Tears welled up in the young woman's eyes. She dabbed at them with the hem of her apron. "I began walking out with Johnny Flynn last spring. He works with his father on the Fletcher estate. He's handsome and fun and treats me like a queen. Here is his picture." She opened the locket and showed us an image of a curly-haired, cleft-chinned man with a broad smile.

Holmes examined it gravely and asked how Kitty had reacted to the arrangement. "She was happy for us, but after months of seeing us together she began questioning everything he said and did. She told me he was not the man I thought he was, that he didn't mean the little compliments he paid me and finally she told me he was keeping a secret from me. I lost my temper. I told her she was jealous of my happiness, and to never talk to me again unless she could prove her accusations. After that I avoided her as much as I could. Then mother started complaining that Kitty was becoming secretive and was never where she was supposed to be. It wasn't until she went missing that I felt bad and wondered if it was my cold shoulder that drove her away."

"Will Johnny Flynn be with you at the funeral this afternoon?"

"Yes."

Sherlock Holmes brought out the lace handkerchief and showed it to her. "Have you ever seen this before?"

The young lady picked up the cloth and examined it. She shook her head and her curls bounced. "It's very pretty, but it's not mine."

"Did you ever see Kitty with this kerchief?"

"Kitty? Where would she get such a nice thing? No, Kitty Cymric never owned a kerchief like this. She had an old piece of calico she carried in her pocket. Now she's dead and I'll never have a chance to make up with her." Kathleen Nebelung burst into tears and hastily excused herself.

Sherlock Holmes let her go. He turned to Dr. Barnes and Constable Chartreux. "Have you heard of this Johnny Flynn?"

The police officer nodded. "I've seen him about with Kathleen. He's assistant groundskeeper with his dad over at the Fletcher estate. Baron Fletcher's family has been at Fletcherford since before Richard II. Johnny is the only son and frankly, the family have pinned their hopes on him. He hangs out with a fast crowd, but he seems more settled since he began seeing Kathleen."

Dr. Barnes shook his head. "I have been the physician for the Fletcher estate for years, both the family and the servants. Johnny's mother and his sisters idolized him since the day he was born. I consider him spoiled. Anything he ever wanted they managed to get him. I remember Joan, his oldest sister, spending all her pocket money to get him some candy he cried for when he was a child. I'm not surprised about his choice of friends. Johnny Flynn never met a bottle or a billiard cue that he didn't like."

"Who is his closest friend?"

"That would be Tim Purcey. I saw him in the courtyard when we came in."

Another knock sounded at the open door and two men came in, somberly dressed. Behind them I saw a coffin made of fresh pine boards resting on a cart. The older man removed his hat and said, "Excuse me, sirs. We're from Murdstone and Marley. We're here to pick up the deceased. There isn't much time to get her ready for the services this afternoon and Mr. Murdstone is waiting back at the shop."

"Of course," said Constable Chartreux. We left him and the undertaker's men to their melancholy task and walked out into the mews.

Dr. Barnes looked at his watch. "My surgery starts at 10 o'clock, so I must be going back. May I offer you gentlemen a ride?"

"I believe I will walk, if Dr. Watson doesn't object. I'd like to take this opportunity to explore Fletcherford while the good weather holds. Watson, you go with the doctor."

"I'd rather stay with you, Holmes."

"Nonsense, I'll be perfectly fine. I'll be back by luncheon." Holmes insisted and finally I agreed. The last sight I had of Sherlock Holmes was as the tall, pale detective watched the undertaker's men carried out the coffin from the shed toward the cart.

There was a line of patients waiting for Galen Barnes at the surgery. I took up a medical periodical in his study and tried to read it. I admit the articles didn't spark my interest and I spent most of the time watching out the front window for Holmes' return. Finally, just as the last patient left and the butler struck the Chinese gong for lunch, I saw Sherlock Holmes come through the garden gate. He looked tired, but his eyes were bright and a smile was on his lips. My heart rose. He looked like his old self. I had to concede that involvement in this case had completed the cure I had begun.

During the mid-day meal Holmes spoke of the local architecture and the general history of the region. When we finished Dr. Barnes pushed back from the table. He looked at the mantle clock and remarked, "The funeral is scheduled for three o'clock. I'll order the carriage to be ready by a quarter to."

"I would like to arrive a little earlier," Holmes said. "The churchyard is quite ancient and I would like to spend some time among the tombstones. One can find such interesting old epitaphs in these small burying-grounds."

"Then I'll make it two-thirty," Dr. Barnes said and thus it was agreed. Meanwhile Holmes and I retired to the long wooden bench with the London papers.

At the appointed time we arrived at St. Bartholomew's. A crowd had begun to gather, but Holmes led us off to the side, away from the freshly dug grave. We wandered through the cemetery, examining a few of the stones, until we fetched up behind the people massed around the newly arrived pine coffin.

It was not a large group, consisting of about a dozen people and, standing off to one side, Constable Chartreux. A short man in robes, the vicar, was fussing with his prayer book. At Holmes' request, Dr. Barnes pointed out the main mourners.

"The round, chubby-cheeked man is Nathan Nebelung, and the woman with him is his wife, Cora. Her brother Birman and his wife stand next to her, and their daughter Katrina Manx is there with Kathleen. The young men at the back are the Nebelung sons. Those men in back of them are old-timers at the "Bell". That young fellow who just arrived and joined the girls is Johnny Flynn."

Johnny Flynn was as good-looking as the picture in Kathleen Nebelung's locket. He was of medium height and broad in the shoulders, dressed in gaiters and a Norfolk jacket suit of grey tweed. When he removed his cap he displayed a head of wavy black hair. Katrina Manx bore a resemblance to her cousin

Kathleen, except that her hair was light brown and her dress was a touch richer, as befit the daughter of a successful haberdasher.

The service was short. After the mourners had filed past and tossed handfuls of dirt on the lowered coffin, the crowd began to disperse. As the young man, a cousin on either arm, started to guide them out of the churchyard, Sherlock Holmes stepped forward.

"Excuse me, Miss Nebelung, I believed you dropped this." He proffered her the kerchief found in Kitty's hand.

"I told you, Mr. Holmes, that that is not mine."

Holmes bowed. He offered the scrap of lace to Miss Manx. "Is this yours?"

Katrina Manx bent over the kerchief. "Yes, that is mine. I embroidered the "K" myself. But how did you get it? I gave it to Johnny last week."

Kathleen Nebelung's face went pale, then red. "You gave it to Johnny? Why?"

Miss Manx blushed. "It was just a little keepsake. We had been talking about the wedding..."

"Wedding! What wedding?"

"I was going to tell you, cousin, but then Kitty disappeared and everyone was upset. Johnny and I..."

Kathleen Nebelung's attitude became arctic. Here face was white again. She dropped Flynn's arm. Her face was a study in anger. She ignored her cousin's explanations and turned to the young man.

"What is she talking about, Johnny?"

Johnny Flynn was staring at the kerchief in Holmes' hand with a sort of sick fascination. He raised his eyes to Miss Nebelung. His expression said it all. The young woman stared at him wordlessly and then she slapped his face. He didn't react. After a moment she turned abruptly and walked away, her back straight and her step firm. She didn't look back. Katrina Manx tugged at his arm.

"Johnny, stop her, tell her. We're going to be married in the spring. You said you wanted something of mine to carry with you. I gave you that handkerchief. How did this man get it?"

"It was found in Kitty Cymric's hand after she was pulled from the well," said Sherlock Holmes.

Miss Manx pulled her hand away from Flynn's sleeve. "You gave my handkerchief to Kitty?"

"No, no! It wasn't that way at all! Listen, Kat, I can explain. Kitty was spying on me. She was carrying tales back to Kathleen. She…"

"Kathleen! Why would Kathleen be interested in what you were doing?"

"Well, Kathleen and I saw each other a little. But, Kat, it didn't mean anything!" The young man's face was twisted in misery. He stammered in his frantic efforts to salvage the engagement. Miss Manx's attitude became as cold as her cousin's.

"It must have meant something to Kathleen. Were you walking out with her all this time? Yes, I can see you were. I wish she had hit you harder. Under the circumstances, please consider yourself released from any obligations to me. Good-by, Mr. Flynn. I never want to see you again."

With that last parting shot, Miss Katrina Manx trotted toward her cousin. As the two women met, we heard a scrap of conversation. Miss Manx said "Johnny never told me," to which Miss Nebelung responded "Then Kitty was telling the truth." They left together, their arms around each other's waists.

Johnny Flynn stared after the two girls forlornly. Sherlock Holmes cleared his throat and the young man looked at him.

"Mr. Flynn, do you want to explain how this kerchief ended up in that poor girl's hand?"

"Hey, mister, I don't know who you are, but I think you've done enough damage for one day. I'm not talking to you. I'm going home."

Constable Chartreux placed a beefy hand on Flynn's shoulder. "I suggest a stop at the police station first, Johnny. This gentleman, Mr. Sherlock Holmes, and I have some questions for you."

"Sherlock Holmes!"

Holmes handed the kerchief to the constable. "Ah, I see you have heard of me, Mr. Flynn. How very gratifying. But I don't think you will have to ask any questions, Constable. I believe I can explain how Kitty Cymric died and the part Mr. Flynn played in her death."

"I didn't kill her! I don't know anything about it!"

There was a stone bench under a yew tree nearby. It was inscribed with the words "Sacred to the Memory of Elizabeth Muffet, who Lived and Died Sitting on her Tuffet." Holmes sat down and pulled the bundle of witness statements out of his coat. He gave the bundle to Constable Chartreux.

"If I am mistaken in any part of this account, I am sure Mr. Flynn can correct me. After Dr. Barnes told Dr. Watson and me the story of Kitty Cymric and her unfortunate fate, I stayed up late last night reading the reports given by the people who knew her. I had a good idea of the facts of the case by the time we arrived at the shed in the mews behind the "Ingbong Bell". I looked over her dress and noted the thorns that remained snagged in the fabric from the bush by the well. I examined the bruises on her arm and determined that they were inflicted by an attacker who was trying to get Kitty to drop the handkerchief she held. Since the kerchief was demonstrably not hers she had to have stolen it. Kathleen Nebelung said that Kitty had been warning her about Johnny Flynn, that he was not the man she thought he was and that he was keeping a secret from her. Miss Nebelung didn't believe her accusations about Flynn and demanded proof. Kitty set out to obtain that proof.

"The kitchen maid had been absent from her duties, even refusing to tell her employer where she had been and what she had been doing. That was because she had begun following Flynn whenever she could. I shared the contents of my flask with Tim Purcey, Flynn's best friend, this morning after Dr. Barnes and Dr. Watson went back to the surgery. He told me that the night Kitty disappeared Purcey, Flynn and a couple of other men were playing billiards at the "Old Oaken Bucket" just north of Fletcherford in the Northern Road. Flynn pulled out this handkerchief and showed it to them. He bragged that Katrina Manx, the only daughter of one of the richest men in Fletcherford, had given it to him and that they were going to get married.

"He put the kerchief back in his coat, then took the coat off and hung it on a peg when he began the next game. A few minutes later, while the men were concentrated on the game, the front door slammed shut. Purcey saw Flynn's coat lying on the floor. Flynn picked it up, went through the pockets, and suddenly ran out that same door. Through the window the men saw Flynn running across the road and toward the woods behind the "Ingbong Bell" a mile away. Purcey thought he saw another figure crossing the field beyond the road, but he couldn't be sure because there was no moon. Flynn didn't return to the "Old Oaken Bucket" that night.

"After Kitty Cymric was reported missing and people began to search for her, Purcey asked Flynn to join him in hunting for the girl. He refused. Purcey joined the search and gave no more thought to Johnny Flynn.

"The bruises on the victim's arm showed that Flynn managed to catch up with Kitty, and squeezed her arm in an effort to make her drop the kerchief. She broke away and ran into the woods. The next few minutes are at the crux of this case. Did Johnny Flynn break off his pursuit and let the girl run away? Then did Kitty fall into the well in the darkness by herself? Or did he follow her into the trees and during another struggle, push Kitty Cymric into the well, thus causing her death?"

"I never went into the trees," said Johnny Flynn. "She kicked my shin and I left her go, then she ran into the woods. I'll roll up my pant leg and show you the bruise. See that? I lost sight of her. It was too dark to follow, even darker under those branches than out in the field. I didn't want to risk braining myself on some low-hanging branch. I recognized Kitty during the fight and I knew she would go back to the "Ingbong Bell" on the other side of the woods. I circled round and stopped only when I reached the mews. I hid in a stable where I could see the back door and waited for her to return. I watched until morning but she never came back. When the alarm was raised I decided to say nothing and went home."

"A very pretty story," rumbled Constable Chartreux. "I think it will be up to the authorities to determine if any part of it is true. Meanwhile, John Flynn, I arrest you in the name of the Crown for the death of Kitty Cymric. Anything you say may be taken down and used in evidence against you."

"I swear it was an accident! You big dumb copper, don't you hear me?"

Sherlock Holmes addressed the policeman. "That bruise could have come as he said, or he may have gotten it when she tried to escape from him in the woods. I draw your attention to the two tiny rosebush thorns that are snagged in the left leg of his trousers just above the gaiters. They are identical to the ones caught up in Kitty's dress. After I gave my last drop of brandy to Tim Purcey I examined the field and the woods where the well was hidden. The dirt had been churned up by the searchers, but I was able to isolate two distinct sets of footsteps. One pair belonged to a man and the other was that of a small woman. They came from the field and ended at the well's edge. A trail left by the man then ran off in the direction of the Fletcher estate."

Johnny Flynn had been glaring at us all. Now he spun around and spat at Sherlock Holmes. Constable Chartreux pulled him back as Flynn vented his fury.

"That miserable brat! She poked her nose into my business and stole my handkerchief! I was just trying to get it back before she could show it to Kathleen. I just wanted to get it back." He suddenly realized what he was saying and fell silent. As Constable Chartreux fastened handcuffs to his wrists he darted murderous glances at us and began to mutter to himself.

"Sherlock Holmes! The great meddler! The famous snoop! Why should I swing for what he says? He wasn't even there!"

His voice died away as he was led out of the churchyard. Holmes stood up. He turned to Galen Barnes.

"I thank you for your hospitality, Doctor, but I think it's time for us to return to the city. I saw by the London newspaper that Inspector Lestrade has been put in charge of the Col. Runcible Spoone case. If he doesn't realize the importance of the awl and the pudding vat, he will never solve it. The next train to London starts in an hour, Watson, and our first stop will be at Scotland Yard."

The Case of the Braided Basket

One summer day my friend Sherlock Holmes and I returned to Baker Street from a walk along London's streets. As I closed the door of the vestibule between the front door and the seventeen steps that led up to our sitting room, I noticed Holmes was bent over something on the hall table.

It was a large oval wicker basket with braided handles at either end. I looked inside and was surprised to see a tiny sleeping infant, with only its head and hands exposed, resting comfortably on a bed of folded cloths.

"What an extraordinary thing!" I exclaimed.

"Might I take it from that remark that you have not seen this child before, Watson? That it is not a patient or perhaps a relative?"

"Of course not, Holmes!" I replied indignantly.

"You may take it as read that it is a stranger to me as well. Since it belongs to neither of us, questions arise. What is it doing here? Where is its mother?"

"She could be visiting Mrs. Hudson."

"Then why leave the basket with its little occupant here in the hall? Wouldn't it be expected that such a young child be kept in near proximity to a parent?"

"Perhaps it relates to a case concerning a client of yours."

"Currently I have no client, but the thought raises definite possibilities. First let me garner what information I can from the available source."

Gently Holmes probed the basket and its tiny inhabitant, turning back cloths and feeling beneath the child. He unwrapped the covers on the infant and took note of what it was wearing. Finally he tucked the last blanket back in place and straightened up from his search. The baby had woken during the examination, but remained quiet, its large brown eyes fixed on Holmes' face.

"The infant is plentifully supplied with material goods, including three receiving blankets, two acting as a make-shift mattress and one as the cover. It is dressed in a nappy, still clean, and a newly-washed lace-trimmed sacque. This cotton bonnet, also laced-trimmed, was tucked inside. The basket is woven of willow withes and the supports and handles have been braided of ash strips, apparently to add strength."

Holmes pulled out his magnifying glass and examined the bonnet and its lace. He also applied the lens to the oval basket. I held out my hand and the baby grasped one of my fingers.

"The cotton of the blankets and the sacque is undistinguished, but the lace is machine-made and similar to that sold at Gammidge's, the People's Emporium. The weaving shows the basket is Japanese and such baskets are also sold at Gammidge's.

"Judging by the state of the nappy and the fact that the infant shows no signs of hunger, we may conclude that it has not been left alone long. Why would anyone leave a young baby in a basket at the home of Sherlock Holmes without even a note of explanation?"

"It must be a case!" I said.

"But what sort of case, Watson? What sort of cases could involve a small baby?

"A kidnapping for ransom."

"There is no note, remember. Please continue."

"An unfortunate birth. Maybe the mother wants you to find the child a good home. Or the mother wants you to locate the father and deliver the child to him."

"Again there are no such directions left with the baby. This island, not to mention Greater London itself, is a very wide field without a compass."

"It could be a missing person. The basket may have been picked up by mistake in a busy neighborhood. When it was discovered that the baby was in it, it was left at a safe location to be returned to its parents."

"But if it was a simple mistake the child could have been returned easily. Again, there is no note with name and address."

"Perhaps the mother was attacked and the child taken away in the confusion. It was dropped here to get rid of it."

"You scintillate today, my friend. Can you think of any other scenarios that might fit these circumstances?"

"I'm afraid I have exhausted all the possibilities."

"Not every one, Watson. I could tell you four more. However, this palaver isn't bringing the child back to its family. Our next step will be to…"

At this point I withdrew my hand and the infant started to make sounds. That diverted our attention. As we bent over the basket again, Mrs. Hudson bustled into the hall from the corridor that led to the kitchen in the back of the house.

"Ah, I see you gentlemen have met our little visitor. Isn't that such a good baby! I put that basket out here just fifteen minutes ago and have heard nary a peep from it."

"Are we to understand, Mrs. Hudson, that you placed this child out here in the hall fifteen minutes ago and left it untended?" asked Sherlock Holmes sternly.

Our landlady put her hands on her ample hips and looked Holmes right in the eye. "I just said so, Mr. Holmes, didn't I, and why should that be a problem? He was asleep until your talking woke him up. I agreed to watch little Bailey Bunting while his mother went to the stores. Her husband is out hunting for work and there was no one else to do it. I was in the middle of putting up preserves and the kitchen was too hot for the baby to stay in for long. I've finished now and the kitchen is cooling off nicely."

I was apologetic. "We…I…just thought that…well, the baby…"

Mrs. Hudson frowned and picked up the basket and its contents with a sniff. She turned back the way she had come. "Not everything in this house is a mystery, Dr. Watson. I sometimes think that you may be spending too much time with Mr. Sherlock Holmes."

The Case of the Callous Collector

"Someone is going to kill me, Mr. Sherlock Holmes! I am certain of it! You must save my life! I'll pay any price for your protection if you will agree to start this very minute!"

I looked with wonder at the agitated little man who sat trembling on our sitting room sofa. His card, which he handed to Holmes when he arrived at 221b Baker Street, stated that his name was Mr. Twain Todd, gentleman. His appearance was unusual, for he looked for all the world as if he had grown to a normal height then been pushed down by a heavy hand until he was left barely five feet tall. His head was large and his curly hair was cut short, so it fluffed out in all directions at the same length. He had no neck to speak of and the rest of his body was squat and blobby. He had short thick legs and very broad feet. He had a wide flat nose and his large pale blue eyes were watery and bulged out of their sockets, indicating a possible thyroid condition. He wore a tropical weight suit with a heavy watch chain bearing a small carved oval of stone slung across his generous stomach. He wrung his wide hands together as he waited for my friend's response.

Sherlock Holmes leaned back in his armchair, fingering Mr. Todd's card and eyeing him closely.

"Watson, please get our visitor a brandy. It is early, but I am sure that Mr. Todd will welcome such refreshment. There, pour him another. Now, Mr. Todd, beside the facts that you ate your dinner last night at the Langham Hotel, have spent some years in

193

Egypt, smoke a hookah for your nerves and only recently returned to England, I know nothing of your circumstances. I cannot decide if I can help you until you tell me your problem."

The little man stared at Holmes with the astonished and suspicious look with which I had become so familiar. "You have heard of my collection and have had me followed, sir. You are part of the plot! Oh, I have fallen into a den of thieves! I am lost!" He staggered to his feet and looked wildly around for escape. He bolted for the door and we sat astonished as he thundered down the stairs and out into the street. I looked out of the window in time to see him bounding down the pavement toward Baker Street Station, his hat clutched in one hand and his coattails flying behind his squat body.

"Now, what do you make of that, Holmes?' I asked as I returned to my armchair. Mr. Twain Todd's arrival had interrupted our post-breakfast cigarettes and I found mine still smoldering in the dish where I had dropped it.

"I must admit that the little exercises in deduction which I always considered a normal part of my detecting method had never produced such a reaction before, Watson. Until he handed me his card, I had never heard of Mr. Twain Todd in my life. Emerging from one of his waistcoat pockets was a receipt for a restaurant meal at the Langham Hotel dated last evening. The paper was twisted but I am familiar with the appearance of many different hotel receipts and easily recognized this as from the Langham. I could read the date from my seat. From another pocket I smelled the distinctive odor of lavender-flavored tobacco that is normally reserved for use in the hookah, a Middle Eastern pipe. Lavender is a well-known fragrance used for calming purposes. Egypt is indicated by the address on his card and the scarab hanging from his watch chain."

"How did you know he recently returned to England?"

"Mr. Todd's card gave an address in a Cairo hotel. He was now here. The man had not had time to order new cards."

"It is all so simple, Holmes. Now that you have explained it, why, anyone could do it."

"So I have been told," replied Holmes wryly. He then picked up a morning newspaper from the stack and opened it.

The rest of that day was spent deep in the details of the Mulberry Bush Farms case and I had nearly forgotten about our agitated visitor until three days later when Mrs. Hudson ushered two gentlemen into our sitting room.

"Mr. Holmes? My name is Rafferty and this is Professor Molesley. Professor Molesley is head of the Egyptology department of Westminster College and I am the author of several books on the Old and New Kingdoms. We have come here to enlist your help in the matter of Mr. Twain Todd."

Mr. Rafferty was a man of thirty-eight, of medium height, a dark-haired man wearing a Savile Row suit. He had a long nose with black eyes set close together and had a ready smile. His arms and shoulders were thick and his handshake displayed a show of strength that surprised me. Professor Molesley was ten years older, clad in black, pudgy and out of shape, with thinning brown hair and the slight stoop of the scholar. The light coming through our windows flashed off the thick lens of his gold spectacles.

Holmes waved them to seats on the sofa and picked up a page of notes from his desk.

"Since Dr. Watson and I were visited by Mr. Twain Todd a few days ago I have arranged to learn more about him," he remarked. "My agents have been swift but thorough. Please correct me if any of my information is wrong.

"Mr. Twain Todd was the last twig of an old family tree rooted in Kent. His father and his before him, indeed many generations of Todds, grew up at Todd Hall. It was a large old house, built in the days of the first Charles, and with enough land for some excellent shooting, hunting and fishing. But he cared for none of that and the house needed extensive repairs by the time Mr. Todd inherited it, fifteen years ago. He turned his back on the estate, sold it all to the highest bidder and departed to sunnier climes to pursue his true life's calling.

"The man packed a bag, made arrangements with his bank, and ended up, after a little traveling, in Egypt. It was there that he began gathering his collection of Egyptian antiquities. He got items from the local markets until he realized the best and rarest finds were still buried in the sands of the Valley of the Kings. He found several knowledgeable men and began financing digs. Questions arose about the legalities of his business, but there was never enough evidence to persuade the authorities to do more than occasionally bring him in for questioning. He was always released, after which he usually moved on to a new city. His men would find something unusual, notify him and in a few days the object would be on its way to a warehouse in East London. Meanwhile Mr. Todd traveled from water-hole to watering-hole, with his base in Cairo. He was always on the look-out for rare bits of the Old Kingdoms and his men saw to it he got them. More than one dealer or digger may have had grounds to complain as to his methods or his prices, but nothing was ever proven

"After fifteen years he decided to come back to England and take stock of what he had gathered. He signed a lease on a large house in Alexandria Square and had all the crates delivered there before he took possession."

"All that is true, Mr. Holmes," said Mr. Rafferty. "The circle of Egyptologists in England is small and upon his return word of his collection spread quickly. Some description of several of the more choice items had been released and drew our attention. In particular, a certain miniature dhow, of unusual design and rarity and found in an ancient tomb, intrigued me. If I can authenticate it, it may fill in a crucial piece of information needed to explain certain manuscripts pertaining to the reign of Imhopen VII."

Professor Molesley now took up the narrative. "My interest in Mr. Todd's collection is centered on a certain ceremonial dagger and sheath, carved from alabaster and covered with symbols pertaining to the lives of the goddess Isis and her son Horus. The workmanship is reputed to be that of Manunetti. It was unheard of that a woman would be allowed to learn the skills needed to produce such an artifact. I am eager to write a paper for the Royal Egyptology Society that would prove she created such a work of art. It will make my name and the prestige to the College will be enormous."

"Both researches promise to extend human knowledge. I fail to see your problem, gentlemen," said Sherlock Holmes.

"The problem is that Mr. Twain Todd is behaving like an old dog in the manger, Mr. Holmes!" exclaimed Mr. Rafferty. "We are both members of the Royal Egyptology Society. In fact, I am currently President. We have sent letters, messages, even stood on his doorstep and knocked on his door and he refuses to allow us to see his collection. Can you imagine possible answers to questions that have plagued scientists for thousands of years locked away and no reason given?"

"What do you expect me to do, gentlemen?"

"We want you to convince Mr. Todd to let us examine at least the items we have described in the interest of research. When Mr. Todd returned to London he brought back two men. Sevilen Ottersby is half-Turkish and acts as Todd's secretary. He worked for Todd for the last twelve years, keeping track of the collection. Baj Jhar is Todd's personal servant. He was hired in Luxor six years ago. We have spoken to them and they indicated that they would each be willing, for a consideration, to let us see the collection. But without Todd's permission we feel such a move would be unethical. We need someone to act as our emissary, to convince Mr. Twain Todd of the benefit to mankind that would come from an examination of his collection of Egyptian artifacts."

"Don't you think that Mr. Todd already knows that?"

"Yes, of course," interjected Professor Molesley. "But if an impartial third party, one with no especial interest in Egyptian historical objects, talks to him, he may be persuaded to open his treasure trove to science. We need a dispassionate, logical voice, Mr. Holmes, and that is why we have turned to you."

"When Mr. Todd was here in my sitting room a few days ago, he gave every sign that he was in fear of his life. Would either of you gentlemen know why he would believe that?"

Mr. Rafferty and Professor Molesley looked confused. "No," they said in unison.

Holmes rose to his feet. "I do not believe I am the one to convince Mr. Todd to allow you to view his collection, but I will meet you at his home this afternoon at two o'clock. Please leave the address with Dr. Watson. I am curious enough about that little man to wish to meet him again."

At the time appointed we drew up to an impressive mansion located on Alexandria Square in Belgravia. Mr. Rafferty and Professor Molesley were already waiting. To our surprise Mr.Rafferty's knock was answered at once by a butler of obvious Egyptian ancestry, dressed in the flowing robes of that region. He had to be Baj Jhar, Twain Todd's native servant.

The Oriental ushered us into the foyer where another man was waiting. Professor Molesley introduced him to Holmes and me as Sevilen Ottersby, Todd's secretary. He, too, was clad in robes, but of a Turkish fashion. He was tall, over six feet, and carried himself with an air of great dignity. His face was swarthy and he cultivated a large thick, black mustache under an impressive hooked nose. He agreed at once to bring us to Mr. Twain Todd.

"Holmes," I whispered to my friend as the secretary led us down a wide hall. "I don't understand. Why are guests being welcomed, after so many previous rejections by Mr. Todd? What has changed?"

Holmes shook his head. "Possess your soul in patience, Watson. I do not know, but Mr. Todd might explain it all to us."

Sevilen Ottersby stopped at a door at the end of the hall and flung it open. Mr. Twain Todd sat behind a huge carved desk, a cup of tea before him. The room was used as an office, with file cabinets, traveling trunks and stacks of papers crowding out the tables and armchairs of the drawing room it had been intended to be. Mr. Ottersby motioned us to chairs and Mr. Todd pushed away his cup. He smirked at us as Mr. Rafferty asked again to see the Egyptian collection, or at least those items he and Professor Molesley were particularly interested in.

"I have allowed you into my home to make my position plain, gentlemen. I will not allow anyone to examine the crates and packages I had shipped back to England from Egypt. In fact, I am not permitted."

Mr. Rafferty and Professor Molesley were astonished. They erupted with protests. "What are you saying? What is to stop you? You know how important the collection is to science! To deny us access is criminal! We demand you lead us to the collection this minute!"

Mr. Todd stilled their clamor with a wave of his broad hand. His voice was smooth and silky with self-satisfaction. "I cannot allow you to see the collection because it is no longer my property. This morning I concluded the final details of a sale of the entire thing to Major Beauregard Stoat of Topeka, Kansas in the United States. It has been agreed that every crate will be delivered without delay to the docks tomorrow to be loaded upon the freighter *Willows* for departure for America. It sails in three days. If you wish to study the items, gentlemen, I suggest that you open negotiations with Major Stoat."

"Where can we find him?" asked Professor Molesley.

"Major Stoat demanded that the papers be signed this morning because he had to catch a train to Southampton at noon. He is leaving on the steamer *Rackham* tonight. He has urgent business in New York and could not wait to accompany his new purchase. I can give you his address in Topeka if you wish it."

"We will never see the collection after it is taken to America!" Mr. Rafferty and Professor Molesley looked at each other in despair. Twain Todd pressed a bell on his desk, pushed back his chair and stood up.

"I believe our business here is concluded, gentlemen, and Ottersby will see you out. I will thank you never to return here or bother me again with your silly interest in my antiquities."

Sherlock Holmes spoke before anyone could say a word. "I beg your pardon, Mr. Todd., but would you indulge me in answering a question before we go?"

"I have heard of your bump of curiosity, Mr. Holmes, and I suppose you want to know why I behaved as I did when we met in your sitting room."

"Yes. Why did you think you were going to die then but now are so calm? Has the threat been averted?"

Todd sat down again. "I have removed the danger to myself."

"In fact, at that time you believed you were threatened by an old Egyptian pharaoh's curse."

"Do not scoff at things you don't understand, Mr. Holmes. I have spent many years in the East and I have seen things there that no Westerner could explain. The threat was real, I can assure you, but now it has been removed."

"By selling the collection to Major Stoat. Now the curse is his problem."

"That is correct. Now, Ottersby, show these gentlemen the door. I am sure that, like me, they are all busy men who have other things to do today."

With that we soon found ourselves on the pavement of Alexandria Square. Mr. Rafferty and Professor Molesley hailed a cab and drove away; each slumped in a corner with a doleful face. Holmes suggested that, since the day was fine, that we stroll back to Baker Street. He wanted to think.

Our walk was interrupted by one of Holmes' Baker Street Irregulars. The young boy, Lane by name, had a message from the barman of a public house that figured in a smuggling ring Holmes had been investigating for months. We followed the child and in the next hours resolved the matter I have written up in my notes as the case of the "Black Sheep", three bags of fuller's earth and the Dame.

Out to an advanced hour the night before, we rose late the next morning. The last of the coffee still remained in the coffeepot when Inspector Lestrade appeared at our door.

"I have come on official business, Mr. Holmes. I'm glad to find both you and Dr. Watson here. I must have your statements as to your meeting with Mr. Twain Todd yesterday." His sharp nose and beady eyes bore into us. Lestrade was only a few months from retirement and his thinning grey hair and wrinkled face told of his decades of service to Scotland Yard. He sat down on the sofa and whipped out his notebook. He poised a pencil over a fresh page and blinked. "Of course, I know what you both were doing from four o'clock on. I read the report Hopkins filed. Good work, by the way."

"Thank you, Inspector. Some coffee? Oh, very well. May I ask why you are so interested in our meeting with Mr. Todd?"

"His body was found strangled and hidden in one of his own mummy cases at his house this morning. You and Dr. Watson were two of the last men known to have spoken to him yesterday."

"My God!" I stared at Lestrade in disbelief.

Sherlock Holmes was no less moved.

"That is a bad business, Lestrade. I found Mr. Todd's personality unpleasant but I would never wish on him an ending such as that. Are we under suspicion?"

"You might have been if you hadn't spent last night in the company of four policemen cleaning up that gang down by the docks. We have enough suspects as it stands. Give me your version of yesterday's events and I'll tell you what other information we have gathered.

Holmes quickly gave a complete account of our encounter with Mr. Twain Todd, both the day before and the first time Todd had come to Baker Street. I concurred in every detail. The old Scotland Yard man wrote it all down and agreed to that cup of coffee. Holmes asked Mrs. Hudson to make a fresh pot.

"I have talked to the houseman and the secretary and bless me if it helps clear up anything," he said. "The servant, Baj Jhar, says that after he let you in at two o'clock, he went back to the kitchen and spent the rest of the time there, preparing dinner. After the meal, he went out and didn't get back until after one. He went to bed and heard nothing. His room was next to the kitchen in the basement. This morning he got up to fix breakfast at six. He came up out of the kitchen at a quarter to seven to lay out the hot dishes in the dining room. He noticed that the carpet in the hallway was disturbed. He followed the marks to the room where the meeting had been held. The furniture was knocked about and papers scattered. There was no sign of Mr. Todd. He called Mr. Ottersby, who came down out of his first-floor room only half-dressed. The secretary walked down the hall in the other direction to the large bare room where Todd's Egyptian collection had been stored.

"The door had been locked but the door jamb was smashed. There was a trio of mummy cases laid out on trestle tables in the center of the room. Mr. Ottersby lifted the lids one by one. The two men were horrified to find Twain Todd's dead body stuffed into the third case on top of a crumbling dry Egyptian corpse at least three thousand years old.

"Ottersby sent Baj Jhar for the police. After the first officer arrived Ottersby showed him that one of the windows on the ground floor had been pried open. Entry had most likely been gained there. Scotland Yard was called in and I have just come from Alexandria Square to see you both. Mr. Ottersby told me you had been there to speak with Mr. Todd yesterday."

"Have you questioned Mr. Rafferty or Professor Molesley?" asked Holmes.

"I sent for the two men and they should be at Todd's house by now. I thought you would like to join me when I questioned them."

"I am always happy to assist the Yard, Lestrade." We went down the seventeen steps of the stairs and out the front door just as Mrs. Hudson stepped out into the hallway bearing a silver coffeepot and three clean cups on a tray. I could hear her helpless protests as I shut the door.

The scene at Alexandria Square when we arrived was very different from the day before. The street had been roped off and several patrolmen were diverting traffic, both pedestrian and vehicular, away from Todd's rented mansion. There was a crush of official carriages and vans around the front door and it took us several minutes to make our way through the crowd of excited onlookers and pressmen on the pavement to the front hall.

Holmes drew out his magnifying lens and examined the rumpled carpet runner in the hall, then looked into the sitting room where we had met with Mr. Todd the day before. It showed quite a lot of disturbance. Piles of papers had been knocked over and files had been tore apart. A broken plate and some chicken bones lay on the floor next to a pair of backless Turkish slippers on the carpet by the hall door.

Holmes paid particular attention to the fireplace. From out of the ashes he pulled two blacken strips, spines from a couple of office ledgers. Carefully he wrapped them in his handkerchief and placed them in his pocket.

Lestrade showed him the room where the body had been found. Here Holmes became animated, walking, crawling and even wriggling on his stomach to examine the crates and the bundles stacked all over the room. Several crates had been opened. On top of a pile of excelsior in one was a small carved wooden boat. He gave equal attention to the two uninvolved mummy cases. Finally, after a quarter-hour of such activity, Sherlock Holmes advanced to the fatal Egyptian container.

It had been stored lying on its back on two rough wooden trestles. Its lid was elaborately painted with a depiction of an ancient Egyptian man. I helped Lestrade open it. Twain Todd's body was stuffed into the box, smashed down and crushing the original inhabitant. His lumpy body was dressed in pajamas wrapped in a garish dressing gown and his feet were bare. The sight of his face was horrible; bloated purple with a gaping mouth and staring eyes glazed in death. Finger marks showed where the murderer's hands had choked the life from the hard-hearted antiquities collector. I helped to sit him up so his back could be examined. The back of his dressing gown was covered with grey powder from the mummy's body. There were no other wounds. We laid him back down, a little clumsily because of the stiffening that was spreading, and I lowered the lid gently to cover the dreadful sight.

"What would you say as to the time of death, doctor?" asked Holmes.

"An autopsy should be able to pinpoint the time better, but by the stiffening of the corpse I would think before midnight," I replied.

The open window was in the back of the room. Holmes looked it over carefully with his lens, especially faint marks on the sill he pointed out to me. Then he examined the marks in the thick dust on the floor around the mummy case, but rose to his feet with an air of disappointment. "A herd of buffaloes couldn't have mussed up the footprints better," he sighed.

A constable led us to the library. After we found seats Inspector Lestrade called for one of his men to bring in the first man, Baj Jhar, the Egyptian servant.

The upset houseman entered and sat down. Lestrade rattled some papers on the table before him and asked the Egyptian to tell his story again. The native wailed and cried about the death of his employer, but after a few minutes he composed himself and began to talk. He spoke in slow, deliberate but clear English tinged with a thick Middle East accent.

"After the meeting the Master told me to go back to the kitchen. I remained there, fixing the meal, until six o'clock, when he ate. The Master always ate early, even in Cairo. Then he would have a bowl of soup or some roast chicken later in the evening before he went to bed. I waited until he rang for the chicken, then my day was over. I would collect the remains of the little meal the next morning.

"The night was fine so I took a walk. There is a pub called the "Grand Vizier" that caters to my countrymen, on the far side of Hyde Park. I went there and played dominos until nearly one o'clock. Then I walked back and went to bed. I didn't hear or see anything until early this morning, when I went to call the Master to breakfast and found the carpet awry and my Master missing."

"How did you get back into the house after your walk?" asked Holmes.

"I have a key to the back door." The Egyptian pulled a brass key out of his pocket and laid it on the table. Holmes picked it up and turned it over. He laid it back on the table.

Lestrade asked for some names of the men in the pub to verify Baj Jhar's story, then dismissed him to wait in the kitchen again with a policeman nearby. He called for the secretary, Sevilen Ottersby.

Ottersby was dressed in his Turkish clothing, a loose white shirt and pants with an embroidered vest, a wide sash wrapped around his waist and sturdy Turkish slippers. A red fez was on his head and his sharp eyes, large nose and ferocious black mustache gave him a wild appearance. But his manner, while guarded in the presence of so many police officials, was civilized and co-operative. He took the chair Lestrade pointed to and nodded to Holmes and me. Lestrade rattled his papers again.

"Now, Mr. Ottersby, tell us about yourself and what you know about Mr. Twain and his death."

"I am the son of an English father and a Turkish mother. My father made sure I got an excellent education in England. I began working for Mr. Twain Todd as his secretary twelve years ago in Ankara where I was visiting my mother. He began collecting Egyptian artifacts a year or so later, after settling in Cairo. I was in charge of packing up the items, paying the workmen or the sellers, and shipping the crates to a warehouse in London. I also kept the records of what was bought, sold or traded. The collection was a mutating thing over time, constantly changing as to inventory and worth as the market changed.

"A few months ago Mr. Twain announced that we were going back to England. He planned to display his collection and become a mover and shaker in the Egyptology community. He wanted fame and prestige after all the time and money he spent gathering the collection together."

"What was Mr. Twain like to work for?"

"I found him to be a selfish man. His collection and his own comfort were his chief interests. He paid no attention to Baj Jhar and me as individuals. Our working hours were long and irregular, sometimes stretching from eight in the morning until after midnight for weeks. Meanwhile he spent his time in various waterholes and resorts, consorting with dubious women and drinking. He refused to accept delay or the possibility of not getting the Egyptian items he wanted. He was stingy and had little regard for others. He paid Baj Jhar a pittance and I had to argue and threaten to quit several times in order to get paid a decent wage. He was excitable and stubborn and suspicious of everyone."

"Why did you stay with him if he was such a terrible boss?"

"Mr. Todd had managed to gather together the most extensive and interesting collection of Old and New Kingdom artifacts outside of the British Museum. The work was exciting. I am half-Turkish and the searching, the haggling; the drama of getting a rare item when it was sought by another determined collector was intoxicating. It became like meat and drink to me."

"You must have been disappointed when Mr. Todd wanted to return to London."

"I had not gone unnoticed by other collectors in Egypt. I had several job offers before we left on the steamship *Grahame*. I planned on setting up the display, then quitting Mr. Todd's employ and returning to Cairo to a better boss and a better wage to begin the excitement all over again."

"Tell us about the trip to England," said Lestrade.

"Mr. Todd spent the voyage home studying tablets that made up a ceremonial necklace he had bought in Alexandria just before we left. Each day he became more agitated and fearful. He told me the inscriptions cast a curse on whoever possessed them, a spell of death. I dismissed such foolishness, but a few strange things did happen during the voyage home. He slipped and almost fell down a steep gangway. A heavy weight was dropped from an upper deck and nearly hit him. On shore in Lisbon he was attacked and robbed of his wallet. He developed a case of food poisoning just before we landed in England. By the time the *Grahame* docked in Southampton he was a nervous wreck and determined to divest himself of everything he had spent his life collecting. He believed it was the only way he could save his life.

"He hated to do it, though. His visit to your rooms was his last-ditch effort to postpone the need for a sale. When you refused to protect him, he arranged to sell everything to Major Stoat. Several men had expressed interest, but Major Stoat offered the most money and a promise to remove the artifacts to America at once. Mr. Todd wanted the collection as far away from himself as soon as possible."

"What happened yesterday?"

"After the meeting broke up, Mr. Todd sent me out to make arrangements for a trip to South Africa. He told me that since the collection has been sold, he had no reason to stay in England. He wanted a total change of scene. He said he had heard of business opportunities in Johannesburg regarding tribal art. I went to three steamship companies inquiring about travel times and hotel connections. I can give you the names of the companies."

"How long did that take?"

"It took all afternoon. I got back just before dinner."

"Did you buy the tickets?"

"No. Mr. Todd wanted to compare the different companies' information before he chose which one to use."

"What did you do after dinner?"

"Mr. Todd and I sat in his make-shift office and went over the pamphlets I had brought back. I also had notes on prices, ports of call, and hotel availabilities. He planned to take his time traveling and wanted to stay at several cities on his way south. As I said, he liked his comfort."

"When did your meeting break up?"

"When Baj Jhar brought in the chicken. I excused myself and went up to my room. I heard the back door close a few minutes later when Baj Jhar left. I came downstairs and went out the back door myself. I saw Baj Jhar turn the corner at the end of the mews. I walked down to the same corner and turned into the park. I walked around for over three hours and then came back. I went up to my room and stayed there until Baj Jhar called me in the morning."

"Can you produce any witnesses? Did you stop at any public house or anywhere else where people might remember seeing you?"

The secretary paused. His sharp black eyes darted at each of us and he spoke slowly. "Well, no, sir. That is, I saw lots of people in Hyde Park. It was a fine night, you remember. I remember a man who ran toward the Serpentine right past me. There were several couples. One lady wearing a bright red hat was with another man in evening dress. One of those people must have seen me."

Sherlock Holmes had some questions.

"Did you speak to anyone?"

"No."

"Were you dressed then as you are now?"

"Yes."

"Did you see Mr. Todd when you returned?"

"No. As I said, I went right up to my room."

"Was the back door locked when you returned?"

"Yes. I had locked it behind me. I have my own key." Sevilen Ottersby placed another brass key on the table next to Baj Jhar's. Holmes compared the two keys. They were identical.

A sergeant opened the door and announced the arrival of Mr. Rafferty and Professor Molesley. Lestrade sent Sevilen Ottersby off with the officer and had Mr. Rafferty come in.

The author and Egyptology Society president walked into the room and began to speak indignantly at Sherlock Holmes..

"This is a terrible, terrible thing, Mr. Holmes. First the stress of Todd denying me access to his collection, then the shock of his announcement that he sold it and it's going away to America and now this! I had nothing to do with Mr. Todd's death, sir. I swear it!"

Lestrade rattled his papers again to gain Mr. Rafferty's attention. "I am Inspector Lestrade from Scotland Yard, Mr. Rafferty. Are you settled enough to answer my questions?"

Rafferty shuddered and made a visible effort to collect his composure. "I'm ready, Inspector. It was just those newsmen outside and some of the questions they yelled at me as I entered the house.... They seemed to think I was a suspect."

"What did you do after the meeting with Mr. Twain Todd yesterday afternoon?"

"Professor Moseley and I left together after Ottersby showed us all out. I dropped him at his place near Westminster University and proceeded to my office at the Society. I sank into a funk there and only realized how late it was when I heard the charwomen working in a nearby office. I left and got some supper at a nearby public house. The food revived my spirits and I began to think about Mr. Todd and his collection. I decided to go back to Alexandria Square and try once more to persuade Mr. Todd to allow me to examine the little tomb artifact I was interested in.

"Do you know what time it was when you got back to Mr. Todd's house?"

"It was just nine thirty. I rang and Mr. Todd answered the door. He let me into the hall. I put forth my case. He chuckled and smiled and, to my surprise, agreed to let me see the model ship. He took me down the hall to the collection room, unlocked the door, and handed me the dhow from an opened crate near the door.

"I didn't know what had changed Mr. Todd's mind, but I didn't waste my chance to check out the dhow. I drew a sketch, made some measurements and wrote down everything I could notice about the little ship. See, here is my notebook." Rafferty pulled a little book from his pocket and handed it to the Inspector.

Lestrade flipped through the marked pages and handed it to Holmes.

"Yes, these notes are very complete," remarked Sherlock Holmes. "How long were you at Mr. Todd's?"

"It must have been over an hour. When I was through examining the model, Mr. Todd let me out the front door. He was alive and well when I walked down the front steps. I was elated at my good luck and walked home, not minding the late hour."

"Did anyone see you return?" Lestrade asked.

"No. The house was silent. The servants had all gone to bed."

Mr. Rafferty was sent off with yet another policeman and Professor Moseley came in.

He was clearly upset and his eyes darted between Lestrade and Holmes as he took his seat before the Inspector. Before anyone could say a word he burst into speech.

"I know I should have reported what happened but the shock was so great! I've been waiting for the police to show up ever since. It's almost a relief to finally be brought here."

Inspector Lestrade dropped his sheaf of papers. He sat up as if he had been galvanized. Professor Moseley drooped and looked about the room with a guilty air.

The Scotland Yard man threw Holmes a triumphant glance and stared sternly at the trembling man before him.

"You may be certain that we know everything, Professor. You would be well advised to make a clean breast of things and tell us all about it now."

"After the cab dropped me near my rooms at the University, I began to walk, turning the events of the meeting over and over again in my mind. I was truly surprised to find that I had wandered back to Mr. Todd's house after spending hours trudging through the streets. I knocked on the front door and rang the bell. No one answered. There was a single light on in one of the downstairs rooms, but the windows were too high for me to see in.

"I finally found one window I could reach. I was desperate to speak to Mr. Todd. I forced the sash open and climbed inside. I shouted, but heard nothing but silence. I clicked on the electric lights.

"Imagine my delight to find the Egyptian collection set out before me! I began to dig into a few crates that had been already opened, looking for the alabaster dagger I was interested in. I never found it, but I did open one of the mummy cases. I found...I found..."

He collapsed, burying his face in his trembling hands.

"You found Mr. Twain Todd's body," said Sherlock Holmes.

The professor nodded mutely. Inspector Lestrade smiled victoriously and motioned to a constable. "Place this man under arrest for the murder or Mr. Twain Todd." Professor Moseley looked up, his eyes wide and his hands fluttering.

"No! No! You can't! I didn't! Please...!"

The accused man was hustled out of the room. The Scotland Yard man smiled at Holmes.

"Well, Mr. Holmes, that seems to clear up everything. I do like a murder where the guilty man confesses early."

"Professor Molesley didn't confess to anything, Lestrade, except a little breaking and entering. You're making a bad mistake, Inspector."

""Nonsense! He admitted to being a desperate man. He broke into the house, searched this collection he's so interested in and when he was interrupted by Mr. Todd, killed him and stuffed him into the mummy case. This is as neat a case as I have ever worked."

"It won't wash, Lestrade. Moseley isn't the murderer. If you will bring back all the suspects I will give you the guilty man and the proof to convict him."

Lestrade lost a little of his victorious air. He knew Sherlock Holmes well enough after all their years together not to question such a firm and declarative statement. Perhaps memories of all the times Holmes had pulled Lestrade's chestnuts out of the fire and given him the credit for cases Holmes had solved passed thru his mind. After a moment he turned to another constable and quietly ordered the four men brought back. In a few minutes Baj Jhar, Sevilen Ottersby, Mr. Rafferty and Professor Moseley were seated before Lestrade's desk.

"Precede, Mr. Holmes." It was a mark of the Scotland Yard man's belief in the integrity and skills of Mr. Sherlock Holmes that he allowed control of the interrogation to past to my friend on Holmes' word alone.

"Mr. Ottersby, you said that you spent the time after you left this house last night walking in Hyde Park. Do you still say that?"

"I do."

"Even if your statement means that you become the prime suspect in Mr. Todd's murder? Even if that fact means that every aspect of your employment with him will be scrutinized, including your handling of his finances?"

I would think it was impossible, but Ottersby's swarthy face faded several shades paler. Sherlock Holmes suddenly produced the two blackened book spines he had found in Todd's fireplace and slapped them down on the desk. Ottersby's eyes locked on them as Holmes continued.

"I have already remarked that I have spent the past few days investigating Mr. Twain Todd's background. The reports I received also included notes on you and the servant Baj Jhar. You

217

didn't spend your free time strolling in Hyde Park, Mr. Ottersby. You have systematically been embezzling funds from your employer for years, beginning back in Egypt. Kickbacks, overpayments, side deals have fattened your wallet at the expense of Mr. Todd. You spent these funds on wine, women and song. These burnt artifacts are all that remains of the second set of books you kept to record your crooked dealings. The construction and materials clearly indicate that they were originally the spines of a day-book and a business journal. They match another day-book and business journal that remains on Todd's desk. Baj Jhar has formed the habit of visiting that pub every night since the three of you moved into this house. He spends a set amount of money each visit, consistent with his salary. You, Mr. Ottersby, on the other hand, spend your free time and more money than you earn being entertained at a certain address not a quarter of a mile from the Houses of Parliament. A rather famous, or shall I say notorious, woman was your hostess last night and one of her employees, a woman, was your companion for the evening.

"You burnt these ledgers after you discovered Mr. Todd's body when you returned to the house last night. You did that to cover your tracks, knowing that his death would mean an investigation."

"And the woman?" I asked.

Sherlock Holmes picked a nearly invisible long hair off the embroidered vest of Sevilen Ottersby. "It must have been an expensive night," he commented. "She was a natural blonde."

"As for Professor Molesley, his story is true in every respect. His shoes and trousers display mud and dust from the streets he wandered through on his way back to here. The evidence is clear to an experienced eye. The shoe varnish found on the window sill indicates that egress was from the outside in and matches the scratches on the professor's footwear. See, here, where the light catches the marks? Here are several pieces of packing straw left on his coat from his rummaging around the collection crates in search of his alabaster dagger."

"He could still have killed Mr. Todd," said Lestrade, loath to let his triumph fade.

"His clothing has not a trace of mummy dust on it. There are traces on the soles but nowhere else. It would have been impossible not to be covered in dust given the force that was necessary to shove Mr. Todd's body into the case. There must have been a cloud of it raised when the murdered man was thrust onto the dried-up body. Professor, what did you do after you found Mr. Todd in the case?"

"I… I was shocked, as I said. I think I pushed the lid back to cover the horrible sight and left through the window I had used to enter. After walking, almost running for a while, I found a cab and went back to my apartment. There I met my landlady, Mrs. Woods, on the stairs. The scullery maid had a toothache and she was tending her. I went to my room. Later the policeman found me and brought me here."

"That leaves us Mr. Rafferty," said Lestrade. Holmes nodded.

"Mr. Rafferty told us a fine story about Mr. Todd's surprising change of heart, of how he allowed Mr. Rafferty to come into his home, examine the model ship, the object of his particular interest, for over an hour and even take detailed notes about it. But there are three witnesses, Dr. Watson, Professor Molesley and myself, who were present when Mr. Todd denied all access to his Egyptian collection and gave a good and legal reason for doing so. He said that it was no longer his property, having been sold earlier in the day. So why would Mr. Todd treat Mr. Rafferty in such a generous manner? What could have changed in the few hours after the meeting and the late-night hour when Mr. Rafferty knocked on Mr. Todd's door?"

"He just had a change of heart," Mr. Rafferty protested. "I am the President of the Royal Egyptology Society. He might have thought there would be some prestige in being mentioned as the former owner of the dhow in the paper I planned to publish."

"Anyone's experience of Mr. Twain Todd's personality would not allow for such a conclusion," said Sherlock Holmes. "It was entirely against his nature. He took great pleasure in turning us out of his house without a glimpse of the collection.

"No, Mr. Rafferty's great desire to examine the little boat that had become his obsession overcame his good sense. He deliberately returned to this house and talked his way in. He attacked Mr. Todd in his office when access to the collection was denied again, knocking over the plate of chicken bones in the process and breaking the plate. He then dragged his victim right out of his slippers to the collection room. When Mr. Todd refused to produce the key, Mr. Rafferty in his mania strangled him there and left his body on the carpet. He went back to the office and ransacked it in search of the key. When he didn't find it he went back and forced open the door. He dragged Mr. Todd's body in and shoved it into one of the mummy cases to get it out of his sight. He then opened several crates until he found the dhow."

"You mean to say that he then spent over an hour calmly making notes and drawing a sketch of the little boat in his notebook in that room, next to the body, risking discovery at any moment by the servants, who may have heard the noise of the struggle?" I gasped.

"Mr. Rafferty's obsession had reached such heights that in his frenzy to achieve his goal such trifles became of no concern. He was past reason. Yet he knew enough not to remove the little boat. That fact will not stand him in good stead later. It happened that he wasn't disturbed by anyone because neither Baj Jhar nor Mr. Ottersby returned during the time Mr. Rafferty was in the house. He was well gone before either man came back and entered through the kitchen door. They were still absent when Professor Molesley entered, found the body and then left."

Mr. Rafferty sneered and said, "You can prove nothing. According to your own words, I should be covered in mummy dust. You can see that there is no dust on my coat or trousers and these were the clothes I wore earlier."

"You have brushed your clothing well, I admit," said Holmes. "But there is one place you have overlooked. A woman would not neglect such a thing, but a murderer in the midst of a busy night might be excused in forgetting such a detail. Lestrade, look at his shoes!"

The President of the Royal Egyptology Society struggled against us, but his bespoke shoes were eventually removed and found to bear quantities of grey mummy dust.

Sherlock Holmes pointed to the footwear. "The murderer cleaned his suit and even washed his face and hands and brushed his hair but his footwear had been merely wiped, leaving the mummy dust lying hidden in the creases across the toes. This may be more of a case for the doctors than the courts, Lestrade. It is possible that Rafferty has a better chance to end up in the authorities' care at Broadmoor Asylum than at the end of a hangman's rope."

The murderer raved and swore. Three strong constables were required to bind him and carry him from the room. Inspector Lestrade carried away his prize in high spirits. He added Sevilen Ottersby to his bag for further questioning about Mr. Todd's finances. The others were dismissed. Holmes and I were left in front of the Belgravia house as the sun began to set over the rooftops of Alexandria Square.

"Shall we walk back to Baker Street again, Holmes?" I inquired. Before my friend could answer, a young woman, dressed like a servant maid, ran up to us from a nearby house.

"Oh, please, sir, you're Mr. Sherlock Holmes, aren't you? Oh, please can you help us? Me wee brother is missing and I'm that worried about him. He ran off in his nightgown two nights before, me mother says, and hasn't been seen since. Such a thing has never happened before and I'm half out of me mind!"

"I would be glad to help you, Miss…Miss…"

"Winkle, sir. Me brother's name is Willy. But I can't talk to you right now. Me mistress wouldn't like it, me neglecting me duties. I'll come to Baker Street this evening, after she's gone out. Thank you, sir, thank you!"

With that she was gone. Sherlock Holmes shrugged. "You have written that I possess only a limited knowledge of Thomas Carlyle, Watson. That may be true, but I do admit to a few relevant lines," he remarked. "One is 'For men must work and women must weep'. Look, the sky grows darker. We shall take a cab."

The Case of the Classic Code

It was a folded sheet of brown paper, without an envelope, and with the words "Sherlock Holmes of London" scrawled on one side. When Holmes handed it to me I could clearly read the lines written on it. They were quite familiar.

"Jack and Jill went up the hill

To fetch a pail of water.

Jack fell down

And broke his crown

And Jill will tumble down after."

"Holmes, what can this mean?"

Sherlock Holmes and I were seated in our armchairs before the sitting room fireplace of 221b Baker Street. The hearth now containing a brightly polished brass fire screen instead of the dingy soot-smudged one that had protected the bearskin rug from the toasty coal fire we had enjoyed all winter. A clear May morning sun sent shafts of light through the newly-cleaned and starched lace window curtains that hung behind our brocade drapes. During our absence of over two weeks on an unusual case that took us from Banbury Cross to Vienna and onward to Morocco, Mrs. Hudson had managed to clean all of 221b without disturbing any of Holmes' files or instruments. The gleaming fire screen was the final touch. I had approved of the results, but Sherlock Holmes had poked around, trying to find a good reason to complain. Despite his best efforts, he had concluded that only the level of dust and the number of spider webs had changed in our absence. Mrs. Hudson had defended her actions on the grounds of sanitation, a difficult reason to refute.

The crumpled brown paper had been brought up by the boy in buttons. He reported that he had found it thrust under the front door as he brought down the breakfast things. Now Sherlock Holmes read the note and handed it to me.

"First, Watson, tell me your impressions of this missive."

I eyed the scrap doubtfully. "It is a dirty piece of brown paper, about 12 inches by 14, with uneven, torn edges. The words upon it were done roughly in pen and ink. The author printed the words clearly, but there are still a few blots from the pen. "Jack and Jill" is a child's nursery rhyme. I cannot conceive any reason in the world why someone should go to the bother of writing it out and shoving it under your door."

"I can think of seven!" Sherlock Holmes declared. He snatched the scrap back and rose to his feet. He moved over to his chemistry table. For some little time his fingers moved among his chemicals and delicate instruments as he examined and analyzed the note. I had finished my post-breakfast cigar before he turned from the eyepiece of his microscope and smiled.

"Each case can be divided into several parts. The first part of this case is finished, Watson. This is a most interesting clue."

"Clue, Holmes? Those are just some lines from a classic old nursery rhyme. They can have nothing to do with any wrongdoing!"

"I beg to differ, my dear doctor. To prove my contention that this is not just the random rendering of a classic poem but instead a clue to evildoing, I point out the one thing that indicates that clearly. It is the mistake."

I picked up the paper and looked it over again. "I see no mistake."

Holmes laughed. "Read the last line again."

I did. "Why, it has been copied out wrong! It should read 'And Jill came tumbling after.' What an odd thing."

"It is the odd things of life that make my work so interesting. Why was this old rhyme pushed under my door? Why write "Sherlock Holmes of London" on it, when my address, due mostly to your own literary efforts, is so well known? Why have it delivered anonymously? Why choose that particular poem? And most intriguingly of all, what is the meaning of that altered last line?"

"It may well be a clue to something, but why must that something be a crime?"

"Because it was delivered to me and my profession is well-known." Holmes picked up his old pipe from the table beside him and tapped the stem on the paper in my hand. "There is a dark story behind that scrap of paper, Watson, and someone has been kind enough to give it to me to decode. I have nothing on hand at the moment except that matter of the Edinburgh Gardens' silver bells. Inspector Lestrade told me yesterday that old Mary Darnley was about to confess. So, barring a call for help from Scotland Yard, I am at leisure to pursue this problem. Please excuse me, my friend. I think this will prove to be a three...nay, perhaps a four...pipe problem and should take up at least the rest of this morning. Perhaps you would like to go to your club, since it is Thursday and Thurston is sure to be there."

"I will leave you to it, Holmes, but I still do not see how this bit of scribbling can be related to a crime."

"Right now neither do I, but after a few hours I may be able to tell to you more." With that, Sherlock Holmes filled his pipe from the tobacco from his Persian slipper, then reached out and took back the note. He leaned back in his armchair and lit his pipe. When rising grey smoke showed the contents were burning finely, I took my hat and cane and left the apartment to that motionless figure.

I played billiards with Thurston on Thursdays, as Holmes well knew, so the day passed pleasantly. After lunch I received a telegram from him, asking that I remain where I was so he could reach me later.

Finally, as the afternoon advanced, a waiter brought me another message, instructing me to enter a four-wheeler Holmes had sent and return to Baker Street. As the cab drove up to our door, I saw Holmes leaning out of one of the sitting room windows waving a telegram form.

"Wait there, Watson," he called. "I'll be right down."

The sun had set and the gaslights were being lit up and down the block. The dancing flames confined in the clear cases set atop tall iron poles lining the street sent out halos of gold that reflected from the glass windows of the buildings around me. I watched them flicker as I contemplated Holmes' words of the morning. How could a child's nonsense rhyme centuries old have anything to do with a crime of the present day? Who would write such a strange note? My thoughts were interrupted by the arrival of Sherlock Holmes himself, who handed the driver a slip of paper and joined me inside the vehicle.

He sat on the cushion next to me and tucked something black next to his other side. Then he reached into his coat pocket and handed me my old service revolver. I was astonished.

"Holmes, what is going on? And where are we going?" I inquired, as the cab lurched toward Marylebone Road.

"We are moving forward on this case, Watson. There may be unexpected developments this evening, and I thought it better that we be prepared. Look, I've bought my stick. Our trusty driver is following my instructions as to our route, in case we are being followed. That is a hazard when mysterious notes are left on one's doorstep. Since even I admit that I cannot be depended upon to foretell the future, I think it best that we talk of other things until we reach our destination."

Whereupon Sherlock Holmes leaned back and began to discourse upon, of all things, agricultural practices of the ancient Babylonians.

The cab we were in twisted through the London streets until we pulled up in front of the Charring Cross Station. Dismissing the driver, Holmes grabbed his black bundle and hustled me through the waiting room and onto the platform, where he shoved me into a First Class carriage just as the train pulled out on the way to Blackheath.

The conductor knocked on our glass door and Holmes bought two tickets. He tented his fingers and regarded me with a satisfied air.

"I have had a most interesting day, Watson. I have spent the time on that scrap of brown paper. The first thing I needed to know was what could be found out about the paper and ink. I examined it carefully. You saw that it was crumpled and had been used. I smelled it and detected the odor of leather. There were blots on the paper from the pen that had inscribed the poem, but there were also several stains that were not from ink. Those proved to be smears of black shoe polish. Its wrinkles indicated that the paper had been fashioned into a rough package around a pair of men's boots and tied with thin string.

"There are four situations in which boots are treated with fresh polish. When new boots are purchased, the pair are wrapped in tissue paper and placed in a shoebox. Then brown paper is wrapped around the box and tied with thin string. This paper was not wrinkled like that. Also, in that case, the boots would never touch the brown paper.

"When a man has his footwear polished by a bootblack, cloth rags are used in the application of polish and no paper of any kind ever comes in contact with the boots.

"When a person stays at a hotel, the employee whose job it is to clean and polish the guests' shoes and boots collects them after they have been left outside the patrons' doors at night and returns them in improved condition by morning. Again, there is no involvement of brown paper.

"But if a pair of boots need repair, a cobbler take on the task. When the boots are picked up, they are wrapped in brown paper into a rough bundle which is tied with string. Therefore the paper on which the poem was written was once used to wrap mended black boots.

"The ink was ordinary cheap India ink, available in all stationary and department stores in England. One interesting point was the pulse points. Pulse points are tiny markers that appear when a tightly-gripped pen is carried across the paper at a very laggardly rate of speed. It comes from the beating of the writer's heart transferred though the fingers gripping the pen transferring ink onto paper. That told me that the letters were written slowly, as if the author was writing in an unfamiliar language. English is not the writer's native tongue."

"Amazing, Holmes!"

"I next proceeded to the paper's contents. I am familiar with over one hundred and seventy different codes and ciphers. I did extensive testing to find out which one was used in this case. It became evident that this was an interpretation code, one depending on the various meanings of each word in the message.

'On one side of the paper was written "Sherlock Holmes of London." Why was it phrased that way? Why not "Sherlock Holmes of 221b Baker Street, Westminster, London"? Since this proved to be an interpretation cipher, the operative word must be "London". Now, Watson, read the first line of the poem."

Obediently I took the paper Holmes handed me. "Jack and Jill went up the hill to fetch a pail of water."

""Now, "Jack" can mean a man's name, or be used as a nick-name for "John", or it can be used as a generic word referring to any man, as in "jack-of-all-trades". "Jill" is often used the same way, either to refer to a woman named Jill, or Jillian or Jewel, or meaning any woman or girl.

"On the face of it, the mention of obtaining water at the top of a hill is ridiculous. Water, unless it comes down from melting glaciers or high sources, is usually found at lower levels, like rivers or lakes or other geological depressions. In the poem, there is not a direct mention of a well. But there is no mention of a waterfall, either. The poem is usually accepted as referring to a well. No one would expect to drill a well on the top of a hill. Why dig through yards of dirt and rock when a water supply could be found at the bottom with only a little effort?

"The exceptions are natural springs. They can appear anywhere. Now the area we are concerned with is London, because "London" was written in the address. I do not believe that restricts us only to the City of London. The City, only one mile square, doesn't have enough scope in regard to hills. It must include to the entire sprawling capital. There are nine elevations in the Greater London area that have the word "hill" in their names. Each has its own unique qualities, but only one is known for its supply of natural springs. There was even talk, a few years ago, of building a spa on the site, to take advantage of the healthful waters."

"Shooter's Hill!"

"Exactly, my friend. It was famous as a medieval archers' practice ground and later, as noted in Samuel Pepys' diary, as a place of gibbets and hanged criminals. We are going to it now. We'll get a cab at Blackheath station, and proceed from there to Shooter's Hill.

"Read the next line, Watson."

"Jack fell down and broke his crown and Jill will tumble down after."

"The phrase "fell down" could mean just that, a collapse to the ground, or a fall from a height. It could also mean the failure of someone to deliver a desired result to his confederates. For example, if the leader of a criminal gang refused to share out the illegal goods in an equitable manner, that might be seen by the other members as a fall from a trusted position. The words "broke his crown" could refer to either the deposing of the chief after such perfidy or a literal attack resulting in a head wound. In fact, it could mean both actions. I think we can assume that something very bad happened to Jack.

"The last few words are the ones changed from the original poem. Originally it read "and Jill came tumbling after." That was written in the past tense. But "and Jill will come tumbling after "is written in the future tense. In other words, it speaks of an incident that has not yet happened. Jill may be a witness to the bad thing that happened to Jack, since they are mentioned together, and now she could be in danger from the same fell confederates. They have not yet done anything to quiet her, but plans may be being drawn up. Our goals tonight are to secure Jill from any threat and to determine the other details of Jack's fate."

"Who could have sent such a warning?"

"For that answer there is a lack of data. It could be that someone knows of Jack's downfall and doesn't want Jill to be another victim."

I thought about Holmes' words as the train rumbled eastward. In spite of my faith in the great powers of my friend, I felt a spasm of doubt.

"Holmes, I fear that this tale you have spun is merely a tissue of suppositions. After all, no matter how clever it is, you have built up this tale over a few words scribbled on a dirty sheet of paper. Perhaps the scrap's delivery at our door was just a coincidence."

Sherlock Holmes folded up the piece of brown paper and tucked it into his pocket.

"Of course it is all supposition, my dear Watson! Every theory is supposition until it is proved conclusively. So far we have nothing for a court of law. But I assure you, I do not receive random mail. Also, there is this telegram."

Holmes pulled out the yellow form he had held in his hand at the window in Baker Street. "After I had spent half the day figuring out the best meaning of the code, I spent some time mulling over possible solutions. I reached back into my files and old scrapbooks for accounts of unsolved thefts and robberies. An unresolved property distribution between gang members is much more likely as a bone of contention than any other crime. There was one case in France that seemed most probable. I sent a telegram to Lestrade at Scotland Yard and asked just one question: "Where are the present whereabouts of Jacques de Vitt?" I got an answer back within an hour. I sent for you, changed out of my dressing grown and aired out the room. It had become quite smoky from my contemplations and I am sure Mrs. Hudson will not be pleased."

"Who is Jacques de Vitt?"

"He was a crafty old lag who was suspected of being the mastermind behind half-a-dozen major jewel thefts, the latest one being the disappearance of the Zenana Diamond from the Musee L'Perse in Paris four weeks ago. The Zenana Diamond is a square marquis-cut stone of the first water about the size of a robin's egg. It is mounted as a pendant in white gold. It has an interesting history. It was a bribe from the Pasha of Kryteronbarr, a province in Persia, to Napoleon I, made in an effort to avoid the Little Corporal's planned invasion of that country. During the burglary a month ago a guard was killed, few clues were found and the Paris police were stumped. The crime had all the marks of de Vitt, but he was supposedly incarcerated in a prison in Tunis at the time.

"Only last week did the government at Tunis confirm that four months ago de Vitt had made a great escape, climbing over his prison's high walls in the dark of a new moon and making his way over the desert to Alexandria. From Egypt he traveled to Marseilles and then his trail disappeared. There had been new reports, however, and so our friend Lestrade was able to send this message in answer to my query earlier today."

Holmes handed me the yellow telegram form. I read it by the light of the electric lamp over our heads. "Jacques de Vitt was last seen two nights ago in company of Jeanette Jacasser, diva of L'Opera Pendule, Greenwich. Woman has not yet been questioned. Mutilated body tentatively identified as De Vitt found on grounds of Brook River Hospital construction Shooter's Hill just this morning. G. Lestrade."

"We are on our way to the scene of the murder?"

"Yes. In a few minutes we will arrive at Blackheath Station. Please arrange for another cab."

It was simple to hail a hansom in Blackheath and travel to Shooter's Hill. The site was one of the highest elevations in the Thames valley, and stood in a peaceful, undeveloped area. Holmes peered eagerly out at the darkness as our cab slowed and stopped.

"We are coming up on the half-finished construction site that will soon become Brook Fever Hospital, a sanctuary for communicable disease cases. Surely you have heard of it, Doctor. It has replaced the proposed spa development designed to take advantage of the plentiful water supply. A most notable feature of this medical improvement is the new Water Tower, built of brick and capable of holding 20,000 gallons of water pumped up from the surrounding springs."

"This is where the body was found? But the police have removed it, surely! What clues can remain?"

"It is always useful to have in one's mind the layout of an important scene involving a crime before one meets with the principals involved. You may stay here. I shall not be long."

Sherlock Holmes brought out his bundle, unwrapped a dark lantern, lit it, and climbed out. The moon, a half-slice of soft grey light hanging over the trees and buildings that stood to our east, did little to dispel the night's sable mantle. I watched the bobbing shaft of light piercing the darkness as the detective moved toward a low wall of fresh dirt and several piles of construction materials. The spot of light fitfully disclosed stacks of bricks, piles of cut lumber, and a partially-built foundation wall. Then it vanished behind an obstruction and I was left to stare into the blackness. I checked my revolver. It was fully loaded. I put it back in my pocket.

It was several minutes later when the light re-appeared and I heard Holmes' footsteps approaching the cab. He spoke a few words to the driver, then re-entered and blew out the lamp. The carriage started up again and soon the sound of the horses' hooves told me we were back on a main road.

"What did you see, Holmes?"

"I saw what I expected to see, Watson. Now we proceed to the fourth part of this case; the endangered diva of l'Opera Pendule of Greenwich. We should just be in time for the second act."

L'Opera Pendule turned out to be a shabby converted music hall on a side street in the city famous for its Royal Observatory. The posters in the cracked display cases by the front doors advertized "Mme. Jeanette Jacasser, the French Phenomenon, in the melodrama 'Lady Grassmere's Secret.'" Inside we bought our tickets from a fat little matron behind a grilled counter and then crossed the cramped lobby to take seats in the stalls. The hall's interior was small, seating perhaps two hundred, and the edge of the stage was only a few rows in front of us. Perhaps a third of the stalls were occupied, and some of the patrons appeared to be asleep. There was no balcony and the walls sported faded red velveteen drapes hung between iron gaslight fixtures. The seats were covered in the same velveteen cloth, worn shiny in spots. The little stage was framed by a flaking proscenium carved with chubby cupids carrying huge roses. The stage curtain was a beige expanse of canvas painted with garish advertisements of local businesses and nationally-known patent medicines. The orchestra consisted of a bald man seated in front of a battered upright piano, an ancient white-haired violinist and a mandolin player who looked barely tall enough to dress himself.

The less said about the performance we saw of "*Lady Grassmere's Secret*" the better. The sets were flimsy, the costumes were ludicrous and the plot was implausible. The only bright spot was Mme. Jacasser, who, while several years too old for the part of the ingénue, did a credible job of making a little sense of her part as the wronged heroine. She was of the type known as "a pocket Venus", with a short curvy figure, a mass of golden hair piled on top of her head and a round face graced with a pair of pouty lips. We stuck it out until the end, however, and after the curtain dropped to sporadic applause, Holmes sent a note backstairs to the star, requesting an audience. He insisted that we remain in our seats a little time in order to allow the bulk of the other actors and stagehands to leave the building. Then we made our way backstage, using the door on the right-handed side leading off from the stalls.

As we walked past the orchestra pit, I glanced down at the musicians gathering their sheet music and packing up their instruments. Only one, the mandolin player, looked back. I was startled to see a mature man's face on his short body, clad in a summer suit of light grey. Straight black hair was parted in the middle over a high forehead. Intelligent dark eyes looked back at me from a rather handsome face. He was a dwarf. He kept watching Holmes and me as we entered the corridor and closed the door behind us.

We stood in a hallway that ran off to our left. It was dark at our end, the lamp by our heads unlit, the mantle broken. The air smelled of greasepaint and wood rot. Dim flaring gaslights lit the rest of the space, which ended in a windowed door forty feet away. Reversed letters on the glass spelled out "Stage Door", clearly visible by the light cast from a street lamp outside in the alley. Beyond the window I saw the silhouettes of several people, moving away to the right. The last of the employees must have just left. Three wooden doors lined the dun-painted walls, and another corridor was visible on the left, running behind the stage.

Halfway down the hallway a man dressed in workingman clothes stood before one of the doors. His hand was raised to the panels. Obviously he had just knocked to gain admittance. He hadn't noticed us in our dark corner. A woman's voice marked with a French accent said, "Who is it?"

"It's Jemmy Phillips," he answered in a rough voice.

"Did Jacques send you?"

"Yeah."

"*Entrez.*" The door opened and the lamplight from within threw the man's face into high relief. He was of medium height, strongly built, with short dark curly hair, a nose that clearly had been broken at least once, and a thick underlip over an unshaven chin. I caught only a glimpse of him before he entered the room, but his demeanor and appearance gave me a sinister feeling of menace. He walked in and the door was firmly shut.

Sherlock Holmes lifted his finger to his lips and gave me a warning glance. Silently we crept down the uncarpeted hall until we stood just outside the dressing room door. The building that housed L'Opera Pendule was old, and everything said within Mme. Jacasser's retreat was easily heard from the corridor.

"Where is Jacques? Did he send you?"

"Yeah, he wants me to pick up that package he gave you."

"He gave me no package."

"Listen, Jeanette, I know he gave you something, and I want it right now."

"I don't know what you talk of. Stop! Leave that alone!" There was a strange metallic slithery sound and then a thump, as if wood had struck wood.

"Where is it? It must be in with this lot. Pick it out!"

"You are crazy! Go! Get out of here!"

"Tell me where it is or I'll break your arm like I broke Jacques' neck!" The woman screamed and Holmes kicked down the door.

I followed the detective in to an amazing scene. Mme. Jeanette Jacasser's dressing room was sizable. The walls were hung with numerous costumes made of thin satin and lace on hooks next to pegs that held feather-trimmed, gauze-covered hats. A tri-fold screen stood in a corner on the right with a couch pushed against the wall just beyond it. A plethora of pillows and throw rugs covered the couch. A window facing the street was opposite the door and to its left was a dressing table and chair, with a round mirror hung over it. The dressing table surface was covered with cosmetic pots, brushes, soiled cotton balls and bottles of lotion. Two gas wall lamps flanked the mirror, which was surrounded with good-luck charms and little mascots tacked to the figured wallpaper. A small wash stand holding a painted tin pitcher and basin was placed in the corner next to the dressing table. In the middle of the room, centered under a gas chandelier, on a worn piece of carpeting, was a round table covered with a square of brocade. Its surface was covered in a dazzling heap of jewels, including ropes of pearls, diamond rings, glittering necklaces of emeralds and rubies, a sparkling stomacher, numerous bracelets and brooches, and at least one gem-laden tiara. Next to the pile was an overturned wooden box, elaborately carved with some of the designs on its surface picked out in silver. Jemmy Phillips stood with his back to us. He was holding Mme. Jacasser's arm behind her back, bending her forwards over the table's edge, with the fingers of his other hand gripping her golden hair.

Sherlock Holmes raised his walking stick and brought it down forcefully on Phillips' shoulder. The man gave a cry and released the woman. She slid to the floor and lay there, motionless. Phillips staggered backward as I trained my revolver on him. He snarled at us both as he clutching his injured shoulder, and only remained upright by propping himself against the wash stand, nearly tipping over the painted tin pitcher that stood there.

"Who the hell are you?"

"My name is Sherlock Holmes."

"Sherlock Holmes!"

"It is gratifying that you recognize me. I shall hold you here for the authorities for the murder of Jacques de Vitt!"

Holmes bought out a set of handcuffs and advanced on the ruffian. He locked one steel cuff on Phillips' wrist and reached for the other. Suddenly Phillips twisted and reached for the heavy box. He flung it at Holmes' head as my friend raised his hands in self-defense. I shouted a warning and moved to the right, seeking a clear field. Before I could aim the revolver, Phillips turned and dove for the window. He crashed through the glass and disappeared into the night. Holmes and I ran up to the shattered pane, but except for glass shards littering the ground outside, there was no sign of the confessed murderer.

My friend raised a silver whistle to his lips and blew several loud, sharp blasts. We heard hurrying footsteps and a policeman appeared out of the darkness. His freckled, ruddy face with its round cheeks and blue eyes, moved from me to Holmes. "Here now, what is all this disturbance? Why, is that Mr. Sherlock Holmes? Do you remember me, sir?"

"Yes, you are Constable Dwoff! Watson, this is the man who found the half-eaten apple that broke open the New Forest Stalking case. I marked you then, Dwoff, as a man to watch. Listen. Jemmy Phillips just confessed to the murder of Jacques de Vitt at Shooter's Hill last night. He attacked Mme. Jacasser and ran off with my handcuff on his wrist. He should be headed for the docks. The *Mother Dobbs* and the *Patched Pate* sail on the morning tide and he's sure to be on one or the other. Notify Inspector Lestrade at Scotland Yard and get the other men to cover the waterfront. You'll get your Sergeant's stripes for this, Dwoff, if you are quick."

The policeman ran down the street and we turned back from the window. I went to Mme. Jacasser. She was still insensible. I pocketed my weapon and lifted her from the carpet. She had removed her costume worn in the play and now was wrapped in a thin flowered kimono. It was just the work of a moment to get her to the couch. I swiftly examined her for injuries. She had suffered no serious harm but continued in a deep faint. As I placed a cushion behind her head, Holmes scrabbled at the pile of brilliants, using his magnifying glass to swiftly study each item and tossing it aside only to return to the heap to search again. He even picked up the jewel box and scrutinized it carefully. After a few minutes, he raised his head and made a gesture of disgust.

"These are merely bits of stage jewelry, Watson. Each is nothing but paste and glass, mounted on brass or nickel. The Zenana Diamond is not here. Yet Jemmy Phillips believed it was hidden in this chest with the other baubles. Why did he think that? It could only be that he has already searched her rooms and did not find it. When Mme. Jacasser returns to her apartment tonight I think she will find its contents have been torn apart.

"Consider that Jacques de Vitt was a hunted man and could not move about safely in public. He could not depend on a hiding place anywhere else. This dressing room has to be the resting place of the diamond. Yet it would seem that Jacques de Vitt did not give Mme. Jacasser the jewel to hold for him after all. How is the woman?"

"She will be bruised, but is not in danger otherwise. Excuse me." I went over to the dressing table and found, among the bottles and pots, a small vial of smelling salts. As I turned to my patient, the mandolin player appeared in the doorway. His dark eyes took in the scene and then he turned to us.

"Will she be alright, M. Holmes?"

"You have the advantage over us, sir."

"I am Henri Souche. I am Jeanette's friend."

"It was you who wrote the nursery rhyme and delivered it to me, wasn't it, M. Souche? Notice, Watson, the mended piece of elastic on our visitor's left shoe. Also, the small size of his feet would explain how a pair of boots could be contained in a sheet of brown paper only 12 inches by 14." Sherlock Holmes motioned the man into the room and gave him his full attention.

The handsome dwarf approached the day bed and gazed on the unconscious woman. "That is true. You are as clever as I have been told, M. Holmes. I have loved Jeanette Jacasser for years, but she feels nothing for me. I am just "le petite Henri", the mascot she cannot pin to the wall by her mirror. She is the only reason I have stayed in England all this time. We grew up together in Avignon, in France.

"Jacques de Vitt visited Jeanette frequently during the last few days. She told me they knew each other years ago, in Paris. He was good to her, but that Jemmy Phillips was a brute. I never liked him. I overheard de Vitt and Phillips talking in the hallway two days ago, before Jeanette got to the theatre. I didn't understand everything that was said, but Phillips was angry. He made an appointment to meet with Jacques last night on Shooter's Hill to collect his "payoff". He made threats against Jeanette if he didn't get his "cut", and I was afraid for her. I followed Jacques, after he visited Jeanette last night, and clung to the back of the buggy."

"You hid among the construction supplies near their meeting place."

"You are correct, M. Holmes."

"You left several tracks, betraying your short stride."

The dwarf smiled ruefully. "I saw what happened. I also heard Phillips tell Jacques just before he killed him that he was sure Jeanette had the diamond and he would come here tonight and get it. If Phillips found out that I had alerted anyone about Jacques' murder, my life would be very short indeed. I wrote the note in code so if it fell into Phillips' hands, he wouldn't understand. Did you have much trouble figuring it out?"

"You gave me a very interesting problem, M. Souche, for which I thank you very much. Do you know where the Zenana Diamond is?"

"No."

"Then we must ask Mme. Jacasser." Holmes motioned to me and I applied the smelling salts. A few moments later the French actress was sitting up, gathering her robe about her and looking at us in bewilderment. When she noticed the dwarf, she spoke to him in French and he answered her reassuringly. De Vitt's name was mentioned and she dissolved in tears. It took a few minutes before she regained her composure. M. Souche introduced us and told her why we were here. After a few more sentences, she agreed to answer Holmes' questions.

Holmes pulled up the chair from the dressing table and positioned it facing the day bed. I stood by the tri-fold screen and Henri Souche sat on the floor by Mme. Jacasser's feet. As she spoke she ran her fingers through his dark hair and patted his head, as one would treat a favorite pet dog. He accepted this attention quietly, but from where I stood I could see the hopeless devotion in his eyes that was invisible to the oblivious young woman.

Mme. Jacasser answered Holmes' questions openly and completely.

"Yes, M. Holmes, Jacques was my friend. I had seen him last three years ago. He returned two weeks ago. I was glad to see him. We met here, after my performances. He was wary, and moved only after dark."

"Did de Vitt ever give you any gifts? Any jewelry or something to hold for him?"

"Jacque never gave me any presents, or anything else. I didn't want him to give me things. Just seeing him and talking about the old days was enough. I knew that he had spent time in prison. I am not a fool. But he was the friend of my years in Paris and always kind to me."

"Tell me about what transpired last night."

"It was like any other visit. He waited in the hall until the play was finished, and I let him into my room. We sat and talked a bit and then he left. He mentioned that he had an important meeting later and had rented a buggy."

"Did he say or do anything unusual?"

"I do not think so. Wait, there was one thing. He was quieter than usual, and before he left for his meeting he brought me a glass of water. That is all I remember."

Sherlock Holmes stood and looked around the room. The flickering gaslight sent sparkles back from the pile of stage jewels on the table. The gauzy cloths of the costumes and the plumes on the hats hung on the walls moved gently in the breeze from the broken window. Absently, he began to place the false jewels back in the silver-painted box. Just as he topped the contents with the brass and paste tiara, a smile broke across his face and he turned to the wash stand. He snatched up the tin pitcher and turned it over. The contents splashed into the basin and we all heard a loud thunk. Holmes reached into the water and turned, something clutched in his hand. He held it out to us and opened his grip.

Water dripped through his long, thin fingers. In the center of his palm was a glittering object, a square faceted diamond with a white gold pendant mount. The gaslight shot beautiful colors off its wet surface. I looked from the gem to Mme. Jacasser and Henri Souche. By a trick of the light, masses of colored light reflected from the precious gem played over his suit, temporarily bathing the dwarf in the tints of motley. The actress in her Oriental robe and M. Souche in his multi-colored garb looked like an illustration of some exotic fairy tale out of a storybook.

"Oh, M. Holmes, is that real?" The woman leaned forward, her eyes as sparkling as the diamond, and peered at Holmes' prize. "How did you know it was in the water pitcher?"

Sherlock Holmes carefully dried the Zenana Diamond with his handkerchief and held it up. "I believe Jacques de Vitt thought he might not return from the meeting. He had no reason to trust

Jemmy Phillips, his disgruntled cohort in crime. He had no secure place to keep the diamond, so he had been carrying it around with him. Rather than risk bringing it to the rendezvous, he had to find a hiding place. He dropped it in the water pitcher. Since the pitcher was made of tin, and at least one third full of water, the diamond would be invisible if someone just looked inside. If he returned unharmed, he could retrieve the gem. If he didn't, it would be discovered by his good friend, Jeanette. He must have trusted you very much, Mademoiselle."

"I think now that he loved me, M. Holmes. He also knew nothing could come of it. He was not a good man, I know, but he was always considerate towards me."

"True love is a rare and wonderful thing, Mme. Jacasser," I said, my eyes fixed on Henri Souche's face. "You must never discount any chance to find it, no matter where it happens to appear or in what guise."

We left Mme. Jacasser and Henri Souche sitting on the couch. The next morning a story in the *Times* announced the apprehension of Phillips, tracked down by the Greenwich police force before he could find refuge on a departing ship. The French Government, in the person of the Ambassador himself, came to our sitting room and with many profuse thanks picked up the recovered Zenana Diamond. He presented Sherlock Holmes with a nice check, which Holmes wasted no time in depositing in his own bank. A few days later we read a small announcement in the *Evening Globe* that said Mme. Jeanette Jacasser, the prima diva of L'Opera Pendule of Greenwich, was giving up her career and returning to her home town of Avignon to marry M. Henri Souche, talented musician and the son of the mayor. Holmes shook his head.

"I believe that we shall not hear from M. Souche again, Watson."

"Why is that, Holmes?"

"With his penchant for communicating via nursery rhymes, it might be that M. Souche's next note could involve a cradle and a tree and that should prove naught to do with either you or me."

The Case of the Bivalve Burglars

For three weeks in October of a year I am constrained by Mr. Sherlock Holmes into concealing for his own personal reasons, I had seen little of my friend the great detective. Circumstances had enabled me to join a small medical practice in partnership with a younger colleague. My efforts allowed me to keep my hand in the healing world while still affording me time to join Holmes when his investigations required my assistance. My partner was keen to advance his professional position and welcomed any opportunity to cover for my irregular absences.

So it was that I was available to Holmes the morning he received Mr. Charles Carroll into the sitting room of 221b Baker Street. Holmes invited him to take a seat near the fire.

"I am a partner in Carroll and Lewis with our offices on the south side of the Thames, sir," said our new client. As he took his seat on the sofa I saw Holmes give him a keen appraisal from head to foot.

Mr. Charles Carroll was a stout man in his mid-fifties, with a thinning head of brown hair and a clean-shaven face the color of rose wine. His nose looked like it was formed from a potato and his pale blue eyes peeked out from behind bags of skin. He had fleshly lips over a set of double chins. He wore a suit of black broadcloth and sported an old-fashioned turnip watch on an Albert chain that hung from one waistcoat pocket across his ample stomach to the other side. Two small seals and an unusual knife hung from the links.

"You must find it very profitable to be able to pick up the oyster trade, after such a lull over the summer," drawled my friend. "Although a vacation spent on the Thames and the Cam, drifting past the great castles and universities of old must have been very relaxing."

"Yes, it was. Wait! How did you know I spent my vacation on the Thames and the Cam?" said Mr. Carroll.

Sherlock Holmes chuckled. "The fresh blisters on your hands have not yet had time to heal. The pattern on the palms is that of a man using a punt pole. Punts are very popular around the stretch of river that runs through Oxford. Leaves from the graceful trees that overhang the river at that point are evident in your pant cuffs and are particular to that area. You are unmarried and live in quite a bachelor establishment, for a wife or competent maid would have brushed off the evidence by now."

"And the oyster trade? How did you know that is my profession, sir?"

"You bring into our land-locked little home an air that smacks of the sea, Mr. Carroll. Plainly you are not a seafaring man, so you must deal with its fruits and the ships that bring in the harvest. On your watch chain is a strange little knife, devised for the shucking of oysters. I have seen such a knife on the brokers who deal with oysters. It is used to test the freshness and quality of the bivalves on the spot, before money changes hands."

"Everything you have said is true, Mr. Holmes. I must admit your words have relieved my mind. I wondered if even such a famous detective would be able to make sense of my problem, but now I am reassured. Mr. Holmes, you must solve my mystery, or I will be forced out of business and left beggared on the streets!'

"Indeed," purred Sherlock Holmes. "Pray tell me of your woe, Mr. Carroll. Watson, get our client a tot of brandy, for I see he is in need of a strengthening dram."

I poured out a drink and placed it on the table by Mr. Carroll's elbow. Before I could regain my seat with my notebook in hand he drained the glass. Silently I refreshed his drink as Holmes filled his morning pipe. The thin smoke from the pipe's bowl veiled my friend's grey eyes as his lids drooped while he listened to our client's story.

"As I said, I am a partner in Carroll and Lewis, the seafood brokers, well-know in the London market and even points north and south," Mr. Carroll began. "Tenniel Lewis and I have been in partnership together for nearly twenty years. We deal mainly in oysters, but during the off months we have a nice little business in whiting and snails, lobsters and other fish. We are strictly wholesale and have a warehouse at the river's edge near the Isle of Dogs to hold our stock until it is shipped out to our customers. We deal in perishables, you understand, and keep complete records of every cask and crate of inventory that goes in and out our doors. If we didn't keep up-to-date information, our stock could easily be overlooked and become spoiled and wasted. We spend a fortune in ice to keep the fish in prime condition. Only constant clear bookkeeping can keep such a business profitable.

"Lewis and I take turns with the business's acquisitions and dispersals. For the past year he has been urging me to sell out my shares to him. He has a family and wants his oldest son to come into the business. The boy wants to get married. I have no other interest in life save the warehouse and as you can see I am still in reasonably good health. I don't want to sell, but Lewis insists there is not enough income on his half to support two households.

"For the past two weeks I have noticed that the accounts on the books and the actual inventory in the warehouse do not square. Numerous casks of oysters have disappeared. I asked Lewis about the discrepancies but he protested that he knew nothing about it. He even took exception to my suspicions and declared that if I continued to suspect him he would insist I sell out to him and his son, or he would take me to court for defamation of character!

"I am of two minds as to whether Lewis is pulling some kind of scheme on me to force me to sell out, or if there is another explanation. I am at my wits end, Mr. Holmes. Can you help me find the thief and save my business?"

"Dr. Watson and I will be happy to look into your case, Mr. Carroll," said my friend. "Can you meet us at your warehouse this afternoon at two o'clock? I think that a survey of the scene of the crime will be most helpful."

"Of course, Mr. Holmes. Thank you, Dr. Watson. Here is the address. Do you wish Mr. Lewis to be present?"

"Yes, that would be most satisfactory," replied Holmes. A moment later the door closed behind Mr. Charles Carroll. Holmes went to his chemical table and resumed an experiment he had begun the evening before. I left for my surgery to see my morning patients and inform my partner that I would need him to cover my afternoon appointments.

I met Holmes after lunch. Together we journeyed over the Thames to the address on the southern side.

Carroll and Lewis's warehouse was situated just west of the Isle of Dogs. The tide had retreated and we could clearly see mud flats exposed under the high pilings of the long wooden building as we approached it from the west. Holmes had the cabby stop and we walked the last fifty yards.

"That is certainly a large warehouse, Watson," murmured Holmes. "The houses and offices on the street's other side are more modest and nondescript, but these on the river's edge are imposing in a silver-grey, well-worn way."

To the left of the Carroll and Lewis establishment was another storage building. It looked deserted. The sign over its door, Surlaw and Company, Import-Export, was faded. Its loading dock door was piled up on either side with flotsam and jetsam thrown up by the river. The wooden building had a pier on the right side between it and Mr. Carroll's business that offered access to the Thames. Only a few feet separated the pier from our client's building. There was a stack of long planks on its splintery surface.

To the right of the Carroll and Lewis warehouse was a brick edifice, the sign over the door reading The Seven Maids Mop Factory. There were clear signs of a thriving business within with sounds testifying to a busy workforce, all concentrating on their various tasks.

Sherlock Holmes smiled. "Now, what do we have here, a welcoming committee?"

Two men who had been standing by the front door to our client's business turned at our approach and came toward us. They were clearly related. Both were just above middle height, with sloping shoulders, long arms and short, thick legs. The elder was dressed in a drab suit, covered by a long rubber apron, with a pair of thick leather gloves shoved into the pocket. The other looked to be his son, clad in corduroys and with a sullen, dissatisfied look on his face that never left it for the entire span of our interview.

The older man thrust out a hand to us and introduced himself. "You must be Mr. Sherlock Holmes and Dr. Watson. I am Tenniel Lewis and this is my son, Bill. Carroll told me you were coming to look into this discrepancy in the books. Bunch of nonsense, if you ask me. If the man isn't happy with the way things are going, he should sell out and find something that pleases him better. I've offered him a fair price. My boy here wants to get married and it's high time he did."

"My girl Alice won't wait forever," muttered Bill Lewis. "She as much as told me she's had other offers. There's Jim Cheshire, always smiling and winking at her at the *White Rabbit*. He's got an ugly puss and I've told him more than once it would be better for him if he just disappeared."

"It's all ridiculous," Mr. Lewis declared. "So what if a couple of small casks of oysters get shoved into a corner and forgotten? Crated oysters on ice can be held for use nearly four weeks after harvesting. I admit they taste best when they are freshest. We've got a successful business but crates and boxes get shifted around. I don't think it's worth bringing in a detective. I told Carroll I'd meet you, Mr. Holmes, but I'm not going to add to this farce by answering foolish questions. He's inside in the office, waiting for you. As for me and Bill, we're going home. My day is done now. Good day to you, sir, and you, sir." With that the Lewis men turned away and marched off.

Charles Carroll was sitting behind a cluttered desk in the small office inside. Two men left as we entered. Our client explained that they were there to pick up a shipment of oysters for a famous London hotel kitchen.

"Please tell me about your neighbors, Mr. Carroll," said Sherlock Holmes.

"The Seven Maids Mop Company has been in business next door since before we took over this warehouse," replied our client. "There has been no conflict between us. Surlaw and Company is another matter. Mr. Gaylord Surlaw and his partner, Mr. Carl Pender, deal in all sorts of merchandise. They import gloves, storybooks, orange marmalade, tiny glass boxes, thimbles, pepper and lots of very clean and neat shoes. They export roses both white and red, tea sets, cucumber frames, canned mock turtle soup and packs of playing cards. Mr. Pender is handy with his hands and constructs wooden chess sets. But during the last few months activity has dropped off a great deal around the building. I haven't seen much of either of them, which is a nice change."

"Why is that a nice change?" asked Holmes.

"Over the years we have been here both of them found many reasons to bother us."

"How did they bother you?"

"At first I thought it was just curiosity, but then they asked to borrow things, like tools or sealing wax. It soon got to the point where I avoided Mr. Surlaw as much as I could and finally, a few months ago, the two stopped coming around."

"They stopped before the oysters began to disappear?" I asked.

254

"Yes."

"Then there would seem to be no connection between your current troubles and them. What about the businesses across the road?" I said.

"None of them have anything to do with shellfish so there is really very little contact between us."

Holmes' next request was a tour of the building. During the walk Mr. Carroll paused by the door of each room and flicked on electric lights that dangled from fixtures hung from the ceiling's rafters.

The large warehouse was divided up into a series of rooms, some stacked with blocks of ice covered with sawdust and stocked with crates and casks of oysters. Others were ice free and filled with empty containers. Mr. Carroll strode among his stock, explaining how the premises were set out.

"You will notice the wide cracks in the floors. That is so the melted ice water will drain out. The water drips out onto the mud flats. These trapdoors are for the larger chunks when we clean the rooms ready to put in fresh ice. We also off-load some of the merchandise out through the trapdoors. When the tide is high, small boats come under the floors and we load or unload the oysters in and out of the different rooms. They can only be opened from the inside and they are all securely fastened. There are only a few windows, up high, because the sun shining through them would hasten the ice melt. Each cask and crate is numbered and labeled. That information is added to the ledgers and is how inventory is kept.

"Our stock comes from many sources but mainly Ireland and France. We sell to restaurants, hotels and public houses. The casks and crates the oysters, lobsters and other fish are shipped in are sent back to us when they are empty. We return them to our suppliers."

"I see there are doors leading outside in the rooms on the river," Holmes remarked.

"That is how the inventory is delivered and sent out by larger boats. Two of the doors lead out to short piers that extend into the Thames. How the casks arrive and leave depend upon the supplier and the purchaser. The keys are kept in the office, on a ring on a hook."

"Are they the only ones?"

"That ring contains the master set. These that I carry never leave my custody. Mr. Lewis and I each have one for the front door but the ones in the office are used but rarely and then only by Mr. Lewis."

"If you will excuse me, Mr. Carroll, I will make an examination of these rooms now."

"Go anywhere you need, Mr. Holmes. I will be in my office when you are finished." Mr. Carroll gave Holmes his ring of keys.

Sherlock Holmes motioned me to follow him and we went from room to room. His magnifying glass in hand, he made a thorough investigation of the warehouse. His energy was amazing. He climbed up the stacks of ice, brushed away the piles of sawdust then brushed them back in place, peered into dozens of empty casks and others full of shellfish. He closely examined each lock on every door in the building, unlocking and locking the ones that lead outside, and ran his fingers over every trapdoor.

At last he straightened up from the last door, on the west side of the building in a room filled with casks of oysters. He examined the casks and the blocks of ice, at one point picking up something from one block's surface. Then he bent and pried slivers of wood off the floor at two places. These items he carefully placed in envelopes from his pocket. He stared up at the rafters for a long time while I stood waiting, the dank of the ice cooling the shellfish soaking into my clothing. Finally he pulled out his watch and checked the time.

"Let us rejoin Mr. Carroll, Watson. I think I have seen all there is to see here."

True to his word, we found our client back in the cluttered office. At the sight of us, our clothes spotted with damp and sprinkled with sawdust, he pulled out a bottle of brandy from a drawer and produced some glasses. When he offered cigars from his own humidor and I accepted one Holmes pulled out his pipe and lit it. For a few minutes we were silent as we warmed up before the electric fire that glowed in the office's corner.

"I have one more question," drawled my friend. "May I see the keys that you keep in this office?"

"Certainly," responded Mr. Carroll. He took down a large ring that hung on a nail near the door and handed it over to the detective. Holmes peered at each key with his lens, then pulled out a handkerchief and began to methodically polish each one in an absent-minded manner. He didn't appear to notice what he was doing, however, because he spoke only about the various suppliers and customers for the oysters of Carroll and Lewis.

Charles Carroll was puzzled by Holmes' distracted air, but he answered his questions politely. When we were finally warm and dry, Holmes handed back the keys and thrust the handkerchief in his pocket. Mr. Carroll escorted us out of the warehouse, exchanging a few last words with Holmes as I hailed a cab. Our horse clip-clopped through the city streets as we returned home in the early evening twilight.

Back in our sitting room, Holmes went straight to his chemical table. He brought out the handkerchief he had used to clean the warehouse keys and the envelopes he had filled during his search. For half an hour he sat on a stool at the table, busy with his instruments. Again as he had many times before he reminded me of some lank, thin bird of prey hunched over his perch, deciding in which direction he would swoop to pluck up his victim. Finally he pushed away from the acid-stained surface.

"Have you any engagement this evening, Watson? No? Then you will be able to accompany me back to our client's business tonight after dark."

"I am always glad to be of service, Holmes."

"That reminds me. Please bring your revolver. When confronting knaves in the dark it is better to be prepared with more than imagination."

We made a simple dinner off the joint and fruit on the sideboard as we waited for the time to pass. The clock had already struck eleven o'clock and the moon was up when we flagged down a hansom and set off for the Carroll and Lewis warehouse.

By prearrangement, a side door was left unlocked for us. Inside, the ring of keys from the office lay on a crate along with two candles and a box of matches. Holmes led the way through the building, unlocking and locking doors behind us. Beneath our feet we could hear the gurgle and splash of the tide coming in. The atmosphere was steeped in the smells of seafood, sawdust, melting ice and the river. Finally he paused before the last room we had examined earlier that day and raised a finger to his lips. Under the door shone a faint, wavering light. Holmes leaned close to my ear and whispered.

"Put out your candle and I will do the same. After I unlock this door, slip in and go to the right. The electric switch will be above your head. Don't touch it until I give the signal. Have your revolver at the ready."

Soundlessly I entered the storeroom and crouched behind a stack of crates. Carefully I laid my revolver on top of the lowest one. I felt rather than heard Sherlock Holmes lock the door and move to the left. My attention was drawn to the center of the room, where two men's faces were illuminated by the light of a single candle. They were seated on a blanket covering another block of ice, with two casks of oysters before them. Also on the blanket were loaves of soda bread, tubs of butter, a pepper pot and a bottle of vinegar. There was a sizable midden of opened shells on the floor at their feet. I watched as the smaller of the two men picked up a knife and sliced into one of the loaves.

He was clean-shaven, with a big nose and a square hat made of newspaper on his head. He wore a white apron under an old jacket. His companion was bulkier, clad in a rusty old evening suit with a shabby white waistcoat. He had an enormous mustache billowing out from his upper lip. His hand was like a flipper as he dipped it into the cask before him and drew out a bivalve. Expertly he shucked the oyster, added some pepper and swallowed it down with a smack of his lips.

"I must say, my dear Pender, even though we have gone through two of these casks tonight, the lure of the oyster never fades. Would you pass me a bit of bread? I have the butter here. There are still several oysters left at the bottom of my cask and I must send them to join their fellows before they grow lonesome."

Pender bent over and watched his companion apply a generous gob of butter to the slice of bread. "You're spreading it too thick, Surlaw," he growled. "There won't be enough to go around."

"But it is only the best butter," protested the other.

"Nevertheless, have a few with vinegar. It will be a nice change for you and the oysters won't mind."

"Did I ever tell you, my friend, that oysters were the particular favorite food of King Henry the VIII? He used to have them boiled with cabbages and pigs' feet. He ate them so often the Ambassador from Spain used to refuse dinner invitations for fear that dish would be featured."

"So would I. What do you have under that handkerchief?"

"What handkerchief?"

"That one, you old fraud. Ah, just as I thought. You have sorted out some of mine, and of the largest size, for yourself. I'll

260

just eat them now, before you can try to talk me out of them."
Noisily Pender gobbled up the treats, butter dripping down his
chin.

"These casks are empty. I'll get two more." Surlaw lumbered
to his feet. At that moment a chunk of ice flew out of the darkness
and knocked over the candle. The flame guttered out on the wet
floor. Instantly the room was dark, lit only by the moonbeams that
glittered through the windows high above and the wavering
reflected lights of the waters showing through the floor cracks.

I stood up, my revolver in my hand, and turned on the light.
The glare revealed Surlaw and Pender, frozen in place, and
Sherlock Holmes standing between them and a door that led
outside.

"Good evening, gentlemen. My name is Sherlock Holmes.
You will notice that my friend Dr. Watson has a weapon trained on
you both. I advise you not to move. He is a very capable shot.
The time has come," said Holmes, "for some matters to be
resolved. Since I have discovered you here, in a warehouse not
your own, in the middle of the night and picnicking on oysters
belonging to my client, I must strongly suspect you two of being
oyster pirates."

Mr. Surlaw drew himself up with a shopworn air of dignity. "I
might point out to you, Mr. Holmes, that I have found you and
your friend over there by that door in a warehouse not your own,
in the middle of the night and threatening to arrest two solid..."

"Very solid," murmured Pender.

"...Englishmen who have every right to be here."

"What?" I was astonished by such effrontery.

For a minute the four of us stood staring at each other. Then Holmes burst out laughing. Surlaw and Pender laughed too, and I watched in amazement as the reprobates settled back on the blanket-draped block of ice and each slapped a knee.

Holmes turned to me. "Watson, put away your revolver. I need to confer with these two gentlemen. It won't take long. Cabs in this neighborhood are hard to find. Please get one and bring it back here."

I was confused, but as always, I did what Holmes asked. I left. Walking through the moonlight, eyes peeled for a carriage, I thought about the scene in the warehouse. Obviously Surlaw and Pender had taken the missing oysters. How had they gotten into the warehouse undetected? What could be their motive, besides a great appetite for the little bivalves? Why did they believe they had a right to be in the Carroll and Lewis warehouse at midnight? What was Sherlock Holmes planning now?

I found a cab and came back to find Holmes standing on the pavement, the ring of keys still in his hand. There were no signs of Surlaw and Pender.

"I'll just return these to their rightful owners at Baker Street at breakfast, Watson."

"Are those two expected also?"

"It will be a jolly little party. The moon is starting to go down. To Baker Street, cabby."

I managed to catch a few hours sleep before Holmes called up the stairs to wake me. I came down to find our landlady fussing with a full breakfast service laid out on the table in our sitting room. There were place settings for six. A fine fire was taking the fall morning chill from the room. She had barely set out the last covered dish when the doorbell rang and she left to answer it.

Up the stairs came our client Mr. Charles Carroll, and his partner, Mr. Tenniel Lewis. There was no sign of Bill. A minute later Mr. Gaylord Surlaw and Mr. Carl Pender entered, their attention immediately fixed on the breakfast table.

Holmes waved everyone to their seats and snapped open a serviette.

Surlaw was reaching for a silver-domed cover when Mr. Lewis said, "Mr. Holmes, Carroll made me accept this invitation to breakfast with you, but I don't know these other gentlemen. What is going on?"

Holmes refolded his square of damask and laid it on his plate. "I can see that Mrs. Hudson's excellent meal must wait to be appreciated until this problem of the oysters is cleared up. Mr. Lewis, you have met these two men before. They hold your son's gambling markers. You were paying off the debt in oysters."

Mr. Carroll's face grew red. "Lewis?"

His partner's face was white. He shot a furious glare at Surlaw and Pender. "You blabbermouths!"

Surlaw shrugged. "What could we do? They caught us in the act and that one was armed."

"So you got rattled, eh?" snarled Lewis. He turned to his partner. "If you had agreed to sell out to me, this never would have happened. Bill bet on the ponies, trying to put together a nest egg to marry on, but he's no judge of horseflesh. These two came to me with a fistful of paper, but I didn't have the cash. I offered them free oysters for a month, but not for resale. When you started to complain, I thought you might get so fed up you would sell your shares to me. Then I could bring Bill into the business, he could marry Alice, and the markers would be canceled by a few casks of shellfish. But you had to consult Mr. Sherlock Holmes!"

Holmes addressed Mr. Lewis. "You took a mold of the room's entrance key on a slab of clay and gave the duplicate to Mr. Surlaw. I found the clay residue on the original key by cleaning it with my handkerchief. I looked for it because there was no sign of any of the locks being picked on any of the outside doors, yet the thieves had to get in somehow. The trapdoors were secured from the inside. I found threads from the blanket they brought frozen to the block of ice they used as a bench, and scrapings of candle wax and butter on the floor boards by the ice block. The deduction was simple. Mr. Surlaw and Mr. Pender were dining by invitation of Mr. Lewis, and felt protected by the laws of hospitality.

"I explained to Mr. Surlaw and Mr. Pender that my client is Mr. Charles Carroll. Half of the warehouse, the business and the oysters belong to him. He was not party to their arrangement with Mr. Lewis. They feasted on Mr. Lewis' oysters for fifteen nights. By any calendar reading that would equal half a month. Tenniel Lewis only has ownership of half the stock. They had eaten all the oysters he could offer them per the contract. I told them that the next one that slid down their throats belonged to Mr. Carroll and they could be charged as oyster pirates."

Gaylord Surlaw looked at the hot dishes on the table with a covetous eye. "I told Mr. Holmes he was as clever as he had been painted. I told Mr. Pender that we must fold our blanket and steal away. We've had a pleasant run. Now we would be trotting home again."

"I invited them to breakfast today because I thought Mr. Lewis might need a bit of prodding to admit his part in this conspiracy. He might dispute my deductions and my account of our meeting. In that case Mr. Carroll would be compelled to take this affair to court where Mr. Surlaw and Mr. Pender would be forced to testify against Mr. Lewis. I asked them if that a wise move for a couple of men just establishing themselves as gambling marker brokers."

Pender pulled on Sherlock Holmes' sleeve. "No courtroom, Mr. Holmes," he muttered. "No police, no lawyers, no constables, no judges, no gaol. You promised."

"I don't think there will be a problem, Mr. Pender," replied Holmes. "I believe that Mr. Carroll and Mr. Lewis are ready to settle the question of oyster ownership this morning. If you desire privacy, gentlemen, you may step into the other room to conduct your negotiations."

Silently the two men, one still with a very red face and the other with a very white one, got up from the table and went into the adjoining room. For a few minutes we heard muttered voices. Suddenly there was loud shouting and a bang as the hallway door slammed shut. Charles Carroll rejoined us as we heard Mr. Lewis stamp down the stairs and out the front door.

"Mr. Lewis offers his regrets but will not be breakfasting with us after all," said our client with satisfaction. "In fact, he has decided to get out of the seafood business altogether. He has a cousin who wants to start a white rose tree nursery. I shall buy him out with a fair price which he can use to invest with his cousin. Bill can work there. Mr. Surlaw, Mr. Lewis considers the debt paid. He asked that you hand the cancelled markers over to Mr. Holmes."

"It seems a shame not to be able to receive the second half of that contract," mused Mr. Surlaw. Carl Pender twitched violently. Surlaw sighed and pulled out a sheaf of papers, which he handed to my friend. Sherlock Holmes walked over to the fireplace and dropped them on the flames.

"There is one more point to clear up before we enjoy Mrs. Hudson's cooking," said Holmes. "Mr. Surlaw, I need the key Mr. Lewis gave you to enter the warehouse."

Gaylord Surlaw looked blank. "The key? That duplicate key? I thought I gave that to you last night."

Holmes smiled and lifted a dish cover. Savory smells emerged. "No, you did not, sir."

The rascal licked his lips and surrendered. He placed the duplicate key on the table and reached for the crumb-dusted baked oysters. I uncovered a generous dish of egg and chopped oyster omelet surrounded by slices of ham. Mr. Carroll picked up the lid of the last dish to reveal smoked kippers in oyster sauce.

Mr. Pender held out his plate.

"Some day you must tell me which was more difficult for you, Mr. Holmes," said Charles Carroll. "To un-dish-cover these oysters or to dishcover Mr. Lewis' plot."

The Case of the Deceitful Death

During my long association with the consulting detective Mr. Sherlock Holmes I had amassed extensive files on many of the cases in which I played some small part. Among these were many unusual stories. One involved a second stepsister where none was expected. Looking into a case of robbery uncovered the fate of a woman named Maria Rapunzel who had run away from her home. But nowhere in my experience did I find a more intriguing and fascinating case as the one that featured the medium and the dead man.

Holmes received a telegram at our rooms at 221b Baker Street one hot summer evening. It was from Scotland Yard Inspector Peck, a police officer who had consulted with my friend on a previous case involving three ships that arrived on New Year's Day in the morning. The telegram message was brief.

"Come at once to 1212 Henning Street, East Nisten. Am investigating odd stabbing case. Who would murder a dead man?"

"Make a long arm and hand me yesterday's issue of the *London Blatt*, Watson," said my companion. He turned the newspaper pages until he came to the article he remembered seeing the day before, which he proceeded to read aloud.

"'Medium Declared Genuine, Sir Oliver Looke tells Royal Academy of Science. Sir Oliver Looke, the eminent astronomer and member of the council that advises Whitehall on important advances in science, has announced that in his investigation of

Madame Fortuna, the noted medium, he has shown that her psychic powers are not faked, as some have alleged.

"Speaking from the steps of Madame Fortuna's home, at 1212 Henning Street, Sir Oliver declared that he will read a paper during the next meeting of the Royal Academy proving that the powers of mediums that endeavor to contact the dead really exist and Spiritualism should be considered an accepted religion.

"'This is a wonderful day,' said Sir Oliver. 'Now everyone can rejoice that their loved ones continue to exist after the death of the body and may be communicated with through the efforts of these humble persons blessed with the power to piece the veils which separate us from the departed. I have heard the voice of my own beloved mother, and touched her hand, through the gifts given Madame Fortuna.' Ha! Claptrap, Watson, pure claptrap!"

Holmes threw down the paper, rose and struck a match for his pipe.

"I've said it before, Watson. This agency stands flatfooted upon the ground. No ghosts need apply. One world is enough. Pah! What have I to do with tipping tables dancing around the room in pitch darkness, floating lights, spooky voices and luminous cheesecloth manifesting as your grandmother's ectoplasm? Spiritualism is famously rife with charlatans, frauds and crooks. Until science can come up with solid, irrefutable proof of its reality, I will continue to class communication with dead people with the existence of vampires, headless horsemen and mermaids.

"But the worthy Inspector Peck has piqued my interest. Go down and hail a cab, Watson, and let us see what mystery haunts 1212 Henning Street."

East Nisten was one of those old neighborhoods that clung to the edges of Greater London, fated to be demolished and replaced by modern houses. A hansom cab ride through some of our more historic districts and over the Thames brought us to our destination. It was a tall crumbling red-brick row house, hastily thrown together in the days of the last Stuart monarch. The neighborhood was under transition. Buildings on either side of 1212 Henning and behind it had already been torn down and the debris cleared away.

We found Inspector Peck waiting inside. He was a tall, thoughtful man with light brown hair and sharp brown eyes who stood to the side in the first floor parlour. I knew little about him except that he was fond of the theatre and boasted a fine tenor voice. Both had came into use during the Three Ships adventure. Behind him were two large windows affording a view of the street. Both were hung with very thick black drapes. On the opposite wall was a large tapestry of a hunting scene hanging over a cherry wood sideboard. On it were three glasses and a pitcher of water. In the middle of the room was a light round table. A simple trumpet and a hand bell stood on its surface. Over the table was suspended an electric chandelier. The table was surrounded by chairs; one of whom held the body of an older man slumped over, his head resting on the table. He was dressed in a drab dark grey suit. Under his left shoulder blade was a small reddish spot. It was the only sign of a wound.

"What did the police surgeon say about the cause of death, Inspector?" asked Holmes.

"That small spot of red marks a wound resulting from the insertion of a long, narrow skewer of some sort through the back muscles. It pierced almost to the heart and filled the sac around the heart with blood. The outer skin closed tight, allowing only a little blood to escape the body. It only took a few moments for internal bleeding to fill the sac around the heart and kill the victim. He probably felt little pain. That is why he never raised an alarm."

"Please continue."

"This house belongs to Madame Fortuna, the famous mystic and Spiritualism medium. We have been following her career for several years. Her real name is Sadie Spector. She started as a fortune teller on the promenade of Brighton and worked her way up to Madame Fortuna, consultant to very important people, including members of Parliament. She is in the habit of using this room for her séances. Sir Oliver Looke just declared she is a genuine medium. You read the story in the *London Blatt*?"

"Yes."

"Well, so have many other people. Over the past year a great many of them wanted to consult the spirits through Madame Fortuna. Among the clients who gathered for a séance here this afternoon was Mr. Fledge Byrd, his fiancé Miss Mina Nestor, Byrd's brother Nead, Herr Schlupfwinkel of Berlin and M. Caspar Bougre of Paris. The others are waiting in another room. This body, sad to say, was all that's left of Herr Schlupfwinkel.

"According to Madame Fortuna, who discovered the death, the sitters arrived for a séance set up at the request of Mr. Fledge Byrd. He had been attending sessions here for nearly four weeks. Each time he wanted to hear from his departed mother, who died six years ago. He was very close to her. Mr. Nead Byrd and Miss Nestor, who was engaged to marry Fledge, usually accompanied him. M. Caspar Bougre was also a previous client. However, Herr Schlupfwinkel had just arrived in London. He had requested that he be allowed to attend one of Madame Fortuna's séances at the earliest opportunity."

"So Herr Schlupfwinkel was unknown to the others."

"That's right. All the clients were admitted by Madame Fortuna's servant, Dormir. Mr. Fledge Byrd asked for this session for a reason. His uncle, Mr. Bailus Schell, travelling in France for his health, had drowned on the Cote de 'Or two weeks ago. Mr. Byrd was most anxious to contact the departed to get information about some papers that were needed in order to settle the estate."

"Was this contact established?" asked Sherlock Holmes with a straight face.

"After the accepted formula, all the clients and Madame Fortuna sat around the table, their fingers spread out and the tips touching to close the psychic circle. According to Madame Fortuna, Fledge Byrd sat at her right and Caspar Bougre to her left. Next to Fledge Byrd sat Miss Nestor and Herr Schlupfwinkel, with Nead Byrd closing the circle. After Dormir pulled these thick curtains over the windows and extinguished the lights, Kura, Madame Fortuna's spirit guide, came through. She was asked to allow the spirit of Mr. Schell to come through. That bell rang and the trumpet sounded and after a lot of knocking and banging in the dark, a message came through the entranced Madame Fortuna. The message asked that Fledge and Nead Byrd return in a week for another séance, when their uncle would be ready to communicate with them and answer any questions they might have. According to Madame Fortuna, Mr. Schell's spirit was still adjusting to the changes brought on by his passing and was not yet strong enough to talk to his nephews directly. After the lights were turned up and nearly all of the parties had left the room Madame Fortuna saw that Herr Schlupfwinkel had not moved. He was discovered to be dead. She sent Dormir for the police. After I arrived I questioned Madame Fortuna who told me this story. Meanwhile the surgeon examined the body. He found something quite unusual. He reported to me what he had found and I realized that this was just the sort of thing you might find interesting. That was when I sent the telegram."

"What was so unusual?"

"Herr Schlupfwinkel was wearing a disguise. See, here are his false Dundreary whiskers and mustache, a grey wig and coloured eyeglasses, designed to hide his true identity."

"Have you established his true identity?"

"I have. After the corpse was stripped of its facial adornments the other clients and Madame Fortuna were allowed to view the body, in hopes that one of them might recognize him."

"And he turned out to be…?"

"Mr. Bailus Schell, the deceased uncle of Mr. Fledge Byrd and his brother Nead."

"You were right; this is just the sort of thing I do find interesting," replied Sherlock Holmes. "Did either Mr. Byrd have any explanation for this deception?"

"None at all, Mr. Holmes. They were adamant that they both believed their uncle was dead. I would point out that it was to contact the spirit of this man that Mr. Byrd requested today's séance."

"One would think that the hereafter would be the worst place to search for the spirit of a living man. Therefore, we may conclude that Mr. Fledge Byrd didn't know that Herr Schlupfwinkel was really his uncle Bailus. Mr. Schell must have been recognized by the murderer before the lights were dimmed and the séance commenced."

"Why would one of those people kill him?"

"That is a good question. Are the sitters still here?"

"Yes. They have been waiting in the next room."

"I want to examine this room first. Then I would like to talk to the others."

"Of course. Besides Madame Fortuna, I have not had a chance to question them myself. I'll have the body removed now."

"Wait a moment."

Sherlock Holmes pulled out his magnifying lens and began an examination of the unfortunate Mr. Bailus Schell. He seemed especially interested in the dead man's hands. He pointed out to Inspector Peck and me the malformed nail of Mr. Schell's smallest finger on his left hand.

When he indicated that he was finished, two constables carried the body away. Holmes was just beginning on the rest of the room when thin grey tendrils drifted in from the hallway. I heard a faint sound of crackling and smelled the sharp odor of burning wood and cloth. Cries of alarum suddenly erupted and there was a rush of people down the hall heading for the stairs.

"Holmes!" I shouted. "The building is on fire! Come away!"

Instead of fleeing like the clients, Holmes ripped the tapestry from the wall over the sideboard and plunged into the mass of smoke and flames, trying to beat out the fire. Loyally I followed him, grabbing the pitcher of water from the sideboard on the way. A couple of the constables and Inspector Peck joined in. Our efforts proved futile, however, for the blaze was far advanced. The heat and smoke finally forced all of us to stagger out of Madame Fortuna's house just as the roof collapsed. The fire brigade arrived, a pair of matched black horses throwing sparks when their hooves clattered across the cobblestones. They pulled the brass-laden red fire engine loaded with firemen close to the building. Tongues of fire and brilliant sparks arched upward into the darkening sky. We collapsed on the curb on the other side of the street and watched as the men fought vigorously against the conflagration. The fire was clearly beyond human control and the building could not be saved. The rest of the block was protected by the fact that the lots surrounding Madame Fortuna's home had already been cleared.

At last it was all over and the crowds moved away from the scene of desolation. As a safety measure, the firemen began to knock down the charred timbers and the friable brickwork by the light of the streetlamps. The sun had gone down long before. The dripping ruin smoldered here and there and the firemen checked to make sure no hot embers survived.

Inspector Peck found us. His face was smudged with soot and dirt, but he swaggered up to Holmes and me as if he was waltzing down Piccadilly.

"There is no reason for you gentlemen to stay," he smiled. "I sent the others home. I have arrested Madame Fortuna for the death of Mr. Schell and the arson of her house."

"You are correct to arrest her for arson," said Holmes. "But she didn't kill Bailus Schell."

Inspector Peck frowned. "Mr. Schell was wearing a disguise. Obviously he was investigating Madame Fortuna's fraudulent business. She saw through the bushy whiskers and killed him before he could expose her tricks. Then she burned down the house, which was slated for demolition anyway, to cover her tracks. There might even be a bit of insurance fraud in it, too. No, Mr. Holmes, I have the right person and no mistake. Thank you for the interest you have shown in this case, but I see little need for you to involve yourself further. We just need to find her servant Dormir. He has disappeared, but I expect we'll track him down soon enough."

There was nothing more to be done that night, so Holmes and I found a cab and returned to Baker Street.

Sherlock Holmes was in a bad humour the next morning. My friend paced around the sitting room, interrupting my breakfast by slapping newspapers on the furniture and banging things around on the mantelpiece.

"Aren't you going to eat anything?" I asked as he threw himself into his armchair.

"Food!" he grumbled. "I am not interested in food. That deluded Inspector Peck has managed to make me as mad as a wet hen. Imagine arresting Madame Fortuna for Bailus Schell's murder! The trouble with that man is that he has too much imagination. Because of that, shall a cold-blooded murderer get away with such a crime?"

The doorbell rang. In a few moments Mrs. Hudson ushered in a middle-aged man. He was tall, with a trim appearance in his dress and footwear that suggested the Continent. His hair was jet black and slicked down with pomade. His eyes were large and pale blue and his nose was thin. He had a strong chin, however, and his mouth curled up at the corners as if he was continually suppressing a natural laugh. Now, though, his air was quite serious as he handed Holmes his card and sat down on the sofa.

"I am M. Caspar Bougre of Paris, France. You must be Dr. Watson and you, of course, are Mr. Holmes, the great detective. I attended the séance at Madame Fortuna's yesterday. Inspector Peck gave me your name, sir, and said you had visited the scene of Mr. Schell's death before the fire broke out."

"That is correct, sir."

"I have come to you, Mr. Sherlock Holmes, to ask you to find Bailus Schell's killer. I knew him for barely a year, but a kinder, more upright man you could never ask to meet. He was only trying to protect his nephew, sir, when he attended that séance, and it was that séance that killed him."

"Do you mean that you believe Madame Fortuna murdered him?"

"No, no! Let me tell the entire story and perhaps you can pick daylight out from the heavy clouds that cover the truth."

"Proceed."

"I am a gentleman of independent means, the son of a chemistry professor connected with the Sorbonne. He made a great deal of money from the patents he filed during his researches into early coal-oil derivatives. I have developed a small reputation from the series of travel books I write. I first met Bailus Schell thirteen months ago at a health spa in Germany. We have met sporadically since, every time our paths crossed during our travels. He was a retired school teacher who had been left some money by his grandfather and so was also independent. He suffered from a heart complaint and had traveled from one watering place to another in search of a cure for over two years. We became friends. Although he had not been home in England for quite a while, he talked a great deal about his family there. His only remaining relatives were two nephews, the sons of his sister. Their names were Fledge Byrd and his younger brother Nead. Their father had been a brewer and upon his death the brothers had inherited the business.

"Nead in particular had written to his uncle regularly. About three months ago Schell told me that Nead's letters became full of news about Fledge's visits to various mediums and the séances he attended. Fledge had become obsessed with getting in contact with his dead mother. They had been very close. Nead even wrote to his uncle about an intimate conversation he had overheard between Fledge and his mother the night before she died six years ago.

"Nead advised Fledge against giving so much attention and money to the mediums but his brother brushed away the warnings. Miss Mina Nestor, Fledge's betrothed, supported her fiancé's actions and would not join Nead in his campaign to bring some common sense to the situation.

"Nearly three weeks ago Nead wrote to say that Fledge had started visiting Madame Fortuna. Her spirit guide, Kura, supposedly was close to establishing a strong link with the spirit of their mother. Fledge started spending a lot of time at her house. He was beginning to neglect the business and Nead felt a crisis was developing. He asked his uncle for help.

"Schell sent a letter of good advice to his nephew, but Fledge sent back a haughty note declaring that, as a grown man he did not believe he needed any advice from "such an old relative". The response hurt Schell very much, although he tried to hide it. I volunteered to go to London and attend a few of Madame Fortuna's séances in order to get an idea of what was going on. I sat in on five séances in as many days, three of them involving Fledge Byrd. He was always accompanied by Miss Nestor. Nead Byrd came twice.

"The man was under Madame Fortuna's spell. He accepted completely every one of her pronouncements, disguised by the trappings of Spiritualism. I am a rational man, Mr. Holmes, and the son of a scientist, and I was dismayed by the power this charlatan held over Fledge Byrd. I admit her tricks were subtle and well presented, but I was never tempted to believe she ever held genuine communication with the dead. Everything that happened could be explained rationally.

"I felt totally vindicated when I discovered that my room at the hotel had been rifled and a man fitting the description of Madame Fortuna's servant, Dormir, had been seen outside my door shortly before. At the next séance I attended several messages were directed to me, repeating details that could have easily been obtained by going through my things.

"I wrote about all this to Schell and he wrote back, asking me to return to the south of France where he wanted to talk over the situation. He met me at the train station and took me off to his hotel. He listened to my summary of the trip and then announced he had a plan.

"I was to stay in the town for several days and keep my eye on the local newspaper. It would carry a message from him. When I saw it, I would know what to do. His instructions were confusing. He was vague on all details. But there was no mistaking his determination, so finally I agreed.

"Two days later I read of his drowning in the Mediterranean Sea.. I was shocked. I went to the police, who told me only that his clothing had been left in a rented bathing chalet. Witnesses had seen him struggling in the water, but by the time rescuers arrived, his body had drifted away. I didn't think this was the kind of news that should be learned from a wire or the newspapers, so I journeyed at once to London to tell the Byrd brothers myself. They were very upset."

"Is that when Fledge Byrd asked Madame Fortuna for a séance in order to contact his uncle?"

"Yes. She made the appointment for yesterday afternoon."

"Did you recognize Mr. Schell when he was introduced as Herr Schlupfwinkel?"

"No. I wasn't expecting to see him, you see. He wore unfamiliar clothes, stooped as though under a heavy burden and had covered his face with that wig and the whiskers. When the police brought us back later to see the dead man's face, I was as surprised as anyone."

"Did you know of Mr. Schell's crooked finger nail?"

"Yes. He told me it was a congenital condition. His father had a crooked finger nail and so did his two nephews. But I didn't notice it yesterday until after the murder. I was sitting several seats away."

"What can you tell me of Miss Mina Nestor?" asked Holmes.

"I just met her the few times we attended the same séance. Fledge Byrd met her when he purchased her father's brewing business. The old man was ill and had to sell. He died soon after. His wife had passed away years ago. According to what was told me by Nead Byrd, Fledge asked her to marry him soon after the sale, but then got the notion into his head that his departed mother should have an opportunity to approve of the union. Ever since then he had been going from one medium to another, trying to contact his mother's spirit. A few times he thought she had gotten through, but the messages were proven false. Madame Fortuna was his latest attempt.

"Miss Nestor supported him in this quest?"

"Yes. She was very eager to get his poor mother's approval. Each time the answer seemed to be yes, she urged him to stop searching and accept that his mother had given her permission. But Nead said that Fledge always found some fault and would look for another medium to investigate. But he did tell Nead that Madame Fortuna was his last try. If she was a fake, he would stop looking. But he told his brother that he felt that he could never marry without his mother's approval."

"That must have upset Miss Nestor."

"It did indeed. According to Nead, she was pinning all her future plans on this marriage."

Sherlock Holmes stood up and fumbled with the pipes and tobacco he kept on the mantelpiece. After a few minutes he turned back to us, his old briar sending tendrils of smoke up toward the ceiling.

"Will you, M. Bougre, help me get all the principals of this case together?"

"Certainly I will. Tell me what to do."

"Invite Mr. Fledge Byrd, Mr. Nead Byrd and Miss Mina Nestor to another séance to be held at the Hotel Stange in Greater Tutam Street this afternoon at three o'clock."

"Who is the medium?"

"Miss Margery Daw, a most amazing woman I met during a case in Canterbury last year. You were visiting Mr. Miller on the river Dee that month, Watson. She has true gifts, I believe, and I think she could solve Mr. Byrd's dilemma. I do ask you, sir, to use a name not his own when you introduce Dr. Watson to the others.

It is now nearly noon. Off you go, M. Bougre, and please do not mention me at all. I will introduce myself to them at the séance."

Our client left and I confronted Sherlock Holmes.

"What are you up to, Holmes? Just yesterday you were telling me that Spiritualism was claptrap. And I've never been to the river Dee in my life!"

My friend just smiled at me and disappeared into his bedroom. I stood fuming for several minutes but when he didn't come back I stamped upstairs to my own room. Again Sherlock Holmes saw things I didn't and knew things that were a mystery to me. He had made me a part of his plans without explaining to me my role. I sat in the armchair by my bed and tried to make sense of what had just happened.

Bailus Schell had faked his own death, for reasons unknown, and in disguise attended a séance in London that included his unsuspecting nephews and his friend. There he had been stabbed to death. When the police were called, the house of the medium had been torched and totally destroyed. Now Sherlock Holmes had invited the two nephews, the friend of the dead man and the betrothed of one of the brothers to another séance where he had promised that an important and pressing question would be answered by spirits conjured up by a medium using otherworldly powers Holmes didn't believe existed.

Had my friend changed his mind about Spiritualism during the last twenty-four hours? It seemed unlikely. Sherlock Holmes' one outstanding characteristic was a cold and logical mind. Appeals to the dead held no brief in his excellent brain. It would be as logical for him to believe in the powers of a medium as it would be to believe that consulting the pigeons outside our sitting room windows would gain us useful advice on the stock market.

And why was I to be incognito? I could think of no answer.

I shrugged and went downstairs. I found Holmes had gone out, but Mrs. Hudson had laid out a little cold lunch for me, *per* his orders. He had also left me a note asking me to come to the Hotel Stange at three o'clock, for he wanted me to be at the séance.

Heartened that apparently I was to play a part in this drama, I arrived at the hotel just at the stroke of three. Inside the manager directed me to room 144.

Room 144 was a plainly furnished room. The bed that it normally contained had been removed and a round table and eight chairs installed. There was a gas fixture over the table and what looked like new thick curtains over the single window. A chest of drawers stood in one corner.

The others arrived shortly after me. Mr. Bougre introduced me as "Mr. Chook" to Mr. Nead Byrd, his older brother Fledge and to Miss Mina Nestor. There was quite a family resemblance between the two brothers. Both were powerfully built men in their mid thirties. Mr. Fledge Byrd was a trifle taller and Mr. Nead Byrd had a thicker head of brown hair. Both had the ruddy complexion of the English Norman-Saxon and their handshakes were firm. I did notice that Fledge Byrd had a habit of twisting a ring on his left hand.

Miss Mina Nestor was a short, somewhat overly plump woman dressed in a welter of furs and satin. Her deep bosom was draped with layers of handmade lace. She appeared to be several years older than her fiancé. She had a broad and plain face and her eyes looked out from under thin brown lashes. As the daughter of one of the most successful brewers in her community she may have been considered a matrimonial prize in her youth, but it was obvious that no man had chose to pluck that prize, and now the years were gathering to her faster than she had expected. The plumes on her extravagant Leghorn hat trembled as she nodded to me. I noticed that she clung to Fledge Byrd's side as he moved about the room.

The door opened behind us and the hotel manager handed me a telegram. I tore it open. All it said was "Start without me. Holmes." He also ushered in a strange figure.

It was a woman, apparently this Margery Daw Holmes had mentioned earlier. She was tall for a woman and wore a simple green gown. It was draped in an unusual fashion with a grab-bag of multi-coloured silky scarves and shawls. Tassels and fringe hung from every edge and corner. On her fingers were many rings and from her ears dangled a pair of earrings that glinted in the gaslight. Her black hair was covered in a paisley scarf and from deep within its folds burned two bright sparks. The woman's face was a map of wrinkles and a massive thick nose spread across half her face.

Behind the manager loomed another guest, an elderly figure dressed in a checked Norfolk suit complete with plus-fours and hiking boots, totally unsuitable for London. His features were obscured by a thick salt-and pepper beard that flowed down his chest like a waterfall. His head was bald with only a fringe of hair surrounding it and his eyes were almost invisible behind black bushy brows. He said nothing, but grinned at everyone.

The woman stood for a moment, dominating the scene. Then she advanced, her arms raised as if in benediction over us all. Surprisingly her voice, when she spoke, was high and thin.

"So, you have called upon the amazing Margery Daw to bring you news of your dearly departed ones. Sit, sit, and sit, everyone. You, sir, Mr. Henlay, that was so kind to bring me here, sit in this chair. You are Miss Nestor. You love this man, heh? This Mr. Fledge Byrd. He is very handsome, but he also has a great question that must be answered. You, sir, are the brother. Sit, sit. This man is French, from Paris. Your name is M. Bougre. You know these people. But this man, this fellow with the fine mustaches, you are a stranger to the others. You will sit by me and be my helper. Please, everyone, sit."

Soon we were all seated around the table. Miss Nestor was given a chair next to the medium with Fledge Byrd on her right and Casper Bougre beside him. I was sitting at the old woman's left with Nead Byrd next to me. Mr. Henlay filled the gap. The extra chair was pushed back to the wall and the curtains were drawn over the window. Our odd leader spread out several sheets of blank foolscap out on the table and took up a sharpened pencil with her right hand.

"I am one who uses what is called automatic writing. My spirit guide, Gallus, uses the pencil and paper. I go into a trance and the messages come through. Please be quiet and do not touch me while I am in trance. You, what is your name?"

"Mr. Chook," I answered.

"You, Mr. Chook, you will make sure that there is always fresh paper under my hand. The messages can be examined afterwards. Now we will begin. Now the lights go."

Mr. Henlay turned off the lights and the room was plunged into darkness. There was just enough light coming in through the curtains to discern the vaguest outlines of our party.

Margery Daw leaned back in her chair and closed her eyes. We looked at her in silence, uncertain as to what will happen next. For several minutes she sat motionless. Then her head dropped down to her chest. One hand held the pencil over the untidy stack of paper. Then she groaned and her body straightened up. Her eyes remained shut but her fingers clutched the pencil harder and the point of the lead began to move.

Swiftly lines were scrawled across the papers. I slid blank pages under the pencil as I removed the filled sheets. For nearly twenty minutes the writing continued with the only sounds being of groans and sighs from Margery Daw. At last her tired fingers faltered and the now-blunt pencil dropped from her cramped hand.

We sat and watched another moment before she raised her head and blinked around the room.

"Well, what happened? Look at all these pages! Gallus must have been busy. Please, someone, turn on the lights and pull back the curtains. That's better. Now, Mr. Chook, let's see what we have, eh? Here, let me have them. I know a lot of it is gibberish, but Gallus drops in a nugget here and there. When I find something, I'll mark it, and when I'm done, we'll string it all together."

The writing on the papers was loose and loopy and I could not see how any words could have been formed in the resultant scribbles. Margery Daw poured over the pile, however, swiftly organizing them into a stack of marked sheets. The rest of us stared at each other as she worked. From murmured comments from the Byrds I gathered that they were not used to holding a séance in this manner. Fledge Byrd twisted his ring. M. Caspar Bougre got up and walked around. Miss Mina Nestor rearranged her hat and wandered over to the window. Mr. Henlay pulled out a corn-cob pipe and lit it.

"How do you know the medium, Mr. Henlay?" asked Nead Byrd. The old man smiled and puffed up a cloud of smoke.

"I just arrived from Rhode Island." The stranger spoke in a strong American accent. "I've been sent by the Providence Paranormal Society to interview Margery Daw. Professor Clausen Fedders, president of our Society, is convinced she is the most powerful medium in England today. I was with her when she was invited to conduct this séance."

"Please, gather around," Margery Daw said. "I will read the messages. Now, the first is from a woman. The writing is hard to read, but here it is clear. "My son, I love you. You are close to my heart. I am so glad to reach you at last. Remember that talk we had the last time we were together? But you must keep looking. You are strong. You will find the right woman and you will have no questions. This one is not the one for you. Not for you, dear boy. Never, never, never." That is all that was written."

Miss Mina Nestor had become more and more agitated as the medium droned on. Now she clutched her fiancé's arm. She turned to him, visibly angry.

"This woman is a fraud, Fledge! How could she deny you the happiness we will have together? Remember our plans. We will travel; we will have a fine home. I will host your parties. Life will be splendid. I don't believe that message came from your mother. That guide, Gallus, must have contacted the wrong spirit. Don't believe him, dear one! We will have a wonderful life!"

Fledge looked at her sadly but he also appeared oddly relieved. "That was Mother, Mina. I shall never forget our last conversation just before she died. No one else knew of that talk. I am sorry, dear, but I cannot marry someone of whom Mother disapproves."

Mina glared at Margery Daw. "Fraud! Fraud!"

Fledge Byrd huddled miserably in his chair, twisting his ring faster and faster.

The medium appeared unmoved. She lifted up another paper. "Here are messages from another. He is newly passed over. He says, "I love you, boys. I always had your best interests at heart. I wanted to show you that this Spiritualism stuff is false so I came to the séance. But I was found out. She stabbed me. The one you love killed me. She carries the proof with her.""

Miss Nestor became white, then red in the face. She rose from the table and backed toward the door. "Fraud! How dare you accuse me of murder? This woman is obviously insane. I deny it all. I will not stay here to hear such lies!" She opened the door to the hall only to be confronted with two constables standing there.

"Don't you dare touch me, you beaks!" she screamed as the policemen put their hands on her arms. Mr. Henlay reached out toward her fancy hat. She shrieked as he drew forth from her headgear a long, sharp hat pin with an enameled bulb at the end the size of a robin's egg. Half of the eighteen inches of its shaft gleamed in the electric lights, but the rest of its length and the tip was smeared with a dark brown stain.

The instant she saw the bearded man holding aloft the fatal hat pin, Mina Nestor collapsed into the arms of her captors.

I heard a stir behind me and the voice of Inspector Peck rang out. "Take her to Scotland Yard. I will be there shortly." The constables disappeared down the hall with their prisoner.

I turned and gasped in surprise. Margery Daw had disappeared into a puddle of garments and scarves on the floor, and Inspector Peck stood in her place. He was carefully peeling a flexible rubber mask from his face. He dropped it onto the pile at his feet and adjusted his collar and tie. The ample dress and the shawls had hidden his normal garb. A black wig, still entangled in the paisley scarf that had helped to disguise his gender, lay under the mask. He pulled out a handkerchief and rubbed off the last of the spirit gum that had secured his disguise.

"I can see that you are confused, gentlemen," he said to us. "I must get to Scotland Yard, as you can see, but I leave you Mr. Sherlock Holmes to explain how this case was solved."

"Mr. Sherlock Holmes!" exclaimed Fledge Byrd.

The removal of a long, thick black beard and the bald cap that went with it revealed Sherlock Holmes. He held up the hat pin and handed it to Inspector Peck as the official left the room and followed the two constables down the hallway.

Holmes picked up the pipe he had dropped on the table and put it in his pocket. "Gentlemen, I think the brandy and cigars, not to mention the armchairs, will be of a higher quality in Baker Street than here. I propose that we adjourn to 221B and there I will tell the sad tale of a woman who counted her chickens before they hatched."

Within half an hour Fledge Byrd, his brother Nead, our client M. Bougre and I were ensconced in the familiar sitting room, drinks in our hands and cigars distributed. Holmes stood before the fireplace with his hands behind his back and with little urging began to talk.

"I was first drawn into this case by Inspector Peck. He posed an intriguing question;

'Who would murder a dead man?' When we arrived at Madame Fortuna's house he explained that Herr Schlupfwinkel was Mr. Bailus Schell in disguise. I examined the body and noted the malformed fingernail which was a mark of the family. You two gentleman have it also."

Fledge Byrd and his brother looked down at their fingers and nodded.

"Before I could go on to examine the house the fire broke out. Madame Fortuna or her assistant Dormir started it. It was their escape plan in case the authorities became suspicious about the séances and wanted to look for trapdoors and hidden wires. Many mediums rig their séance rooms with such devices to help them produce the illusions that convince their clients their contacts in the other plane are genuine. I caught a glimpse of the control panel in the séance room when I tore down the tapestry in an effort to fight the fire.

"The building could not be saved, however, and Inspector Peck arrested Madame Fortuna for arson. He also charged her with the murder of Bailus Schell. I did not believe she was responsible for that. Why would she kill a complete stranger? He had done nothing threatening to her. Even if she had seen through his disguise was that fact alone enough for her to murder? No, Madame Fortuna had many sins against her, but Bailus Schell's death was not one of them.

"This morning M. Caspar Bougre came to me and asked that I find Mr. Schell's killer. I agreed. He told me something about Mr. Schell's relationship with his nephews and a little about Miss Mina Nestor's engagement to Mr. Fledge Byrd. I found especially interesting his account of their trek through the ranks of mediums of London, trying to get in touch with Mr. Byrd's mother for her approval of the marriage. Mr. Byrd was an adult, well passed his first youth, and I found it unusual that he would depend so much on his dead mother's endorsement of the union. Even when he seemed to achieve it, and Miss Nestor urged him to accept the message as genuine, he would demur and continue to search. This told me Mr. Fledge Byrd had deep-seated reservations about the engagement and was really looking for a way out of it. Another sign of his reserve was the twisting of the ring on his finger. He was unconsciously fighting the addition of a wedding ring."

Mr. Fledge Byrd nodded again. "I thought I loved her when I asked her to marry me. She was so alone, so vulnerable after her father's death. Her mother had died years before and she had no other family. But after the engagement was announced she became so clinging and so helpless that I could only foresee a future of more and more dependence that would be unsupportable over time. No marriage could survive burdened with such constant fear. A man wants a helpmeet, not a child to constantly comfort."

"It was her fear that you were her one and only chance for a home and an escape from spinsterhood that drove her to such lengths. When she recognized the family mark on Herr Schlupfwinkel's hand as it was spread out next to hers on the séance table, she panicked. She must have already sensed your hesitation. All her great plans would be ruined if your uncle could persuade you to not go through with the wedding. She struck out with the only weapon she had, the lethal hat pin.

"Later that night, back at your hotel, she wiped the instrument clean. But Dormir had escaped his mistress's arrest and had seen something during the séance that convinced him Miss Nestor was the culprit. He sent her a message to meet him outside the lodgings. He planned to blackmail Miss Nestor in order to get money to leave England. But the woman surprised him by thrusting the same weapon into his chest. She left him dying in the alley where they had met and got back to the hotel just in time to be notified of the upcoming séance. She had no opportunity to clean the hat pin. The best she could do was shove it back into her hat.

"The news of the finding of Dormir's body came just as Inspector Peck and I were leaving Scotland Yard. His death formed another link in the chain. I knew of Inspector Peck's acting talents from our co-operation in a previous case. He was more than willing to impersonate Margery Daw, a character he had originated for a Policeman's Frolic earlier this summer. He played through our script wonderfully. I must say that the stage lost a fine actor when Bantam Peck took up crime-solving.

"Shattered by the refusal of Mr. Byrd's "mother" to allow the marriage, Miss Nestor had no defense when she was accused of the crime of murder. When I plucked the fatal hat pin from her hat, still stained by Dormir's blood, she collapsed. Inspector Peck shed his disguise and the rest you know."

A second round of brandy seemed called for, so I circulated the bottle. The somber Byrd brothers were disinclined to stay after Holmes' revelations, so they soon called for a cab and went back to their lodgings. M. Caspar Bougre paused at our door and clasped Sherlock Holmes' hand warmly.

"Make up your bill, Mr. Holmes, and I'll be around tomorrow to pay it. Now I feel my friend Bailus Schell can rest in peace. What a horrible woman!"

"She was afraid," said Sherlock Holmes. "She lived in fear of abandonment and a lonely old age. When she met with Dormir she killed him on impulse, driven by a fear of discovery. Fear drove the woman into crime and it was her fear of capture that allowed us to prove her guilt.

"Come for breakfast tomorrow, M. Bougre. We will present you with a table that will offer no ghosts, spooks and messages from the other side, only nourishing dishes to eat. You will rise up satisfied while the table remains in place. There will be no chance that it will dance around the room. Of that you may have no fear!"

The Case of the Hesitant Heist

It was a morning in late May when I heard my friend Mr. Sherlock Holmes make a surprising statement.

"It appears that I now will have the time and leisure to pursue my interests independent of the hasty need to replenish my bank account, Watson."

"Why is that, Holmes?"

"By this show of the high regard in which Sir Kilkenny Kattz held my services." Holmes leaned back in his armchair and lazily waved a slip of paper in my direction. I poured out the last of the coffee.

"Is that the check for the fight club case?"

"Yes and it is a most generous sum for such a slight investigation."

"Slight investigation! For two weeks you posed as a down-and-out bare-knuckled boxer, a punching bag for every tough and hoodlum that villain Striker could throw against you. It amazes me that you survived without permanent damage. I never knew in what condition I would find you whenever you returned to Baker Street."

"Ah, but I had a few tricks to turn away the worse of the blows offered me. You were most helpful when it came time to expose Striker's diabolical plan to Sir Kilkenny."

"We were both lucky Striker was better with his fists than with a pistol."

Holmes rose and impaled the rest of the post to the center of the mantle with a jackknife he kept there for that purpose. Then he carefully placed the knight's check in his notebook.

"After I deposit this at my bank this morning, Watson, what do you say to a little trip to …yes, Mrs. Hudson, what is it?"

"There is a young woman here to see you, Mr. Holmes," our landlady announced as she gathered up the breakfast things.

"Bother all young women! I am seeing no new clients. Put a sign in the window, if you please, Mrs. Hudson, that Mr. Sherlock Holmes has retired to the country and will not return until fall."

Mrs. Hudson was unperturbed. "I will send her up," she said and exited in a flurry of skirts and clinking china.

A moment later a young female stepped into our sitting room. Her round face and figure held no promise of great beauty but there was a sweetness evident in her green eyes. Her round nose was held in place by a wave of freckles over a cupid bow mouth. She was dressed in a street dress of dull green with a narrow-brimmed hat of the same colour perched upon her head of tight reddish curls. One hand was gloved in the same shade as her dress and in the other hand she clutched the matching glove along with her reticule. As I got up to offer her a seat on the sofa I realized that she came up just to my shoulder. She smiled timidly at me as she sat down then transferred all her attention to Sherlock Holmes.

"You are very kind to agree to see me, Mr. Holmes."

Holmes had turned away to the mantelpiece and was pretending to examine the knife he had just thrust into its surface. From where I stood I could see his face. It was a mask of irritation. Our landlady seldom went against any of his wishes and this violation was out of character for her. But his customary courteous attitude toward women prevented him from throwing the young lady out on her ear without hearing her case. After a pause and a glance at me he ran his eye over her. She looked back at him bravely, tugging at the third finger of her gloved hand. When she tried to speak he raised a hand.

"You were born in Belfast, Ireland five and twenty years ago. Your parents brought you to London when you were ten years old. You work as a children's nurse and live with the family that employs you. Not a rich family. Your master is an up-and-coming merchant, dealing in spices and fruits...a greengrocer who uses part of his private property as a warehouse for his stores. This is not your day out, but your problem cannot wait and you have arranged with another servant to exchange shifts so that you might travel to Baker Street on the Underground and ask for my help. You are satisfactory in your work and so your mistress has agreed to this plan. Your problem involves someone with whom you are very close.

"You did notice, Watson, the faint traces of her Irish accent, which she has worked so hard to overcome. The older child of the family, one of two, I think, has marked her dress with traces of chalk from the nursery which she has failed to completely brush off her skirt. The marks are at the exact height for a toddler to reach. At her age, she would not be head nursemaid, but assistant to an older woman. There is a stain on the glove she holds in her hand of Madson's Baby Food, a popular canned formula for babies. So there is a second child as well. The splash occurred this morning, as she was bidding farewell to the infant. She could not take time to clean the glove or exchange it for another.

"Such a profession demands that the nursemaids live on the premises. She carries a faint aroma of apples and pears, cinnamon and coriander that marks her employer as a greengrocer who uses part of his property as a warehouse for his stores. Thus he has shown himself to be thrifty and sensible. He has married a woman also sensible enough not to want to cause discord with a valued and trusted servant. Monday mornings are not the customary time that servants are allowed absence from their jobs so arrangements were made with her mistress and the head children's nurse to be allowed to leave the house. The return ticket of the Underground line is peeking out of her pocket and nothing less than the peril faced by a close relative or a lover would be so important as to bring around such climatic upheavals in the life of this ordinary young member of the working class."

"Oh, Mr. Holmes, you are correct on every point, although I cannot tell how you knew all that. My name is Morgana Dyne and it's my brother Alan that I am worried about. I saw him last Thursday, my regular night out, and we were to meet again yesterday after church. I waited outside St. Christopher's for two hours, until I had to go back to the house to help with the little ones' lunch, but he never showed. I'm worried because he said he had some kind of job set up for Saturday night. He wouldn't really tell me much about it. I'm afraid something has gone wrong. And I didn't like the looks of that man that Alan met at the café just after I left."

I could see that despite himself Sherlock Holmes was interested in her story. He filled one of his pipes from the Persian slipper by the fireplace, struck a match to light it and leaned back against the mantle.

"Please tell me your story. Leave nothing out. The smallest detail may be important."

"My brother Alan Dyne had a harder time adjusting to our new life in London than either my parents or I. He is a few years older than I and early on fell in with a rough crowd. My parents couldn't handle him and he finally moved out. We lost track of him. I suppose I tried to be extra good and diligent as a daughter as a result of the trials he put our folks through. After I left school I went to work as a children's nurse. I enjoy the work. Our parents died four years ago. Two years later I took a job as a second nursemaid for the Waddys of Empire Square.

"Mrs. Waddy had a little boy, but the second nursemaid had unexpected quit to get married. It's a good place and I adore the children. Mrs. Sands is in charge of the nursery.

"I had heard nothing from my brother until about six months ago when he walked up to me after church on Sunday."

"How did he look?" asked Holmes.

"He was thin. He didn't grow much after he left so he's no taller than I. He was well-dressed in a sporting way, but his eyes looked harder. He was more reserved than I remember and his hair was sprinkled with early grey, like our father's was. He took me to a pub called the "Jewel and Bottle". He had heard about our folks. He gave me a wad of five pound notes. I tried to refuse the money but he insisted, and rather than cause a scene in public I accepted them. I've never spent any of them. See, here they are in my handbag."

She opened her bag and held it out to Holmes. I could see a number of notes folded over and tucked inside. It looked like forty pounds.

"I arranged to meet him after church each week for an hour or two, my only free time except for my half-day on Thursday. Twice on Thursdays he found me when I came out of the Waddys' home and treated me to dinner at the "Jewel and Bottle". Last Thursday was one of those times.

"He looked more worried than he had before and spoke of "making a big score" on Saturday. I thought he meant wagering. I knew by then that he moved in questionable circles. He never told me, but a woman knows. It is the major reason I never spent any of the money he gave me. He talked rather mysteriously about "if something went wrong". I became upset and cautioned him against taking risks. He laughed and assured me he was an "old hand" and the job he was to do was "a cinch".

"It grew late and I had to leave. He said he was meeting someone. Just as I reached the door of the pub, a big, swarthy man pushed past me coming in. I looked through the window outside and saw that man join my brother at his table. My brother had an unhappy expression on his face. Then I had to hurry off."

"What did the man look like?"

"As I said, he was big and had an olive complexion. He had broad shoulders and was dressed in an expensive suit, like those that Mr. Waddy wears. When he brushed past me I noticed the cufflink on his left sleeve. It was shaped like a horseshoe made of tiny rubies."

Sherlock Holmes stopped fiddling with his pipe and sat down opposite from the young woman.

"I heard nothing more from my brother. When he didn't show up at St. Christopher's I decided something had happened to him. I spoke to a policeman on the street but he said my brother was a grown man and missing one appointment with me didn't warrant an official investigation. There is another to whom I may have gone for advice, but he is presently out of the country. That is when I resolved to seek your help. I had followed your adventures in the Strand Magazine, you see."

Sherlock Holmes raised Miss Dyne to her feet. "I will look into your little problem," he said, patting her hand. "Might I suggest that you put that money in a safer place than your handbag? Deposit it in a bank or give it to your mistress to hold for you."

"Would you hold it for me, Mr. Holmes? I'm afraid anyone else would have too many questions about how I came to have it."

"Of course. Put it in the safe, Watson, and write her a receipt. Goodbye, Miss Dyne. Please give me your address so I may send you word of my investigation. If you hear from your brother, I ask that you let me know at once."

She handed him a slip of paper and turned toward the door. I tucked the receipt into her hand and murmured farewell. Holmes moved over to the window and watched as the faithful little woman trundled toward the Underground station.

"There is a sister a man might be proud of, Watson. And a constant reader of yours! Her problem does present interesting features. What was the job that was "a cinch" yet could "go

301

wrong" enough to make a rogue brother worry his sister? What is Dyne's connection with the other man with the horseshoe cufflink? How did Dyne get that money? And most importantly, where is Alan Dyne now?"

"What are you going to do, Holmes?"

"First I shall deposit my check and then take a stroll over to the "Jewel and Bottle". There must be a beginning for every old hound to follow and the barkeeper there will put me on the scent. No man, even in a city as big as London, goes through his routine of life without leaving traces. I would be a poor investigator indeed if I could not uncover the course Mr. Alan Dyne has been covering."

My duties to the patients at the surgery kept me busy until late in the evening. It was after eight o'clock when I returned to 221b Baker Street to find Sherlock Holmes ensconced in his armchair, wreathed in a cloud of grey tobacco smoke. After I opened a window to make the atmosphere tolerable, I noticed that he held his pipe with barked knuckles. There was a cut near his eye and one side of his head was bloody.

"Good heavens, Holmes," I exclaimed. "What happened?"

"My investigation has led me down some dark paths, Watson," he drawled, as I brought out bandages and antiseptic. He winced as I cleaned his wounds.

"The moment I walked into the "Jewel and Bottle" I recognized the barkeeper as an associate of the suspected fence and gang leader Jay Farr. Farr was thought to be one of the men involved in the Pyemann swindle of two years back, when Lord

Simon Sympell was tricked out of possession of his family's most precious asset, the famous painting "Pomegranate Heifer".

"But that case went to trial and the prosecution's case fell apart when the witness who saw the transaction on the waterfront never appeared to testify!"

"And that witness has not been seen since, my friend. Mark that fact. Alan Dyne has gotten himself mixed up with a dangerous bunch."

"What happened next?"

"I was recognized and two other rather bulky gentlemen invited me into the back room. There I was introduced to Mr. Farr. He is tall and has an olive complexion. He was wearing a fine suit. However, his face has a thickness and cruelty about it that will never be concealed by any pretense of gentility. His cufflinks are ruby horseshoes. Ah, yes, just like the man Miss Dyne saw taking to her brother in the "Jewel and Bottle". We chatted about my career and his for a few minutes, then I was invited to give up my current investigation and leave town for an extended period of time. After a suitable amount of persuasion I pretended to agree, but to make sure I realized the gravity of the situation the head bruiser used his club to knock me out. Yes, that tender spot over my ear. Is it still bleeding?"

"My God, Holmes," I murmured as I parted the hair and examined the cut. "No, it is not bleeding now. Here, sit still while I clean it up and apply a bandage. Then what happened?"

"I awoke on a dirt path near the river behind some decaying warehouses. I was sprawled out in the mud. I managed to reach the nearby home of one of my Irregulars, who helped me back to here. I insisted that he leave me two blocks away, and I got in without alerting Mrs. Hudson. I knew consulting another doctor would raise the alarm so I've been waiting for your return. The tobacco acted as a bit of a painkiller. I think my adversary will believe I have dropped the case. Now he will be less likely to guard against me and my search for Alan Dyne may continue."

"Continue? Man, you must go straight to bed and stay there!"

"I'll rest tomorrow, Watson, I promise, but in exchange you must follow my orders. We need to spread the rumour that Sherlock Holmes has left the country to investigate another case."

"That will be simple enough to arrange. You have frequently gone abroad to work for foreign clients."

"The underworld must be convinced that I have left London. Jay Farr will attribute it to our little discussion and think that he has scared me off. That is of no matter as long as I am left free to move about the dives and joss-joints near the river."

"What is so important about the river, Holmes?"

"During my meeting with Mr. Farr I noticed that the soles of his shoes were marked with the oily black ooze that is left by the retreating Thames. He had recently walked along some boardwalk or steps that are regularly submerged by the high tide. There was also the faintest odor of decayed fish, not something often encountered near St. Christopher's Church, located as it is so far from the water. It is a clue that bears following. Give me your shoulder, old fellow, and I'll rest now. Tomorrow will be a busy day."

I determined that Holmes had no serious injuries besides some smaller cuts and bruises. I left word at the surgery that I would be unavailable for the next few days and spent the night on the sofa in the sitting room, ready to assist if I was called upon. With the thought of what my friend had endured, I made sure my trusty service revolver was near at hand.

The next morning Sherlock Holmes stayed in his bed. He sent for Wiggins, the clever little lieutenant of the gang of street urchins he sometimes employed to assist him on some of his investigations. Mrs. Hudson had been told that no one was to learn of his injuries or current location and fussed over him, bringing up hot soup and allowing Wiggins open access to Holmes' room.

The little street Arab was in and out, reporting by late afternoon that the rumour of Holmes' departure to the Continent was common currency in the haunts of the criminal element of the city. The afternoon papers carried a short squib about Mr. Sherlock Holmes' engagement by the family of Mr. Thomas Tucker, the promising young tenor who was reported missing after a concert given the week before at La Scala. According to Wiggin's report, this story alone seemed to reassure the criminal element that he had left for Italy by boat-train early and was safely away from them.

At Holmes' direction I traveled to Empire Square that evening and was given a cup of tea by the kitchen staff while I waited for our client to descend from the nursery. The housekeeper offered the privacy of her sitting room for our meeting. Miss Dyne, dressed neatly in a black uniform and white collar and cuffs, poured the tea. I noticed the glint of a silver chain around her neck as she leaned forward to hand me my cup. I was able to reassure our client that her case was progressing without giving her much information. . When I returned to Baker Street the street lamps were just being lit. Holmes was dressed to go out.

He was wearing black, including a worn fisherman's sweater and old boots. He motioned to similar garb laid out for me.

"Change into that old slop, Watson, and don't forget your revolver. Our adventures lead us to the river tonight, and we must be able to blend in with the population as well as the darkness. No cab, I fear, but a healthy stroll will invigorate us. Wiggins is below, ready to guide us. The Irregulars have been busy. Here, man, wear this."

He shoved an old tweed cap into my hand and covered the glaring white bandage on his head with another. Down in the street Wiggins saw us come out on our step from across the street and casually strolled away.

We followed, giving no sign that we knew of his existence. We trod a serpentine path through the London streets, doubling back on ourselves and taking several dodges through public walkways and dark and noisome alleys to evade any followers. Big Ben had tolled eleven before the boy ducked into a shadowy doorway only a few yards from the Thames. I could hear faraway raucous music drifting across the water and smell the stench that rose off the river.

"Where are we, Holmes?"

"We are in Blackyards, at the top of a set of steps that will take us down to a rowboat. Here is a light. Wiggins has descended and is down there waiting for us. Watch your step."

The work of a few moments had the three of us down the rough stone staircase and into the little boat. With Sherlock Holmes at the oars we pulled out from the landing and proceeded across the Thames to the southern shore. The tide was only an hour from its height and the banks were lined with various shadowy vessels preparing to raise anchor at midnight. Lights from swaying lanterns gleamed in broken lines across the estuary and the murmuring waters carried the sound of anonymous men as they shouted to each other while the last preparations for casting off were completed. Raucous but muted music sounded from some place on the other side. We remained silent as our boat approached the far bank and crept along the soggy, moss-covered stone barricades that protected the ancient foundations of the buildings above us from the water. Finally Holmes shipped oars at the bottom of another set of stone steps that rose out of the river to a square structure that loomed overhead. The hurdy-gurdy music I had heard earlier was now loud and with it blended the sound of men talking and women laughing. It was coming from the building above our heads.

"That is the notorious public house called the "Camel's Breath". It is another of the many enterprises in which Mr. Jay Farr holds an interest. If you had a shilling, Watson, for every smuggled jewel and every poor man shanghaied to foreign lands that has passed through the back doors and secret hatches of the "Camel's Breath", you could write your little romances from a mansion next door to the Duke of Denver."

"You amaze me, Holmes!"

He gave me a hand up and we stood on the lowest step above the water. Wiggins was left in the boat, tying the boat's rope to a ring set into the wall. Holmes held up his lantern and showed me a set of worn limestone steps going upwards. I listened to the sound of river water lapping around our frail vessel as he whispered to me.

"The tide has been coming in for some time. These stairs lead to a stone wharf that runs most of the length of this building, the "Camel's Breath". I believe these steps, exposed in a few hours by the retreating tide, and covered with the resulting slime, supplied the mud that Mr. Farr carried on his boots.

"There is a narrow extension build onto the back of the public house, supported by posts fixed to the wharf below it. Have your revolver ready, Watson. Now, up we go."

The steps we had to mount to reach the wharf were indeed slippery and coated with a noxious film. Carefully we reached the flat expanse of the wharf and silently stepped on the worn surface. The stone staircase continued upward to the street.

We found ourselves among crates and barrels and coils of rope. Obviously this platform was used to load cargo and receive shipments from other vessels when the tide was full. There was a solid brick wall against the back of the wharf. An iron ladder led up to a door on the end of the extension over our heads, and I could detect several lines of faint light that revealed square holes cut into the floor of the edifice above, covered by crude hatches. Lights showed across the water from the back windows of the "Camel's Breath" and the unseen hurdy-gurdy player started up another tune.

Holmes silently mounted the ladder and swiftly picked the lock of the door at the top. I followed. In an instant we found ourselves standing in a large room. It was filled with boxes and casks stacked against the walls and extending into the floor space. Strong pulley systems equipped with ropes hung from the beamed ceiling over the hatch covers. In the middle of the space was a man huddled on a dirty divan, a single candle burning on a crate beside him. Sherlock Holmes bent over the prisoner and released the gag and metal bands that bound him. A grey-hair man with a familial resemblance to our client looked at us in amazement. I helped him to a sitting position.

"Who are you? Are you from Farr?" the man stammered.

"No. Your sister sent us. Are you Alan Dyne? Then come along."

Willingly he stumbled down the ladder, his muscles stiff from the fetters, and we headed for the stone steps. Suddenly there was a commotion above us, and a furious voice was heard from the room overhead.

"He's escaped! The door is open! Lift the hatches! There they are! Get them, boys! Bring me back Dyne alive and toss the others in the Thames! Go! Go!"

These orders were followed by a string of horrible oaths.

Bodies dropped from the hatches, armed with cudgels and knives. Holmes, Dyne and I found ourselves cut off from the steps and faced with four ruffians, each armed to the teeth. As we backed up against the blank brick wall of the structure I pulled out my revolver and pointed it at the largest attacker. My handgun was clearly visible from the light that streamed through the hatch above us.

"Stand back, man, if you value your life! I'll shoot if you come any nearer!" I exclaimed. Besides me cowered Dyne but on his other side Sherlock Holmes displayed another revolver to the crowd. The sight of two determined men pointing pistols at them made the brutes hesitate. Above us I could hear one last man climb down the iron ladder and join our pursuers.

"What's this? What's this? Why are they still standing?" A tall, well-dressed man with ruby horseshoe cufflinks pushed his way to the front. At the sight of our weapons he stopped. He started when he recognized Holmes and his aggression faded away. He gave my friend a sickly smile.

"Why, it's you, Mr. Holmes! I thought you were in Europe."

"That is what I wanted you to think, Mr. Farr," said my companion. His voice was smooth and unhurried, as if he had just met the criminal on a street corner. He motioned to the other men with his revolver. "You needn't introduce me to your friends. In fact, I think this wharf is getting crowded, don't you?"

At a gesture from their leader, the other men retreated up the ladder. Above I could hear the hatches being replaced and their footsteps fade away as the men re-entered the "Camel's Breath". The only source of light now came from Holmes' lantern. He shown it into Farr's eyes and the big man blinked. His face was indeed thick. His nose, his lips, even his eyelids were turbid and protruding. His fingers were like sausages as he clenched his hands in stifled fury. Holmes kept his revolver trained on Farr as he addressed Alan Dyne.

"Is this the man who kidnapped you, sir?"

"Yes. The entire plot was his idea."

"Will you testify to that in a court of law?"

Jay Farr turned his furious gaze to Dyne. I could see murderous promises in those hooded eyes. I felt the little man shrink back farther into the shelter of my shoulder.

"I...I...I must think of my sister, Mr. Holmes. She would not be safe if Scotland Yard was brought into the case and neither would I. That has been made abundantly clear to me during the past few days. I'm sorry, sir, but I have made plans to move to America and the wait for a trial would only delay me."

I could see the beginnings of a triumphant smile creep across Farr's lips. He relaxed and thrust his thumbs into his waistcoat pockets. He rocked back on his heels and crowed at Sherlock Holmes.

"You have no case, Mr. High and Mighty Detective. I suppose Mr. Dyne will want to leave with you and your friend, but we two have no more business together. Good night, sir. Next time you visit the "Camel's Breath", come in the front door and I'll treat you to a proper drink." With a sinister laugh, he turned and climbed up the ladder. A moment later, we could hear him enter the pub accompanied by a great gust of laughter from its denizens.

Sherlock Holmes said nothing as we descended the stone steps and rejoined Wiggins at the boat. Again Holmes took the oars and our craft crossed the river to our starting point. It was more difficult now, as the tide was nearly full and many ships, large and small, were making their way down the water toward the sea. Mocking hurdy-gurdy music followed us across the water. In the uncertain lights bobbing on the river's surface I studied Holmes' shadowed face, trying to see how the escape of his enemy had affected him.

He was disappointed, I was sure. But the rescue of his client's brother from prolonged imprisonment must have given him solace. Alan Dyne had spoken of a plot. What could it possibly have been? Why had Jay Farr kept one of his own operatives captive? What else did Mr. Dyne have to tell us? And I wondered if he would even tell us anything, after seeing his marked reluctance to talk to Scotland Yard?

We landed at the other set of steps and Holmes hailed a cab, leaving Wiggins to see to the rowboat. Within an hour the three of us were seated before a fire at 221B, drinking coffee Holmes brewed over his Bunsen burner. I checked Mr. Dyne for injuries and found nothing serious. As he was supplied with a plate of meat and bread from the ever-ready sideboard supply, the little man looked immensely more comfortable than he had first appeared to us in that crowded, candle-lit room.

He dug into the food with relish. Obviously his rations had been short since Saturday. When he finished and I removed the plate and water glass, I put a glass of brandy before him. He eagerly drained it. Then Sherlock Holmes began.

"You have been hard-used the past few days, sir, but it is still evident from your appearance that you began as a second story man. You were never apprehended, but became proficient as a safe-cracker about three years ago, feeling it was a safer way to make a living. Within the last year you developed a small business as a turf accountant. Slowly and surely you are transitioning into a legitimate businessman. But your unsavory past wouldn't let you go. Jay Farr, leader of a ruthless gang and one of your former employers, told you he needed a safe to be opened. Since it wasn't his safe, you were reluctant. But he forced you, possible holding your sister's safety over you, and Saturday night you broke into that safe. Where was it?"

"How did you know all that about him?" I wondered aloud.

"You know my methods, Watson, and my sources. Despite his efforts to keep a low profile about his career, Alan Dyne has left a history among his fellows. Nothing Scotland Yard can use to their advantage, but enough to make him a person of interest. Now, Mr. Dyne, who's safe did you open and what did you take from it?"

"Well, you seem to know so much already, Mr. Holmes, I suppose it can make little difference if I tell you the rest, as long as I don't have to talk to the coppers."

"You have my word."

"All you said was true. When the bookie job looked like it was working, I decided to find my sister. I wanted to reconnect with my family. I knew I had been a disappointment to her, but by my making good as a turf accountant, I could redeem myself in her eyes. I didn't want to say too much, however, because the break from my old life wasn't complete yet.

"Farr found me several weeks ago. He had me followed and learned about my sister. He set up this job and threatened something would happen to Morgana if I wouldn't go through with it. Saturday night he gave me directions to the law offices of Palmbranch and Hawkes in the City. The safe took me a little time, but finally the tumblers fell into place and the door opened. I searched through the papers inside. Farr told me to look for an envelope with a certain postmark and return address. I didn't find the envelope, but I did find the letter it had held.

"I had to read the letter to determine if it was the one he wanted. I was surprised to find that it was from Abraham Rabb, an old member of Farr's gang. He was writing to his lawyer to confirm plans set out that would let him surrender to Scotland Yard when he returns to England. He had been living in a small village in France since he fled arrest years ago for a series of assaults and robberies. Now he was dying. The doctors told him he had only a few months to live. In these last years he had married and his wife led him to the Church. To save his soul, he told the lawyer, he must confess his sins. A priest was not enough. He believed he must make amends to the British authorities also.

"I brought the letter to Farr. He was enraged that I had read it. It upset his plans to have this information known to anyone outside his inner circle. He had me taken and tied up, brought to the storeroom behind the "Camel's Breath" and held prisoner. I overheard him plotting with others to meet Abe Rabb's boat, to grab the sick man and find out everything he had spilled so far. Apparently Abe Rabb had been in on several large jobs Farr had arranged over the years. Then we both would disappear, knocked on the head and thrown into the sea some moonless night. I think he didn't kill me at once because he didn't want the police to stumble across my body and start an investigation before Rabb could be silenced. The ill man's information will be fatal to Jay Farr and his thugs."

"When is Abraham Rabb due to return to England?"

"He booked a cabin on the cargo steamer *Persian Princess* from Lisbon. It is due to berth at Alexandria Dock at nine o'clock tomorrow night. His lawyer arranged a hotel room nearby and will meet him there the next morning to accompany him to Scotland Yard."

I filled Dyne's glass again as Holmes leaned back in his armchair and puffed his pipe, his eyes closed and his forehead marked in concentration. When the little man began to nod off, I guided him up the staircase to my room, where he wearily stretched out on the bed. Soon he was asleep, exhausted by his recent adventure. I left him snoring and returned to the sitting room.

Holmes was where I had left him. The hour was quite late and I curled up under a blanket on the sofa. In a few minutes I, too, was asleep.

When I awoke, the sun was just breaking over the buildings across the street. I went upstairs to check on our guest. The bedclothes were thrown back and the room was empty. A hastily-scribbled note and a sealed envelope were on my desk. I met Holmes in the hallway coming up the stairs as I came down, the papers in my hand.

"Dyne is gone, Holmes!" I exclaimed. "His note asked that we not look for him, that he had friends that will smuggle him out of the country. He left a letter for his sister."

"I know, Watson. He crept down the stairs soon after you fell asleep. His cat burglar skills are still keen, but my ears are keener. I followed him as far as his lodgings and then to the waterfront. I waited until the sloop cast off. Alan Dyne is safe, away from Jay Farr and his gang. Now I can see about Abraham Rabb."

"What will you do?"

"I'll take that letter to Miss Dyne. I still have arrangements to make. We will meet tonight."

I spent the day catching up at the surgery. That evening I came back after dinner to find instructions left by Holmes. I put my trusty service revolver in my pocket and took a cab down to the Alexandria Docks.

The *Persian Princess* was already docked, her decks busy with men and cranes. Huge cargo nets filled with crates and bundles swung out over the waterline as the holds were emptied onto the pier. Then the crates and barrels were carried by burly men into the custom sheds. From the deck of the *Persian Princess* there stretched a long gangplank down to the pier. Two men, clipboards in hand, were just making their way down it. The scene was lit by flickering gas lights and oil lanterns.

I walked toward the nearest shed. As I passed a pile of crates, I heard a hiss. I turned and saw Inspector Bradshaw motion me to join him in the shadows.

"You are just in time, Dr. Watson. The custom officials have finished their on-board inspections and are leaving the ship. Where is Holmes?"

"Isn't he with you?"

"He came to Scotland Yard and talked to me earlier today. He was very mysterious but insisted that I and a picked squad of men meet the *Persian Princess* tonight at nine-thirty. He gave me some very complicated instructions. Sometimes your friend can be quite exasperating, Doctor. Does he think we police have nothing else to do but lurk about on piers and wait for…"

Bradshaw stopped whispering. The officials had gone into a low building. The *Persian Princess's* passengers and crew began disembarking. Several people, including four men and a woman, came down the gangway carrying their grips and valises. Two seamen carried down a trunk. Behind them came another man. He was a hunched, thin figure, wrapped up in shawls, and stumbled as he made his way down to the pier. He reached the seamen with the trunk and was handing them a few coins when running footsteps were heard. There was shouting and a closed carriage galloped up to the group from the street. Several toughs appeared and began struggling with the group by the trunk, trying to force the invalid into the cab. Bradshaw blew his whistle and sprang out of his hiding place with me close behind. Half-a-dozen policemen emerged from their stations behind the piles and stacks of crates and casks around us and joined in the melee.

One or two of the gang I recognized from our encounter the night before. I maneuvered myself close to the invalid and tried to hold off his attackers. The police managed to quell and take prisoner the entire group, but not before Abraham Rabb and I were thrown into the carriage against our wills. As soon as the door banged shut behind us, the driver whipped up the horses and we bolted off, down dark and narrow London alleys and around anonymous corners. I sat up and searched for my revolver, but my pocket was empty. It must have been lost during the fight. I started to say something, but the well-known voice of Sherlock Holmes sounded in my ear. "Say nothing and follow my lead." I stared at the man in the opposite seat. Why was it I could never penetrate Holmes' disguises? Just then we swerved around one more corner and the carriage stopped. The door was pulled open and a familiar voice silkily invited us to join him.

Holmes was still wrapped in the shawls that hid his face. He shakily put out a hand and Jay Farr took it to help him down the step. Instead my friend's strong, thin fingers gripped Farr's hand. He reached out with the other hand, gripped the criminal's coat collar and jerked him into the carriage. I slammed the door shut. Instantly the carriage lurched again and we rattled down the street.

Between us Holmes and I fitted Jay Farr's wrists with the detective's handcuffs. Holmes tied his ankles with his cravat and when Farr began to yell, I stuffed my handkerchief into his mouth. When he was satisfied his prisoner was secure, Holmes pulled up the shade, thrust out his head and shouted at the driver.

"Scotland Yard, Constable. They will be expecting us."

The carriage slowed to a trot. As we proceeded toward our goal, Holmes threw off the encompassing shawls and pulled out his pipe. I stared from our prisoner to my friend in wonderment.

"What happened to Abraham Rabb, Holmes?"

"He is safe, Watson. By now Inspector Bradshaw will have released him from that travel trunk in which he was willing to hide in order to evade his old cohort. I joined the ship from the pilot boat. I carried a letter from his lawyers and sought out Rabb in his cabin. It didn't take much convincing to get him to agree to my plan. I had arranged with Bradshaw to engage with whoever tried to interfere with Rabb's disembarkation. I had two men carry the trunk down the plank then wrapped myself in extra shawls and followed it. The trickiest part was substituting Constable Rock for the original cab driver. The Scotland Yard man was in place before Farr engaged the cab."

"What if Jay Farr had asked for another cab?"

"There were four cabs circling the "Jewel and Bottle" and two more lingering near the "Camel's Breath", each manned by a policeman. Farr had to pick one of them."

Our prisoner struggled. Sherlock Holmes plucked the gag from his mouth. Farr's face was red and his eyes glared at us both. "I'll have you arrested for this assault, Holmes! You have no case against me! This is illegal!"

Holmes chuckled. "There is a pile of warrants waiting for you at Scotland Yard, Mr. Farr. Your reputation precedes you. But you have been most elusive. Many well-planned raids on your organization have failed to dig you out of your burrow. It will be quite a feather in Constable Rock's helmet when he deposits you at Scotland Yard's gate. He has arrested you with the anonymous help of two public-spirited citizens. He'll most likely get his sergeant's stripes for this.

"It's all quite legal, I assure you. As we speak Metropolitan's finest are rounding up the last of your gang. Abraham Rabb and your own men will build a strong and study case against you, Mr. Farr. How long will your organization stand when your men are confronted with the police's proof of your robberies, assaults, thefts, and murders? The image of rats deserting a sinking ship comes to mind. Lesser sentences offered to your men for confessions, stolen goods recovered from your hiding places, Abe Rabb's sworn statements; all combine to put you in the shadow of a cell door or a rope, Mr. Farr."

Jay Farr began to spew out more dreadful oaths and Holmes stuffed my handkerchief back in his mouth.

Miss Morgana Dyne sat on our sofa in the sitting room of 221b Baker Street the next afternoon, holding the letter her brother had left for her. Holmes had just finished telling of our adventures on her behalf and she looked at us both in wonder.

"That is amazing, Mr. Holmes! So Jay Farr and his men are safely in custody? They pose no threat to either my brother or I?"

"That is correct, Miss Dyne."

"Your story helps make sense of this letter Alan left for me." She held out a small shiny object in her palm. "He left me this key to a box in a downtown bank with instructions to use the contents for my own benefit. He had earlier arranged to transfer most of his wealth to another bank on the Continent. He must have had grave doubts about the job Jay Farr insisted he do for him. I am very grateful to both of you gentlemen for saving my brother from that horrible man."

"What are your plans now, Miss Dyne? Or will it be Miss Dyne for much longer? Could that gentleman waiting in the street below have his own ideas of what your future will bring?"

"Mr. Holmes! How did you guess?"

"Dr. Watson will tell you that I never guess, Miss Dyne. I have known since our first meeting. While you told me your story, you repeatedly pulled and rubbed the third finger of your left hand. When I bid you farewell, I took care to pat that hand and felt the lump hidden under your glove. It felt exactly like an engagement ring. You had not yet informed your employer and so took pains that it not be visible during working hours."

"I noticed a thin chain about her neck when I went to talk to her," I exclaimed.

"Just so. That is where she carried the ring while in uniform."

Miss Morgana Dyne smiled. "I can see I have no secrets from either of you gentlemen. I told Mr. and Mrs. Waddy yesterday and they have given their blessing. His name is T. Edward Lawrence and he has spent the past year in Toronto, Canada, working as a clerk for the Canadian Pacific Railroad. We agreed to keep the engagement quiet while he established a place for us in that city. Now he has returned on the steamship *Oasis* with a promotion and we will marry. The money my brother has left for me will help to start us off nicely in our new faraway home."

Sherlock Holmes took out the forty pounds she had previously deposited in his safekeeping and offered it to her but she waved it away.

"Keep it as your fee, please," she said. "My brother, wherever he may go, and I will both count it as well-spent. My fiancé waits below. He has a special license and we have a four o'clock appointment at St. Christopher's Church. Goodbye, Mr. Holmes. Goodbye, Dr. Watson."

With another smile and another handshake she was gone. I picked up one of the newspapers delivered that day and noted something on an inside page.

"Holmes! That young singer, Thomas Tucker, who disappeared after his La Scala debut, has been found!"

"Eating supper in the company of a notorious lady of the evening, well-known to the police and to the minor local royalty."

"Exactly! How did you know?"

"Watson, think of those many countries and three continents. Weren't you once a young man yourself?"

Also from MX Publishing

MX Publishing is the world's largest specialist Sherlock Holmes publisher, with over a hundred titles and fifty authors creating the latest in Sherlock Holmes fiction and non-fiction.

From traditional short stories and novels to travel guides and quiz books, MX Publishing cater for all Holmes fans.

The collection includes leading titles such as *Benedict Cumberbatch In Transition* and *The Norwood Author* which won the 2011 Howlett Award (Sherlock Holmes Book of the Year).

MX Publishing also has one of the largest communities of Holmes fans on Facebook with regular contributions from dozens of authors.

www.ingramcontent.com/pod-product-compliance
Lightning Source LLC
Chambersburg PA
CBHW051237260626
47162CB00002B/477